THE CASH COUNTESS

THE CASH COUNTESS

SAMANTHA HASTINGS

Scribbling
Pens

Printed in the United States of America

Paperback: ISBN 979-8-39347-310-5

First Edition: July 2023

Scribbling Pens Press

Salt Lake City, UT

Edited by: Meghan Hoesch @ Precision Editing

Cover art by: Scribbling pens

Layout Formatting by: Michelle Martin

This is a work of fiction. The characters, names, incidents, places, and dialogue are either products of the author's imagination, and are not to be construed as real, or as used factiously.

To Stacy Moon

PRAISE FOR SAMANTHA HASTINGS

Secret of the Sonnets "will keep readers turning pages" - *Publishers Weekly*

"This Shakespeare-connected mystery takes on the challenge of living up to the many excellent Regency romances available. Challenge met and exceeded!" - *Historical Novel Society*

A Novel Disguise is "wildly enjoyable" - *Publishers Weekly*

"Class differences, prejudice, and the lack of women's rights drive this enjoyable mystery." - *Kirkus Reviews*

The Marquess and the Runaway Lady "VERDICT Combining the Regency season with the runaway woman trope makes for a delightful story." - *Library Journal*

"In England, as on the Continent, the American woman was looked upon as a strange and abnormal creature … Anything of an outlandish nature might be expected of her. If she talked, dressed, and conducted herself as any well-bred woman would, much astonishment was invariably evinced, and she was usually saluted with the tactful remark: 'I should never have thought you an American'—which was intended as a compliment."

—Jennie Jerome Randall

---

*W*hispers followed her around like the wind.

Miss Cordelia Jones was used to people staring at her. She was a Jones, after all. Her clothes were made in Paris by the house of Worth, and her five-strand pearl necklace cost half a million dollars at Tiffany's. She was a member of one of the richest families in America, and until last month, one of the most sought-after social connections.

She slowly walked out of church behind her mother, who seemed impervious to the insolent looks. Gentlemen turned their backs to them. Matrons whispered behind their hands. And young ladies whom she had once called friends greeted her with cold stares instead of smiles. Miss Eva Astor, niece of *the* Mrs. Astor, the head of New York society, openly sneered at her. Alida and Julia Wilson both had tears in their eyes as she passed them, but they did not wave or acknowledge their long friendship in any way. Even Lucy Miller, who was illegitimate, glanced down as they approached.

Lucy's betrayal stung the deepest, like a barbed fishhook caught underneath her skin. Cordelia had never once held Lucy's parentage against *her.*

Cordelia's younger sister, Edith, tugged on the sleeve of her dress. She glanced back at her. Edith was only twelve, six years younger than she, and her sister's head barely reached her shoulder.

"What?"

Edith leaned closer. "Why aren't my friends talking to me?"

"It's church, you're supposed to be silent," Cordelia whispered.

Edith squeezed Cordelia's hand, which was already being pinched by her too-tight gloves.

"I'll tell you when we get home."

This answer finally satisfied her sister, for Edith released her vise-like grip. Cordelia saw Stuyvesant, her best friend and the man that she loved. The pressure moved from her hand to her heart, squeezing it tightly. He was standing in the back of the church. Stuyvesant was no longer the scruffy boy next door, with dirt on his nose and messy brown hair. He was all man—tall, broad, and handsome, with his recently grown sideburns and new gray suit. He had changed so much in the last year at college. Cordelia's throat felt dry, her pulse quickened, and she felt a bead of sweat slide down the back of her neck.

Surely he would not cut her.

Every step closer to the door, Cordelia's corset seemed to tighten. She felt as breathless as she had that morning, when the maid tightened the contraption to make an eighteen-inch waist— the number her mother insisted upon. She clutched her reticule with one hand and pulled the double veil down from her hat to cover her face.

To hide.

She felt ashamed. She wouldn't, couldn't, look at Stuyvesant. Instead, Cordelia followed her mother's footsteps out of the church and into their carriage.

The ride to their home was uncommonly quiet. It was as if the very architecture of New York City looked upon them in silent condemnation.

Cordelia felt relieved when the carriage finally pulled up in front of their home on Fifth Avenue called the "Château." The architecture was styled after a French castle, with spires, balconies, and impressive stone steps. Her room was called the "tower" because it was circular and the roof pointed. The footmen opened the door to the carriage and helped both Edith and Cordelia down and then their mother, who walked into the house without acknowledging either of her daughters.

Edith squeezed Cordelia's gloved hand once more.

"Come to my room," Cordelia said.

They gave their wraps and hats to the butler and climbed the stairs to the third floor. It wasn't until they were safely inside, with the door closed tightly, that Cordelia talked. "You know how Father hasn't come and seen us for a few weeks?"

Her little sister shrugged her shoulders. "He's sailing on his yacht."

Cordelia yanked off her gloves and set them on the bureau. "Yes, darling, but it's a bit more than that," she tried to explain gently. "You know how Mother and Father used to argue?"

"Even the servants know about that."

"Yes," Cordelia said with a sigh. "Well, they decided not to be married to each other anymore... They got divorced."

"Why?" Edith said, folding her arms and giving her elder sister a wide-eyed look. Edith resembled their mother, who was still considered to be one of the most beautiful women in New York society. Edith's hair was golden, her large eyes bright blue, and her expression precious. She had not yet bloomed into womanhood, but she was still lovely enough to make strangers stop and stare.

Unlike Cordelia, who did not resemble her mother very much at all. Her hair was a nondescript shade between dark blonde and light brown, which her mother called "mousy." Cordelia's eyes were ordinary and such a dark blue that they almost looked black. Worst of all, she'd gone sailing with her father frequently as a child and not worn a hat. Her face was covered in freckles, and no matter how many products her mother purchased to eradicate them, Cordelia's freckles stayed obstinately on her face. She folded her own arms across her ample chest—the only part of Cordelia's body that her mother did not find fault with.

She swallowed, wondering how much she should tell her little sister about a certain actress named Suzy Velvet (if that really was her name). Her father's previous "indiscretions" had at least been discreet, but he was so enamored with Suzy Velvet that he had entertained her openly in the city. Mother not only decided to divorce him (a major social taboo) but to sue him for infidelity. Something that no one from their elite social circle, the *Four Hundred*, had done before. Women usually lost everything when they divorced their husbands: their home, their fortunes, and their children. But Mother hadn't. Because she sued Father and won, she'd kept it all. Unfortunately, fashionable society did not condone liberated and financially powerful women.

"They decided that they would be happier apart," Cordelia said at last.

Edith shrugged again. "Father was rarely here anyway. That doesn't explain why my friends wouldn't talk to me."

She struggled to find the right words. "I'm sure it had nothing to do with you, Edith. It's just some gentlemen don't allow their wives or children to associate with people who are divorced."

"I'm not divorced."

"But our parents are."

"That's not fair!" Edith nearly shouted and stomped her foot, acting more like a child than the young woman she was becoming.

Cordelia walked over to her sister and put her arm around her shoulders. "I know, darling; but you are about to return to school. I'm sure everything will be the same there. Hopefully in a few months we'll get back to our normal lives, and our friends will be able to talk to us and invite us to parties again."

"Is that why you haven't worn your new dress yet?"

Cordelia thought longingly of the gorgeous green satin gown from Paris that managed to make her look pretty. It was an original from the house of Worth and practically a work of art. Not that her mother thought she looked good in it. Mother told her that she had no taste in clothes and could never appear beautiful, no matter what she wore. The words had cut at the time, but now they had lessened into a dull sting. She would never be a beauty like her mother, but that didn't mean that she wasn't attractive. Or that her worth was measured by her waistline.

"Yes, Edith," she said with a sigh. "I haven't received any invitations since the divorce, so I've had no opportunity to wear my new gown."

"Then, how will you get a husband?"

Cordelia blinked. "Excuse me?"

"A husband," Edith said matter-of-factly. "You're eighteen years old now and you should be 'out.' If no one will invite us to parties, how will you find a husband?"

Cordelia recovered her composure enough to laugh. "I am much too young to get married yet. I plan to go to university first. Mother had me take the entrance exams to Oxford and I passed them. And even when I do find a young man to marry, we will be engaged for two or three years before the wedding."

"Good," Edith said. "I shouldn't wish to lose you yet."

Cordelia hugged her little sister and assured her, "You won't."

Edith returned the embrace and then left the room. Cordelia locked the door behind her. She needed to be alone. Her head ached from the weight of her hair and the awful day. It was the first time they'd appeared in public since the divorce, and surely it would get better. She didn't care that it was only the afternoon; she took out the dozen hairpins that kept her hair in a loose bun on top of her head. Cordelia shook out her long hair that reached past her waist. Her head still pounded. She needed fresh air. Cordelia opened the double doors that led to a small balcony, barely large enough for her to stand on. She placed her elbows on the stone railing and rested her head in her hands.

Cordelia did not know if she could survive another Sunday like this one. Perhaps she ought to ask her mother to take them all to Paris for the rest of the summer. Somewhere that society did not know about the divorce.

In the fall she would be at Oxford University as a student. Without her mother or her father. It was a heady thought.

"You look like Juliet," Stuyvesant called across to her from the door to his own balcony. It was scarcely four feet from hers, but there was a two-story drop between them. At nineteen, he was already taller than his father and had broad shoulders, with lean, muscular arms. His wavy brown hair was supposed to be slicked back, but it fell forward across his brow, giving him a roguish look. He grinned at her and she forgot about her headache. Her body felt so light that she thought she might float. Stuyvesant still loved her. His feelings had not changed.

"Would that make you Romeo?"

"Of course," Stuyvesant said, leaning over his own railing toward her, with one arm outstretched. "Juliet, Juliet, let down your hair so that I may climb it."

"I think you mean Rapunzel, Romeo."

"Very well, if you won't let down your hair, Juliet," he said with a laugh, "I'll just have to jump over there."

"You can't," Cordelia nearly shrieked. "It's too dangerous."

Stuyvesant ignored her, swinging one leg over his own stone balcony and then his other. With only one hand holding on to the rail, he reached for Cordelia's balcony. She grabbed his hand with both of hers, holding them tighter than Edith had held hers at church. Stuyvesant swung his legs across and over the balcony. He stood close enough to her that their shoes were touching. Oh, how she'd missed his nearness. The smell of his cologne and aftershave. The way the heat of his skin made her heart flutter.

"You nearly gave me a heart attack," she teased. "You could have talked to me just fine from your house."

"But I couldn't have kissed you from that distance."

Stuyvesant tentatively put a hand on her waist, pausing before leaning in, as if waiting for permission. Cordelia smiled and that was all the encouragement he needed. He leaned closer to her and gently pressed his mouth to hers. His lips felt soft, warm, and entirely marvelous. They moved over hers until she opened her mouth to him and the kiss deepened. It wasn't their first kiss or their second, but something about this kiss was special. Magical. The happily-ever-after ending that she hadn't dare to hope for.

After what seemed as long as an hour, but as short as a blink of the eye, the kiss ended.

Stuyvesant's arms were around her shoulders and he leaned his forehead against hers. Running his fingers through her hair, he said, "That kiss was certainly worth risking my life over."

A laugh bubbled out of Cordelia and found its way to her lips. It felt wonderful but unpracticed. She hadn't laughed in weeks. "I'm glad, but don't do it again. I'm not sure if my heart could survive another scare like that."

Stuyvesant grinned. "Do you realize this is the first time we've ever been alone together?"

"Mother makes certain of that," Cordelia said, but instantly wished she hadn't, for Stuyvesant's smile faltered.

"About that—"

"Don't," Cordelia said, pressing her finger on his soft lips that she'd just kissed. "I can't bear for you to scorn anyone in my family."

Stuyvesant's hand covered hers and he gently kissed her finger as he took it away from his mouth. "I would never censure you or any member of your family. I don't care that your parents are divorced. I have loved you since the first day I saw you. You had just moved in next door, and you wore a little blue coat with a matching beret hat."

"I've only loved you three years, not fifteen."

"Someday you'll catch up with me," Stuyvesant said, and kissed her temple. "Cordy, I'm leaving on a trip to South America tomorrow and I'll probably be gone several months, but I want you to know before I go that you are the girl for me. The only girl for me. And I mean to court you when I come back and marry you when you turn twenty-one."

"That's in three years. I should be done with university by then."

"Exactly. Set the date and start planning."

Cordelia couldn't help but smile. "I hope you intend on asking me more romantically for our official proposal, Romeo."

"Rapunzel, I risked my life to climb over to your tower because you refused to let me climb your hair. What could possibly be more romantic?"

"If you remembered my name."

"I love you, Cordelia Violet Jones."

"And I love you, Stuyvesant Eugene Bradley," Cordelia whispered and then pulled his head down to hers for another kiss. Stuyvesant's hands moved to her waist and he pulled her closer to him.

A knock on her door broke their reverie.

She pulled back from Stuyvesant. "Who is it?"

"Your mother. Now open this door at once."

Cordelia's throat constricted. She felt as if someone had a hand on her neck and was choking the air out of her. She looked at Stuyvesant, who was silently laughing. He gave her a quick kiss on the cheek and then preformed his acrobatic move to cross from one balcony to the other. One of his feet slipped, causing his legs to dangle. He was holding on only by his strong arms. Her heart dropped in her chest.

"Cordelia Violet!" her mother's voice rang loudly through the door.

She couldn't move until she saw him safely reach the other balcony. Stuyvesant managed to get one foot back up and pulled himself over the railing onto the safety of the other side.

"Do not keep me waiting!" her mother yelled loud enough for every mansion on Fifth Avenue to hear.

Stuyvesant scrambled to his feet and waved for her to go to her mother. Cordelia blew him one last kiss.

"See you soon, Rapunzel," he called and walked into his house.

Cordelia waited until his door closed before dashing into her bedroom and unlocking her own door for her mother. Mother did not say a word but strode purposely into the room. She was still wearing the same green silk gown with a black lace overlay that she'd worn to church. It clung perfectly to her mother's ample curves and narrow waist. Not one golden hair was displaced on her head. Her mother's cold blue eyes looked at her with patent disapproval. Cordelia turned from her mother and picked up one of her old dolls off the bureau, foolishly seeking comfort and love from it like she had as a child.

"You are too old to be playing with dolls," her mother snapped. "You are about to be married. You are no longer a child and I cannot allow you to behave like one."

Cordelia dropped the doll and its porcelain face shattered on the marble tiled floor. She felt cold all over. "Excuse me?"

"Do not make me repeat myself."

Dozens of thoughts whirled through Cordelia's mind. Did her mother know about Stuyvesant's visit? How soon would they be married? In only two years, instead of three? New York society deemed any engagement less than two years unduly fast. Surely she would have at least a Season before there was a formal proposal and announcement. Would her father be invited to her come-out party? To the wedding? Cordelia hadn't seen him in over two months since before the divorce. He seemed to have washed his hands not only of her mother but Cordelia and Edith as well.

"I did not think that I raised a dullard."

Her mother's comment stung, but Cordelia was trained from her first words to subject herself to her mother's iron will. To never fight back. Her mother demanded complete obedience. Cordelia swallowed and straightened her posture. "I assumed that no wedding announcement would be made until after my come-out. Stuyvesant just turned nineteen and I am barely eighteen."

Her mother laughed. It wasn't a happy sound but sharp and cruel. "Foolish child. You are not going to marry Stuyvesant Bradley or any young man from the *Four Hundred*. No one in New York society would have you. You're only passably pretty, and even your impressive dowry is not enough to overcome our family's current social dilemma."

Cordelia held her breath. She was determined not to cry. She hadn't sobbed when her father left. She hadn't wept when her friends stopped calling and social invitations ceased. She would not break down now.

"If not Stuyvesant, who do you intend for me to marry?"

"I have given this matter a great deal of thought," her mother said. "The only way for you, Edith, and me to re-enter society is for you to marry an English lord... Even Mrs. Astor, the undisputed leader of fashion, would not snub the mother-in-law of an English aristocrat, and whomever she approves of, the rest of New York will accept without question."

Cordelia shook her head. "I am only eighteen years old. I am much too young to be married yet. Besides, I've passed the entrance examinations to Oxford University, and I thought the plan was that I attend there in the fall with a chaperone. You've always told me how important my education is. How a woman's mind is equal to any man's."

"I don't ask *you* to think," she said. "*I* do the thinking."

"It's 1893, Mama!" Cordelia burst out. "This isn't the Middle Ages. Arranged marriages are a thing of the past."

Her mother's beautiful features contorted with anger. "You will do as you are told."

"But it is *my* life. And if I am only 'passably pretty,' why would an English aristocrat wish to marry me in the first place?"

Her mother smiled, a cold, calculated one. "If you weren't so young and foolish, you would know that most English lords are desperate for money. There have been many marriages between American heiresses and Europeans with titles."

Cordelia *had* heard of them. The newspapers loved to publish articles on "cash for coronet" marriages. They called American heiresses "dollar princesses" and tried to sell papers by pretending it was a modern fairytale spectacle. But Cordelia was not fooled. She knew firsthand the misery that lay beneath the glitter and gold of the upper class. The sadness behind the smiles. And what little happiness could be found in a marriage based on money like her parents' had been.

"I will not do it," Cordelia said, shaking her head. "You cannot make me marry a complete stranger."

Her mother clutched her chest where her heart should have been, but Cordelia thought it was empty underneath.

"Do you not care about your family? Your own mother? Your sister? What chance do you think Edith will have at school if you do not restore our place in society? And when she comes of age? She will be censured and despised. All because of your selfishness."

"Perhaps you should have thought about that before you divorced Father."

Her mother rounded on her. "You are a child. You know nothing. You understand nothing. I am your mother. You must be guided by me. And you will not leave this room until I have your word that you will marry whomever I select."

"Then I shall stay in here forever."

"We will see about that," her mother said, and opened the door to the room. She stepped out and called for a footman. "Peter, see that Miss Cordelia does not leave her room and that no one else goes in unless it is one of her governesses."

The tall footman bowed and walked to her door to stand as a sentry.

"I'll give you some time to come to your senses and realize your duty," her mother said, and the footman shut the door.

Cordelia fell to her knees, lacking the energy to stand any longer. She picked up the broken doll. More than half of the doll's face was now a jagged hole. The only facial feature that remained was one blue eye, permanently open. Cordelia cradled her broken doll against her chest, crying for the loss of her childhood and her own dreams. And for Stuyvesant.

2

---

*T*here was no service said over his father's body. The seventh Earl of Farnham was buried in the Petersley Church graveyard, with nary a soul save for Thomas and the rector, Mr. Ryse. Thomas watched the two burly gravediggers shovel dirt onto the simple wooden casket until it could no longer be seen.

Mr. Ryse was a stout man of middling years, with thinning brown hair and a trimmed beard. He was a remote relation of the Ashby family and had spent more time at Ashdown Abbey than his father had. Mr. Ryse placed his hand on Thomas's shoulder. "'Tis a bad business."

What an understatement, Thomas thought. His father had shot himself in the ash grove adjacent to the house, leaving Thomas with a title, a heavily mortgaged estate, staggering debts, his mother, and his ward, Penelope Hutchinson, to provide for. Thomas barely had enough cash to pay for his father's burial, as no one in the village of Petersley would give him credit. Not that he could blame them. The debt to the butcher was two years overdue and the wine merchant hadn't been paid in five years.

"How are you holding up, young man?" Mr. Ryse inquired, still holding Thomas's shoulder with his beefy hand.

"Well enough," Thomas lied. He was only twenty-one years old and his family was depending on him to save them. But how? His father had already pawned all the family jewels, sold their 18,000-volume library and both the Raphael and Van Dyck paintings. The only item left of value in the entire Ashdown Abbey was the silverware. Thomas tried to picture himself paying the butcher's bill with silver forks and spoons.

"At least you didn't lose Ashdown Abbey," Mr. Ryse said in a reassuring tone.

Thomas could feel the blood draining from his face. He felt as if he was going to be sick. He did not know how he could possibly save his home. It was already mortgaged past what it was worth, and he would still have to pay all of his father's outstanding debts.

"I didn't mean to frighten you, Thomas," Mr. Ryse said quickly. "I only meant that twenty years ago your father's property would have been forfeit to the crown. Suicide is a crime, after all."

Thomas gave him a polite nod, but in his heart, he didn't agree. Taking one's life was a terrible act of sorrow, desperation, and temporary insanity. His father had gambled away his fortune, and once the money was gone, so were his father's so-called friends. Thomas felt deep grief that his father had seen no other course of action.

The gravediggers used their shovels to pat down the newly turned soil over the mound. There was not a grave marker yet and Thomas did not have enough money to order one from the stone mason. His grandfathers had large ornately carved monuments inside the chapel, but they weren't disgraced earls. His father's grave looked strangely blank without one. Thomas turned to Mr. Ryse and thanked him before shaking his hand. He left the graveyard without another glance backward.

Untying his horse, Thomas swung up into the saddle and began the short ride home.

From a distance, Ashdown Abbey looked more like a medieval castle than an estate house. Once the home of a monastery, the abbey had been sold in 1539 by King Henry VIII to Thomas's ancestor the first Earl of Farnham. The front façade had four tall, circle stone towers with pointed roofs. Two separate wings flanked the main house, making the structure U-shaped. The wings did not have towers, instead eight arched and pointed eaves, with several narrow windows underneath. Once stately and formal gardens surrounded the house on two sides, with a large, rectangular man-made pond reflecting the west wing of the house. To the south stood the ash grove.

The closer Thomas got to Ashdown, the more dilapidated it looked. The roof was missing shingles. The gardens were over-grown and full of weeds. The windows were dirty and in desperate need of replacing. The stables in need of a coat of paint. The entire estate looked like an abandoned ruin. But his mother and his family's ward, Miss Penelope Hutchinson, lived there, as well as a handful of dedicated servants who had remained despite the fact that they hadn't been paid all year.

Thomas would pay them. He would fulfill all of his father's debts.

He rode his horse into the stables and was surprised to see his valet, Edwin Thayne, there. Thomas dismounted and led his horse by the bridle to the stall where he stood.

"What are you doing, Thayne?"

"Isn't it obvious, Mr. Thomas?"

"You're mucking the stall," Thomas said. "But that isn't your job. Where is Gerald? And the other grooms?"

"Gone, sir."

"Gone?" Thomas repeated stupidly.

"They left after breakfast to find new employment," Thayne explained.

Thomas nodded dumbly, fiddling with his shirtsleeves. He didn't blame them. Ashdown Abbey was doomed. As the eighth Earl of Farnham, he had no way to pay all the debts. His tenants couldn't pay their rents because of several bad harvests and he had no other source of income. He had been trained for no profession, only three years of classical studies at Oxford University that had been cut

Penelope's inheritance. Which he did. Money was like sand in his fingers."

"Have you made Penelope an offer?"

Thomas shook his head. Penelope was the most beautiful girl he'd ever seen, and he'd always planned to marry her but not immediately—in some distant future. He was only twenty-one, after all.

"Then you are not honor bound to marry her."

Thomas shrugged his shoulders. "But my father wasted her inheritance."

"And you won't be able to pay her back unless you marry well," Oliver stated. "You should do what I have done."

"Marry an American heiress."

"Precisely."

"I didn't know that you married Lois for her money."

"Not entirely," Oliver said, blushing. The only sign that he felt discomfited by their conversation. "I was smitten from the first time I saw Lois. She was like a revelation to me of how wonderful a woman could be. But I never would have married her if she hadn't had money, and she would not have chosen me if I was not the heir to a dukedom."

"I could always marry an English heiress."

"Not a bad idea, Thomas, but there simply aren't as many of them. Plus, most of the English heiresses come from the lower classes and you'll have to deal with the vulgar parents on a regular basis. They'll be expecting you to host them whilst in town. You won't be able to show your face in London."

"I hadn't thought of that."

"American girls are an entirely different breed from their British sisters. They're prettier, wittier, and come with more than enough cash to solve your every financial difficulty," Oliver said. "I have never made a better decision in all of my life than when I married Lois."

"Even if I could get enough credit to go to America," Thomas said, "what woman in her right mind would want to marry me? I have little more than a title to my name."

"Americans love titles and they'll pay millions for them," Oliver stated. "Once you're married, your wife's dowry is money in *your* pocket. Lois's parents still send her a yearly allowance. You'll never have financial difficulties again and you'll be able to dower Penelope. I don't doubt that she'll marry well, with her looks and a respectable dowry. And you'll have enough money to bring Ashdown Abbey back to its original glory."

Thomas sighed. "I don't know. It seems morally wrong to marry a young woman for her money—even an American."

"If you don't, you're facing bankruptcy. Your estate will be foreclosed on. Your tenants will lose their farms, which have been in their families for generations. Your mother and Penelope will be homeless. And your family name will be smirched forever. It is time to grow up, Thomas."

He swallowed uncomfortably, his throat dry.

"Not only will your family be ruined and homeless, but all of your staff who have stayed on to help you, despite irregular wages, will be uprooted. Poor Mr. Hibbert's been here since my mother was a little girl. What is he going to do now? Mrs. Cook and the housekeeper, Mrs. Norton, who have devotedly stayed without pay? They are all senior members of your staff, which means they will have to find new positions at another house and start again from the bottom. And despite their vast experience, they aren't getting any younger. It may prove impossible to find another position for many of them. You owe it to them, to your mother, and to your family's ward to try and marry an American heiress immediately."

Thomas mulled this over in his mind. "I suppose you're right."

"I'm always right," Oliver said with a smile. "It's a burden."

Thomas attempted a smile, but it was a pathetic one.

Oliver put his hand in his coat pocket and pulled out a stack of papers. "I've booked you and your valet passage on the *Queen Adelaide* for this Saturday. Lois has written you letters of introduction to several prominent New York families. And here is a bank draft for one thousand pounds—as long as you're careful, it should see you through until the marriage. I suggest a very short engagement. I'll do my best to hold off the foreclosure on Ashdown Abbey until you arrive back home."

"But my mother—" Thomas began. "My father's suic—death is so recent."

"Miss Hutchinson will take care of her. You don't have time to dawdle. You have to marry immediately."

Oliver placed the papers in Thomas's reluctant hands. "Trust me, you have no other choice."

"Thank you."

"You're not grateful yet," Oliver said knowingly, and clapped Thomas on the back. "But you will be soon. American girls are full of snap and dash; you'll be swept off of your feet."

"I thought men were supposed to do the sweeping off of feet," he said. "Shall I have Hibbert make up a room for you?"

"No, no. I told Lois that I would take the afternoon train back."

Thomas smiled with relief that his cousin would not be staying. Not that he didn't enjoy Oliver's company, but he was embarrassed at the lack of servants and the general state of disarray that the house was in. Oliver literally lived in a palace that not only was twice the size of Ashdown Abbey but had three times the servants. There was nothing in Birkhall Palace that was not made of the very finest materials, and Ashdown Abbey paled in comparison.

He walked Oliver to the front of the house, where the hired coach was waiting. His valet, Mr. Thayne, playing the role of a footman, opened the door for Oliver. Thomas watched the hired coach depart down the gravel drive until it turned onto the road.

"Thayne," Thomas said quietly. "Would you please pack our things?"

"Where are we going, sir?"

"New York City."

3

$\mathcal{A}$fter four weeks, Cordelia hated everything about her bedchamber. She hated the circular walls that were made of blue silk. She despised the floor installed with the finest Italian marble. She loathed the moldings that were gilded with real gold and the Venetian mirrors that hung over her bureau. She no longer sat on the expensive brass and mahogany furniture but on the cold floor. She lived in the finest prison on earth. All she could do was stare down from her balcony at the people below, living their lives.

Hoping. Praying to see Stuyvesant's handsome brown eyes and infectious smile. Waiting for him to return home to her.

The Wilson twins had come to see her twice. It was impossible not to recognize the sisters even from afar. Alida was tall and thin, with light blonde hair and Julia was short and curvaceous, with dark brown hair. Both times they'd come to visit, they'd been ushered inside. Her mother must have talked with them, for Cordelia was never called from her room. A half hour later, the twins had left. After two visits without seeing her, they must have given up trying. Neither Wilson girl was overly fond of her mother, who had called Julia "plump" at Cordelia's eighteenth birthday party.

Lucy Miller came five times during the first week of Cordelia's confinement and was rebuffed each time by the butler. Her mother had never approved of their friendship. Every day since, Lucy walked down Fifth Avenue at ten o'clock in the morning with her maid and waved up at Cordelia. Lucy's bright red hair and infectious smile were the only light in her life. All Cordelia could do was wave back. She longed to shout to her friend. To beg for help, but if she made a scene, her mother would no doubt restrict her from the balcony, and Cordelia couldn't bear not to have any sunlight and fresh air.

She stood up, her long hair falling loose past her waist. Cordelia tiptoed across the room and gently opened the door, hoping that no one would be on the other side. But the footman stood as sentry, guarding her exit. The expression on his handsome face was one of pity, but also of resolve. Peter would not let her out and she couldn't blame him. If he did, he would lose his position and be sent off without a reference. He didn't say anything, but he didn't need to. She closed the door.

Cordelia had to get out of her blue room or she would go mad. She flung open the double doors to her balcony and leaned over the railing, breathing in the fresh air. Her long hair tumbled over the ledge and she laughed—a hysterical little laugh.

She was truly Rapunzel now. She was locked in her tower and forced to stay there until her handsome prince came to save her. Or rather, until she promised to marry whomever her mother selected.

If only he wasn't in South America. Stuyvesant would have loved to play the role of the handsome prince. Cordelia gave another hysterical little laugh that turned into a sob. In her heart she knew that he would help her if there were some way to get him a message. A letter. She fell to her knees and buried her face into her hands. She didn't have a paper or a pen with which to write one. She, Cordelia Violet Jones, heiress to over two million dollars, did not have enough pennies to purchase a stamp.

Cordelia grabbed a fistful of her hair. She had to escape this room. If she could make it to Lucy's or the twins' house, they would help her get a letter Stuyvesant. He would surely return immediately from his trip if he knew she was in trouble.

She looked across at the balcony Stuyvesant had climbed over to see her. If only he could climb over now. Or that she could climb to him. But Stuyvesant was much taller and stronger than she was and that was before she'd been locked in a room for over a month with no exercise. And even if she could get to the opposite balcony, the doors would be locked. Stuyvesant's entire family was out of town. There would most likely be a few servants left to watch the house, but whether or not they would be near enough to hear her or help seemed doubtful.

Cordelia sat up and wiped off her wet face with the edge of her sleeve. Her tears were not helping. She needed to use her mind. Pulling herself to her feet, she looked over the balcony—it was over a twenty-five-foot drop. She would be dead if she attempted it. What she really needed was a ladder. Something besides hair to climb down on.

Stumbling back to her room, Cordelia pulled the coverlet and the satin sheets off her bed. She tied them all together with knots and the end she secured to the balcony. She threw her makeshift ladder over; the bottom did not quite reach the ground, but she could jump the last three or four feet. Her long hair fell forward—it would only be in the way, so she quickly braided it and went back into her room for a ribbon. Her eyes fell on her jewelry box and her five-strand pearl necklace. She would need money. With shaking hands, she clasped the pearls around her neck and placed diamond earrings in her ears.

Cordelia walked back to the balcony and put one leg over the top of it. She held her breath. Her heart was racing and her hands were sweaty. What if she fell? What if she slipped? She resolved only to think of Stuyvesant. The feel of his finger gently tracing her collarbone until she was weak in the knees. The pressure of his mouth on hers, parting her lips with a gentle lick of his tongue. She could do this for him. Holding on tightly to the material, she lifted her other leg over the balcony to the small ledge on the other side. Gripping the sheet even tighter, she stepped off the ledge.

For a second, she felt weightless.

Finally free.

Her weight pulled against her arms and hands, and she began to slide down the sheets to the first knot, the second knot, and finally to the bottom of the coverlet. Her legs dangled beneath her, not quite far enough to reach the cement sidewalk below. Before she could prepare herself for the drop, her fingers slipped.

Cordelia's feet hit the sidewalk, but the force of the impact caused her to fall forward onto her hands. She took a deep breath and tried to get to her feet, but one of her ankles refused to hold her weight. Both of her hands were scratched and bleeding. She reached for the wrought iron fence and pulled herself to her feet. Shifting her weight onto the foot that wasn't sore, she dragged her other foot behind her and managed to walk around the block and out of sight of her home, when a police officer came up to her. He was a burly man, with a black mustache that reached from one side of his face to the other.

"May I be of assistance, miss?" he said as he looked from her bloodied hands to the fortune around her throat.

"No, thank you, Officer," she said. "I had a little accident is all."

"I'll help you home," he said, and offered her his beefy hand.

"No! No, thank you. I'm perfectly able to take care of myself."

"What's your name, miss?"

"What does it matter?"

The police officer pointed to the pearls on her neck. "You're either a thief or a runaway. Either way, I can't let you go."

"I'm not a thief. My name is Miss Cordelia Jones and I fell on the pavement. My jewels are mine and I have done nothing wrong. You cannot detain me."

"Jones, is it?" he said. "Then your house would be the one just around the block. The Château, isn't it?"

She pointed down the street. "It is, but I am not going home presently. I am visiting Miss Alida Wilson and Miss Julia Wilson. Their home is only three houses away. Much closer than mine."

"But you are going back," the police officer said, and he took her elbow. "Don't make this more difficult than it needs to be, Miss Jones. We will pop round your house and check your story. If everything is how you say it is, then you'll be scot-free to visit whomever you wish."

She limped slowly back to her prison and tried not to cry. The police officer knocked on the door and it was opened by the butler, Mr. Winkworth. If the sight of Cordelia's hands covered in blood and her being accompanied by a police officer surprised him, he showed no sign of it on his stoic face. He held open the door for them and said in his deep voice, "Please come in."

The police officer stepped forward, but Cordelia hesitated. "I do not want to come inside. Mr. Winkworth, tell the police officer who I am."

The butler blinked twice before turning to pull the cord for more servants. He was calling for reinforcements, and once they arrived her chance of escape would be lost.

"Please, sir," Cordelia begged the officer. "They have told you who I truly am. If you must return me to a parent, please take me to my father, Mr. Rowland Jones. Please! Do not leave me here with my mother. I am being locked in like a prisoner."

The burly police officer stepped back from her, unsure of what to do. Cordelia fell to her knees out of desperation and exhaustion. She clasped her sore hands together and begged. "Please! Please help me!"

"Quiet, Cordelia," her mother said sharply.

Her mother walked down the last stair and toward them. She looked beautiful, elegant, and unruffled in a pink afternoon-tea gown that emphasized her tiny waist. "Winkworth and Peter, escort Miss Cordelia back to her room. And Mrs. Rinkhart, see that her injuries are tended to."

Mr. Winkworth and the footman Peter each took one of Cordelia's elbows and lifted her up to her feet. She tried to push them off, even though she did not blame them for their part in her incarceration. The two men were stronger than she, and in less than a minute they had forced her arms down and frog-marched her into the house.

Cordelia's whole body sagged. If she couldn't fight them off, she was not going to walk willingly to her prison. The servants would have to drag her there. Winkworth's and Peter's fingers dug into her arms, but she resisted like a deadweight. Finally, Peter let go of her arm and she crumbled on the stairs.

"Please, Miss Cordelia," he said in an undertone. "I'll lose my position."

Cordelia lifted her head. "I can't walk."

"Then let me carry you."

She nodded in defeat. Peter put one arm underneath her legs and the other around her shoulder, lifting her off the stairs. She closed her eyes as he carried her up the next two flights of stairs to her blue silk room. Peter set her on a chair. Her eyes flickered back open and she saw the butler, Mr. Winkworth, untying her sheets from the balcony.

"Good heavens," Mrs. Rinkhart exclaimed and covered her mouth with her hand. "That's how she got out."

Mr. Winkworth, his face still expressionless, carried the wrinkled sheets. "I'll send up one of the maids to make her bed."

"Very good," Mrs. Rinkhart said, and walked over to the bureau where there was a pitcher of water and a basin. She brought them both over to the chair where Cordelia was sitting. The housekeeper dipped a white cloth into the water and then took Cordelia's right hand and gently began to wipe off the dried blood.

"Do you mind if I look at your legs and feet, Miss Cordelia?" she asked. "So I can ascertain if there are any injuries there."

"I think I might have sprained my ankle."

Mrs. Rinkhart lifted up the now dirty white skirt and tutted over her bruised knees. She then pulled off Cordelia's shoes and stockings, exclaiming when she saw the size and color of Cordelia's left ankle. "Dearie me! How you walked at all on this ankle is beyond me. I'll fetch some cold compresses and send for the doctor. Your ankle might be broken."

The housekeeper stood up, and before she reached the door, it was opened by Cordelia's mother. "How did she get out? Did one of the servants help her? I want that person out of my house at once!"

Mrs. Rinkhart bowed to her mother, shaking her head. "No one helped her, ma'am. Miss Cordelia tied her sheets together and climbed out of the window. Her ankle is either sprained or broken. I am going to get some cold compresses now to reduce the swelling."

"Very good. You may go."

Mrs. Rinkhart bowed once again to her mother and left the room. Her mother looked at the open doors to the balcony and then back at Cordelia.

"I did not expect you to be so obstinate," her mother said in a placating voice. "You've always allowed yourself to be guided by me in the past. I have selected your clothes, your bedroom furnishings, even your friends. Except for Miss Miller, whom you know I disapprove of. But you must trust me once more. I know what will make you happy."

Allowed?!

Cordelia's mother had never given her a choice as a child. Well, she was a child no longer, and she was an adult and would make her own decisions. "Even though you are my mother, you don't care about my happiness. You are selfish. You only care about *your* happiness. About *your* place in society, and I will not be sacrificed for it."

"Then we are much alike, Cordelia, for you only care about yourself. If you cared for your sister or for me, you would marry for our sakes."

"I do not want to get married to anyone yet! I am only eighteen."

Her mother clutched her chest. "I did not think that I raised such an ungrateful, obstinate little beast. But mark my words, you will not leave this room until you do as I say."

Mrs. Rinkhart and the sneering maid re-entered the room. Her mother rounded on them. "She is never to be left alone. Do you understand me?"

"Of course, Mrs. Jones, someone will be with your daughter at all hours of the day."

"The doors to the balcony must be kept locked."

Her last piece of freedom was being taken away.

"Yes, ma'am."

Mrs. Rinkhart took a key off of the chain on her belt and locked the door to the balcony. The maid roughly placed a cold compress onto Cordelia's ankle. Cordelia felt tears of anger and ignominious defeat fall down her hot cheeks. She would not bend to her mother's will. Stuyvesant would arrive home in another month, and he would come for her.

She knew he would.

4

Thomas watched Penelope from the other side of the dinner table. Even dressed in a somber gown of black bombazine she was breathtaking. Her luxurious chestnut curls framed her perfectly oval face. Her large brown eyes, with their thick inky-black lashes, were the stuff of sonnets. Her pale cheeks had only a hint of color, and her pink lips looked soft and inviting. Not that Thomas would know. He'd never kissed her. Never even held her. He was left wondering what might have been.

Did he love her?

Thomas was not sure that he knew what love felt like, but there was a pain in his chest when contemplating what might have been between them. He'd considered leaving without a word. But that was cowardly and he did not wish to be a coward. No, he would do what his father never did. He would face up to his responsibilities and accept the consequences of his actions.

His mother stood up. "Come, Penelope, we will adjourn to the sitting room."

The ladies always left after dinner and the gentlemen drank port and smoked, but it seemed like such a silly protocol when Thomas was the only gentleman present. Penelope stood and gave him a gentle smile—the pain in his chest increased. Thomas found his feet.

"Penelope, might I have a quick word with you, alone?"

Thomas half expected his mother to protest, but instead, she smiled broadly and left the room. His mother thought he was going to propose to Penelope. What a coil he was in! There was nothing left to do but to cut it.

He walked over to where Penelope stood on the other side of the dining room. They were the same age, and for many years they'd been the same height, but now he was a good head taller than she. She'd grown quite lovely in different directions, but he was trying very hard not to notice those tempting additions.

"There is something I need to tell you, Pen."

"You don't need to stand on ceremony with me, Tom," she said, with a smile that nearly did him in. She took his large hand into her two small ones and held it.

"You have always been my greatest friend and my closest companion. It was the wish of my parents that we would someday marry, but it cannot be."

Penelope's face fell. "You do not wish to marry me?"

Thomas exhaled. "It's not that. It's just, Pen…I can't marry you. I have to marry an heiress, or we'll lose everything."

She held his hand tighter. "We could be happy somewhere else. You could sell Ashdown Abbey."

"There is nothing of worth left to sell, and my father's debts are so great that if I don't marry an heiress, I'll be headed to debtor's prison before the year's end."

Penelope finally released her hold. With regret, he let his hand fall to his side. This would be the last time he touched her. When he came back home, he would be a married man.

"My father cheated you of your dowry and I swear that I will repay you every farthing," he said, but she was no longer looking at him but at his feet.

"You mean your wife will provide my dowry."

"Yes."

"Are you to be married soon?"

"I'm leaving for America tomorrow and I won't come back until I have a bride." This time it was Thomas that could not look her in the eye.

And before he knew what she was doing, Penelope pressed her soft pink lips, even softer than he'd expected, to his cheek. "Good-bye, my sweetest Tom."

Then she opened the door and left the room.

"Goodbye, Pen," he whispered, placing a hand against his breast-bone and the tightness there.

5

---

*C*ordelia's French governess, Madame Raubier, brought her breakfast tray every morning. She would stay with her until luncheon, when Frau Gruber, her German governess, arrived. Frau Gruber spoke in German with Cordelia until dinnertime, when either her mother or Mrs. Rinkhart came to sit with her. At bedtime, the sneering maid, Miss Mabel Davis, would come in and sleep on a cot in the corner of the room. She never spoke to Cordelia or even glanced in her direction. But somehow the maid never fell asleep before she did. For whenever Cordelia sat up in her bed, the maid bolted up in her cot and did not lie down again until Cordelia did.

After another week, a small pianoforte was brought to her room so that she could keep up on her music lessons. Music became the only respite for her soul. She played the keys for hours, sorrowing with Chopin, triumphing with Mozart, and despairing with Beethoven. Stuyvesant loved to hear her play and he had a beautiful baritone voice. Occasionally, she could even convince him to sing while she accompanied him. Cordelia squeezed her eyes closed and pictured him standing beside her at the piano.

But when she opened them, he was not there. She slumped in her seat.

One week turned into two weeks. Two weeks became a month. One month became two months, for a total of three months of confinement. But still no word from Stuyvesant. He should have been back from South America already. Why had he not called? Why had he not broken down the front door and come to save her?

Cordelia felt desperate. Unconsciously she bit her fingernails down to the nubs until they bled. But the pricks of pain in her fingertips were nothing on the ache of her heart. She was drowning in feelings of hopelessness. Powerless against the strong wave of her mother's will.

Her mother would not relent.

Her father never visited.

The summer ended and Edith was sent back to school.

Cordelia *had* to get a letter Stuyvesant. Wherever he was in the world, he would come for her if he knew she needed to be saved. He would place his strong arms around her and she could lay her head against his broad chest. Safe at last.

During Madame Raubier's lesson on the history of the French Revolution, she carefully tore a blank page out of her book. Cordelia waited two more days before slipping a pen and inkwell into her pocket while Frau Gruber read Goethe. Frau Gruber asked Cordelia to write an essay about *The Sorrows of Young Werther.*

"I cannot write an essay without a pen."

"*Ich dachte, ich habe einen Stift,*" Frau Gruber said, her plump hands on her ample hips.

"*Nein,*" Cordelia lied. "You didn't give me a pen."

Frau Gruber's eyes looked Cordelia up and down before opening her box and giving her another pen and inkwell. She watched Cordelia write the essay and then carefully counted the papers to ensure that Cordelia had not kept any. Cordelia did not touch the pen or the inkwell in her pocket until Mrs. Rinkhart left and Mabel came into the room. She quickly shoved them both underneath her pillow. Mabel helped Cordelia undress and put on her nightgown.

Cordelia lay down on her satin sheets and watched Mabel take care of her clothing before lying down on her cot.

"Mabel."

"Do you need something, Miss Cordelia?" she asked, a hint of impertinence in her tone.

"I need you to deliver a letter for me."

"I'm afraid that you'll have to ask Mrs. Rinkhart to do that, miss."

Cordelia sat up and like a shadow, so did Mabel. "Tomorrow is your afternoon off, is it not?"

"Yes, miss."

"If you promise to deliver my letter next door, I will give you my diamond earrings."

"If Mrs. Rinkhart or Mrs. Jones find out, I will lose my position."

"My diamond earrings are worth more than you make in a year —ten years, even. You could start a new life with them."

Mabel did not speak for several minutes. Cordelia knew the maid was not asleep, for she was still sitting up in her cot.

"I'll do it, miss."

"Thank you, Mabel." Cordelia leaned back against her pillows and sighed in relief.

She did not sleep well that night and woke up the next morning at sunrise. She took out her stolen pen and ripped piece of paper and began to write:

My dearest Stuyvesant,

You will not believe what I am about to tell you, but please trust that this is no jest. My mother is keeping me locked in my room until I promise to marry an old English lord, but I could never marry another man, when you hold all of my heart. Please come at once, or if you cannot get past the front door, seek help from my father. He has not visited, but I pray he has not completely disowned me. I fear if I stay in this room much longer, I shall run mad. I am growing weak and pale. Please, my dearest friend and darling love, please help me.

Always Yours, Cordelia

She blew on the paper until the ink dried and she folded it up. Corking the ink, she stuffed both underneath her mattress. She tiptoed to the cot and placed the letter in Mabel's hand.

"I'll need the diamond earrings before I'll take this."

"Fine," Cordelia whispered. She tiptoed back across the room and took the diamond earrings from her jewelry box. Her father had given her the earrings for her sixteenth birthday. Back when he still lived at home and loved her.

The sound of footsteps approaching her room brought her back to the present. She dashed back to the cot and handed over the diamond earrings without another word, then rushed back to her bed and crawled into it. She pretended to be asleep, when Madame Raubier entered the room with her breakfast tray, but she couldn't quite suppress a smile on her lips. Her heart beat rapidly and she had to clench her hands to stop them from shaking. It had been several months; Stuyvesant had to be back from South America now and he was going to save her. She knew it.

6

---

*O*liver had been right, Thomas realized as he disembarked
from *Queen Adelaide*. Once the first-class passengers on the
ship had learned that he was the Earl of Farnham, they'd gone out of
their way to befriend him. He'd received Cuban cigars, French
wines, and countless invitations from perfect strangers. The night
before, he'd received card after card with names and addresses.
Every one of them eager to assure him that he'd be most welcome,
should he choose to call on them. He would have been flattered had
he not known that the title was hollow. His estate was in ruins, and
the cash in his pocket was borrowed.

Thayne carried his trunk and Thomas found them a coach for
hire to take them to the Waldorf Hotel on the corner of Fifth
Avenue and Thirty-Third Street. One of his new "friends" had
recommended it. The coach stopped in front of an enormous,
opulent building that rivaled or surpassed any site in London. A
porter ushered him inside to an octagonal room that was as ornate
as a palace. Everyone in the room was dressed finer than he'd ever
seen. The ladies were all dripping in jewels, from their ears to their
necks, to their wrists, to their fingers.

Once again, when Thayne mentioned that Thomas was the Earl

of Farnham, the staff went out of their way to accommodate them. Thomas was led to an elaborate corner suite, with floral wallpaper, cornice moldings, and a painted coffered ceiling. There were chairs, a dining table, and even a piano. The adjacent room had a bed fit for a king and he had his very own bathing room with a water closet. A luxury he'd never before experienced.

"Will these rooms be satisfactory, my lord?" the porter asked.

"Yes, thank you. That will be all."

Once the porter left, Thayne sat down on Thomas's trunk and laughed. Thomas joined in his mirth.

"To think a couple of weeks ago I was mucking out the stalls, and now we're sitting in a grand hotel like blooming kings."

"I did not expect America to be like this."

"Me neither, my lord."

Thomas felt his color rise. "You don't need to call me 'my lord' all the time, Thayne. It wasn't that long ago that we played together as children."

Thayne stood up, as if recalling his duty. "But we grew up, my lord. You are no longer Master Thomas and I'm not Edwin, the gamemaster's son. And thanks to you, I am an upper servant and ever so grateful to be called Mr. Thayne, or simply Thayne. Most blokes have to work for years before they reach my current station."

"Of course, Thayne. I meant no offense."

His old friend almost smiled. "You're just not used to being an earl yet, my lord. But I'm sure and certain that you'll learn your place, just like I've learned mine."

Thomas nodded. "Will you prepare my tan suit, Thayne? I have some calls to make this afternoon."

"Yes, my lord," Thayne said, and took the trunk to the bedroom and began unpacking it.

Thomas washed his face and hands in a sink with running water. What luxury! After, he took out the letters of introduction from his cousin's wife, Lois. There were four of them: Mrs. Astor, Mrs. Vanderbilt, Mrs. Fish, and Mrs. Jones. He rested while Thayne meticulously pressed his clothes and prepared his shoes. He needed to look his best if he was going to make the right impression; everything was riding on his ability to find a rich wife.

He visited Mrs. Astor first, for her house (mansion, really) was across the street from the hotel. He gave a servant the letter, and it was a few minutes before he was ushered into a room where a middle-aged woman sat. He bowed to her and made polite conversation. She asked searching questions about his title, his estate, and his ancestry. Thomas glided over the details of his father's death as he fidgeted with his hands. He didn't need all of New York society to know that his father had committed suicide.

Mrs. Vanderbilt's mansion was even more opulent than Mrs. Astor's, as were her cold manners. Mrs. Fish was the kindest of the three and asked him to attend a party she was hosting the very next day.

The last house, Mrs. Jones's, looked out of place in New York City. It was just as large as the other mansions on Fifth Avenue, but the architecture resembled a French château on a taller and narrower scale. There were towers and gables, with Victorian gingerbread trim on the roofs and balconies. It reminded him of a castle in a fairytale.

The butler took Thomas into a sitting room that was positively crowded with overstuffed pieces of furniture. He took a seat on a chair that was trimmed in gold. He didn't have to wait long before Mrs. Jones came into the room. Even though she had to be close to twice his age, she was beautiful. It was impossible not to stare at her flawless face and the ruby choker at her throat. Matching ruby earrings hung from her ears, dripped from her wrists, and dotted her fingers. Thomas remembered to stand up. He did so awkwardly and bowed to this woman who wore more jewels than a queen.

"Lord Farnham, I am so glad you called."

"Mrs. Jones, I am pleased to make your acquaintance."

"Please sit down, my lord."

Thomas sat on the edge of his chair. With the other New York matrons, he'd felt at ease. Much like he was talking to his mother, but this shapely woman did not remind him of his mother at all. He glanced nervously out the window.

"What drew you to New York, my lord?"

Thomas glanced at his hands before he looked up at her face. "I'm only here for a visit."

Mrs. Jones gave him a warm smile. "How long do you mean to stay?"

"That is…I…I'm not sure how long I will stay…I'm hoping to… um…make new acquaintances. Lois—Lady Rutledge is my cousin's wife, and she suggested that I make the trip."

"Your cousin is Lord Rutledge?"

"It is an honorary title," Thomas admitted, fiddling with his hands. "My cousin Oliver Keeler is the heir to the Duke of Oxenbury, and so he carries his father's secondary title, the Earl of Rutledge."

"She will be a duchess someday, then. How delightful. I suppose the Oxenbury estate is quite large?"

"Very. My uncle's main seat is Birkhall Palace in Norfolk, but he owns several other smaller estates."

"And what is your estate called?"

"Ash-Ashdown Abbey."

"An abbey? How fascinating. It must be a building of great antiquity."

"My ancestor purchased it from King Henry VIII. Although there have been more recent additions to the building."

Mrs. Jones gave a high, false laugh. "I should hope so. I doubt you wish to live as a monk."

"No. No. I am very fond of young ladies… I mean I hope to make many new acquaintances during my visit."

Her smile widened. "Well, I am delighted to be one of your new acquaintances, and I should like to introduce you to my daughter Cordelia. She is about your same age."

"I should like very much to meet your daughter," Thomas said, and he was telling the truth. If the daughter was half as pretty as the mother, he would count himself lucky. And he did not need to ask what the daughter's dowry was to know that the Joneses were dripping in dollars. Everything about the house was as expensive as it was ostentatious.

"I am sure she will be just as eager to meet you, Lord Farnham. Perhaps you could grace us with your presence for dinner tomorrow night?"

"I'm afraid I already have a previous commitment with Mrs. Fish."

"The day after?"

Thomas felt himself blush. "I am engaged for that evening with Mrs. Astor."

Her studied smile faltered. "Lord Farnham, may I be frank with you?"

"Of course, ma'am."

"I am eager to see my daughter well married to a man of character and consequence such as yourself," Mrs. Jones said.

Thomas did not know how to respond to such bluntness. "I-I-I am flattered, ma'am."

"My daughter's dowry is two million dollars," she said, folding her arms. "And I will continue to give her a yearly allowance of twenty-five thousand dollars to pay for her clothes and pocket money."

Two million dollars, plus twenty-five thousand dollars a year in pocket money? Thomas clenched his teeth to keep his jaw from dropping. These sums were beyond his wildest dreams. "You are very generous."

"Let us not beat around the bush. Do we have a bargain?"

Thomas blinked. "Excuse me?"

"Will you marry my daughter Cordelia?"

"I have not even met her."

"That is of little consequence. Will you marry her in exchange for the terms which I have stated?"

A silent debate raged inside of him. He was unlikely to find such favorable terms from another American heiress. But he'd never even met the girl. Was something wrong with her? Was she simple?

Or shrewish? Or unattractive? Why else would her mother refuse to even let him see her first?

Did it even matter? He'd hoped to find someone whom he could like—a friend. But how could he love her, when his heart was already full of Penelope?

Penelope.

His mother.

Mr. Hibbert.

Mrs. Cook.

Mrs. Norton.

Mr. Thayne.

And all the other servants and tenants were depending on him to save their homes. He couldn't afford to be fastidious. "I would be most honored to marry your daughter, if she is willing to marry me."

Mrs. Jones gave him a glittering smile. "I shall have my lawyers call on you at the Waldorf Hotel in the morning to go over the particulars and to sign the papers regarding the financial aspect of our agreement."

Thomas swallowed and began to cough. He cleared his throat. "Excellent."

"Shall we plan on a November wedding?"

November was only a little over a month away. Thomas could hardly believe his good fortune. He would be back in England before the year was over. He'd not only be able to pay the mortgage bills but pay them off. He could afford to hire enough staff to properly take care of the house, the stables, and the gardens. He'd be able to hire a foreman to repair the house, with plenty of money afterward to buy books and start a new library.

"A November wedding would be perfect, ma'am."

"Then I will send out the invitations immediately and notify the newspapers," Mrs. Jones said as she stood. She held out her gloved hand and Thomas eagerly kissed it.

7

*T*wo weeks passed since Cordelia gave Mabel the letter, but there was still no sign of Stuyvesant. He must not be in New York City. The letter had probably been forwarded to him at Harvard. Surely he would have started the fall term already. That was why he was taking so long to come. He hadn't received it yet— or he was on his way. She pictured him bouncing his knee impatiently as he sat in the first-class car on the train. Eager to get to her as quickly as possible.

She wished he was already here, and not even Chopin's preludes could console her. Frau Gruber yelled at her in German more than once to pay attention, but her mind kept wandering past the walls of her house. Peter brought in her dinner tray, followed by her mother. Frau Gruber bowed and excused herself. Peter set the tray on the table before leaving the room.

"This has gone on for long enough," her mother said through clenched teeth. "It has been nearly five months."

It felt like an eternity.

"I will not marry without love."

"Love," she scoffed. "You know nothing of love. You think your childish infatuation with Stuyvesant Bradley is going to last?"

"Y-yes," Cordelia said, but her stomach flip-flopped and she felt a flicker of doubt. Why had he not come for her already?

"He's already forgotten you," her mother said with a cruel laugh. "His newest love is sailing and his father bought him a yacht. He left this morning for a trip to the Middle East and will be gone for the rest of the year. Mrs. Bradley called yesterday to tell me how he's taking a year off from university."

"You're lying," Cordelia said, swallowing heavily. But the expression on her mother's face was not one of deceit but of triumph. Her mother smiled like a cat licking cream from a bowl. Cordelia's insides crumpled as she sat down. Her heart and lungs seemed to have fallen to the bottom of her stomach. Still, she did not want to believe it: her handsome prince was not coming to save her.

"Men are such changeable creatures. You of all people should know that. Your father's proclivities with females of a certain class…"

"Stuyvesant isn't like Father."

Or is he? a small voice said from the back of her head. He had abandoned her just like her father had. Was his love for her so weak that it could not withstand five months? Had he met someone new?

"Then, why hasn't he come to visit you?" her mother pressed. "Why haven't any of your friends come to visit you?"

Her friends *had* visited, but her mother had turned them all away. She wondered how many mornings Lucy had walked by at precisely ten o'clock before she realized that Cordelia was no longer able to come out onto the balcony and wave to her. A week? Two?

Cordelia stood and walked over to the locked door that led to the balcony. "It's not my fault if they haven't visited. It's yours and Father's. You have disgraced our family. Made us all figures for public ridicule. You've dragged our family name through the courts and the papers, and if I am friendless, it is your fault."

"I know it is and I am giving you a chance to make it right again, for all of us. For yourself. Your sister. For me. Even for your father… Please, my darling daughter. Trust me once more."

For eighteen years Cordelia had tried to please her mother, but it had never been enough. She was never pretty enough. Smart enough. Or good enough. Cordelia used to believe that her mother was hard on her because she wanted her to be strong like her. But she finally realized, after her many months of incarceration, that her mother did not want her to be strong. She wanted to subjugate Cordelia to her own will.

Cordelia looked down at the locked doors in front of her. She couldn't live like this any longer. She couldn't be a prisoner in her own home. If she pretended to be willing, her mother would let her leave her room. The house. She could get help from her father. Or perhaps an aunt or an uncle. Surely her mother hadn't found an English lord already. And even if she had, their engagement would be for at least a year, possibly two or three.

"All right," she whispered.

"My darling girl," her mother said, and embraced her. Cordelia felt as stiff as a stone column. Her body refused to respond. Her mother stepped away.

"May I leave my room now?"

"Yes, of course."

Cordelia sprinted to the door of the room, opened it, and ran into the footman, Peter, who was standing in front of the door. He turned toward her but did not stop blocking her way.

"Peter, Miss Cordelia is now allowed to leave her room," her mother said from behind her.

The footman stepped aside and apologized. Cordelia ran down the hall, out of breath after only a few hobbled steps. Her broken ankle was slow to heal. She carefully walked down each stair. She twirled around in the great entry and was about to leap into the ballroom, when she saw an enormous stack of letters. They were small envelopes that appeared to be acceptance cards. Was her mother having a party? Perhaps a come-out ball for Cordelia?

Her curiosity overcame her and she walked over and picked one up. She wasn't surprised to see Mr. Jacob Astor's letter on top. The seal was already broken. Cordelia took out the small card and read:

Mr. Jacob Astor and his wife would be delighted to attend your daughter's wedding...

Shocked, she dropped the letter. She fell down to her knees to pick it back up and continued to read:

...in New York Grace Church on November 9, 1893.

She was to be married in less than three weeks to a complete stranger. Her mother had outmaneuvered her again. All hopes of going to university faded.

"So, you've seen your wedding invitation," her mother said. "They turned out rather well."

Cordelia glanced up at her mother in disbelief. "You can't make me marry him. I won't say yes."

"You already promised to marry the man of my choice."

She crushed the invitation in her hand like her mother had crushed her dreams. "How can I marry someone that I haven't even met?"

Her mother folded her arms. "Easily. If you met him, you would only beg him to end the engagement, which I will not have."

"But what will I have?" she asked, her voice close to tears.

"A second chance," her mother said. "You had better take it, for society will not give you a third."

Cordelia had escaped one jailer only to be consigned to another.

8

$\mathcal{T}$he morning of her wedding arrived and Cordelia could not stop crying. She curled up in a ball on her bed and refused to allow Mabel to dress her. She wished she could hold Stuyvesant's hand and that he would comfort and protect her; but he had not come.

"Please, Miss Cordelia," Mabel pleaded. "Mr. Jones has arrived. It's time for you to go to the church. You're going to be late for your own wedding."

"I don't care."

Mabel muttered something that Cordelia couldn't understand and she left her room. A few minutes later her mother arrived.

"Cordelia, get up this instant!"

Her body responded out of habit.

"Come, Mrs. Rinkhart, bring the dress in," her mother commanded. "Mabel, take off her nightdress and help her into new underclothes. Cordelia, if you will not help, you can at least hold still."

They stripped off her clothes and put on her new lace lingerie. Then they tied her corset so tightly that Cordelia gasped for air. The maids took the wedding dress from Mrs. Rinkhart and carefully put it on her. The sleeves were puffed and tightened at her wrists. The neck was high and choked her. Cordelia could barely breathe. The gown's bodice was made from Brussels lace and there was a full satin skirt. The train was over five feet long and embellished with real silver and seed pearls. The dress was exquisite. If only it didn't mean that her life would be over.

Her mother directed her to sit down, then clasped her five-strand pearls around her neck. Mabel plaited her hair and twisted it up into a bun on the top of her head, leaving only a few short curls around Cordelia's face. Mrs. Rinkhart brought in a wreath of orange blossoms and carefully placed it on Cordelia's head. She smiled at Cordelia, with tears in her eyes as she patted her hands.

"I always knew you'd be a beautiful bride, Miss Cordelia."

"Thank you, Mrs. Rinkhart," she said with a choked voice. The housekeeper was the only person who had ever told Cordelia that she was beautiful. The only person who had ever shown any affection for Cordelia without expecting something in return.

When Cordelia was a little girl, she'd called her "Rink" and Mr. Winkworth "Wink." She would miss both Rink and Wink more than she'd miss her own mother and father. They had been the only constants in her life.

"Don't dawdle, Mrs. Rinkhart," her mother snapped. "Help me put on the tulle veil. We are unconscionably late already. I only hope that Lord Farnham doesn't leave before we get there."

Cordelia sincerely wished that he would.

Mrs. Rinkhart and her mother carefully arranged her long white veil, while Mabel and Cynthia each took a hand and pulled on the tight white gloves. They then put on her stockings, attaching them with golden garters, and then her slippers. It seemed like everyone in the room was pulling and tugging at her from different directions.

Her mother took her elbow and helped her to her feet. "Your father is waiting outside. Edith and I will follow in the carriage behind you."

Cordelia took one step and then another. Even walking felt

surreal. As if it was all some elaborate nightmare and she was her mother's puppet. They walked out of her room. Peter was still standing guard by her door; her mother wanted to make sure she didn't run. But Cordelia had nowhere to run to. Mrs. Rinkhart followed behind them, holding the bottom of her long train as they stepped down the grand staircase.

Edith stood waiting in the entry, tapping her little boot impatiently, her golden curls surrounding her angelic face. She wore a peach-colored dress with a high lacy neck. The shade should not have suited her, but it did. In her gloved hands, she held flowers. She gave Cordelia the bouquet of orchids and whispered, "My friends say that he's only marrying you for your money. Is that true, Cordy?"

Cordelia swallowed painfully. "You look very beautiful, Edith."

"Your dress is very pretty, too, but your face is all red and puffy," she said in brutal, childish honesty.

"Quiet, Edith!" their mother commanded. "Cynthia, get a sponge for her eyes, and Mabel, bring some more powder for Miss Cordelia's face. Immediately!"

Mrs. Rinkhart carefully raised Cordelia's veil. She took the sponge from Cynthia and gently wiped away Cordelia's tears. Next, Mabel brushed the white powder underneath Cordelia's blood-shot eyes.

"That'll have to do," her mother snapped and pulled the veil back over Cordelia's face. "Hurry. We are so late!"

Mr. Winkworth held the front door and as Cordelia passed, he gave her a warm smile. Peter opened the door to her father's carriage and helped her inside to the seat next to him. Mrs. Rinkhart carefully handed up the train so that it wouldn't get dirty from the pavement. Peter closed the door and the carriage jerked forward. She looked at her father. He smiled at her. He was wearing a black top hat and a long black coat, with a peach bowtie that was the same color as Edith's dress. He looked much too young and handsome to be having a daughter getting married.

"Please, Father," Cordelia said, taking his arm in both of her hands. "I do not want to marry the Earl of Farnham. Mother is forcing me to. Please, you must help me. You are my father. Please put a stop to this."

Her father patted her hand. "This marriage is for your own good, Cordy. If we were to jilt him now, you would have no hope of finding an eligible connection."

"I don't want to find an eligible connection. I am only eighteen, Father. All I want to do is go to college at Oxford. I don't want to go live in some country estate in the middle of nowhere."

He squeezed her hand. "Country life is rather tedious. Say, I'll purchase you a nice house in London for a wedding present. How does that sound?"

Cordelia shook her head and bit back another wave of tears. "I do not want your money. I want your help!"

"This is only a case of pre-wedding jitters," he said calmly, as if she hadn't spoken. "Even your mother cried a few tears before our wedding."

It was no use talking to her father. He thought a present could solve any problem. He'd never stood up to her mother when they were married, and now that they were divorced, she doubted he'd ever side with his daughter against his former wife. Her father would always take the easiest approach. The one that caused him the least amount of effort or discomfort. He didn't care about her. Not really. Not beyond giving her money.

The carriage pulled up in front of the church, where crowds of spectators stood waiting and watching. She saw women pushing each other to get a closer look. A man lifted his daughter onto his shoulders so that she could see Cordelia, the newest cash countess. Cordelia didn't smile. She didn't wave. She allowed the footman to help her from the carriage. Her father took her arm and they walked into the church.

9

Once she and her father entered the church, Cordelia was ushered into a side room. She had barely stepped through the door, when she was hugged by three different people at the same time. All of whom were wearing that same unflattering shade of peach. Her mother must have chosen it so that her attendants did not outshine her at the wedding. Not even Alida, the beauty of their group, looked well in it.

"Why did you not return my letters?" Lucy demanded, her voice on the edge of tears.

"We've been so worried about you," Julia said with a sniff.

"Why wouldn't you see us?" Alida demanded. "I nearly raced up the stairs to your room to see you."

Cordelia bit her lip to try to keep in her own tears. She hugged her friends tightly and shook her head. "My mother wouldn't let me. I've been a prisoner in my house for nearly six months. There was always a servant at my door who kept me from leaving."

She sniffed as she looked at Lucy. "I have never received even one of your letters, and I was not allowed any paper to write to you."

How she wished that she would have sent the letter to Lucy for help, instead of Stuyvesant. Her father was one of the richest and most powerful businessmen in the world.

Lucy threw her arms around Cordelia again and squeezed her tightly. "I never doubted you for a moment. For weeks, no matter the weather, I have walked by your house every day at ten o'clock, hoping to see you again."

"I tried to escape from the balcony like a fairytale, but I twisted my ankle and was caught."

"Brilliant!" Alida said, and then her eyes widened. "Not brilliant that you were caught, but brilliant that you escaped."

"Is your mother forcing you into this marriage?" Julia asked.

Cordelia couldn't speak; all she could do was nod. If she spoke, tears would begin to stream from her eyes again.

"She can't do that," Lucy insisted. "You are eighteen years old. You are an adult."

But Lucy knew as well as Cordelia how little power an unmarried young woman had. Lucy was forced to live with Mrs. Stewart, who was cold and uncaring but undoubtedly respectable. Something Lucy's birth mother, the famous opera singer, was most certainly not. Both young women were subject to the whims of their wealthy parents.

Julia placed a reassuring hand on Cordelia's shoulder. "All you have to do is say no during the ceremony. The bishop is a man of God. He will not let them force you."

"Why wait for the ceremony?" Alida insisted. "Let's all escape now in our carriage. It would serve that uppity English lord right, as well as your harpy of a mother."

"Alida!" Julia said in shocked accents. "You shouldn't say that about her mother."

"Well, it is true," Cordelia said.

Julia covered her mouth with her hand, and Alida and Lucy laughed loudly. Cordelia even managed a half smile.

"Should we go out the window and give those newspaper reporters a really great story?" Alida asked. "Or go the more conventional way through the door and then burst from the church at a run, all four of us holding hands?"

Lucy pointed out the window. "It will be hard to escape with the crowd out there."

Cordelia's eyes followed her finger. The crowd had trebled in size since she had left the carriage. She watched police officers in their bowler hats try to keep the spectators off the stairs of the church. Their carriages were completely surrounded by people of all classes. Everyone wanted a glimpse of an American princess, but she was nothing more than a prisoner. Foolishly, she still hoped to see Stuyvesant in the crowd—rushing to save her. But she did not recognize his tall, broad frame. The painful ache in her chest for the last three weeks dulled to numbness. He hadn't truly loved her after all.

"Oh dear!" Julia said, shaking her head.

"They'll make way for us," Alida insisted. "And if they don't, I will push our way through the crowd. I am not afraid."

Cordelia didn't doubt it. Alida might be fashionably slim, but she was tall and strong. Always the best at any sport.

"I would be ruined if I ran," Cordelia said, touching her puffy, swollen cheeks. "This is my second chance to rejoin society."

Alida folded her arms and huffed. "Ruined is better than being married to a complete stranger."

"Will I be ruined too?"

They all turned around to see that Edith had entered the small room. Cordelia could tell that her sister was trying to act like a grown-up, but her lower lip trembled.

"Why would you be ruined, Edith?"

Her little sister sniffed, but two tears fell from her angelic blue eyes. "Mama said that if you don't marry the English earl, our family will never be able to go out in public again... Is that true, Cordy? Will I lose all my friends? Will I have to come home from school?"

Cordelia hated both of her parents equally in that moment. She hated her father for his affairs. She hated her mother for making Cordelia pay the price for both of her parents' sins. She wanted nothing more than to run away with her friends, but like herself, Edith was blameless. But New York society, particularly the *Four Hundred*, did not care about the truth. Or about a little girl's feelings. They were quick to gossip, to scorn, and to exclude.

She no longer cared if they snubbed her. Her friends, her true friends, still loved her. They would stand beside her, no matter what her decision was. All but Stuyvesant. He had proven not to be a true friend or a true prince. He hadn't loved her enough.

Cordelia wrapped her arms around her little sister and pulled her close. "I love you and I promise that you will never be ruined."

"But—" Alida began, and her mother walked into the room.

"Why are you not ready, Cordelia?" she demanded and then turned to her friends. "You are her attendants. Why have you not put on her veil and arranged her train?"

Lucy looked to Cordelia for guidance. Cordelia nodded slightly. She was marrying for love after all—the love she felt for her little sister.

Julia and Lucy gently picked up her long veil and covered Cordelia's face. They each took a side of her gown and made sure that every ruffle and flounce was perfect all the way down to the lace on the back of the train. Alida kept her arms folded across her flat chest and glared at them mulishly, but she didn't say anything.

"I suppose you want Lucy to go first," her mother said.

"Yes," Cordelia said.

Lucy would be her first attendant.

"I shall go last," Alida said. "And if you should change your mind, I'll happily hold your train and run out the door with you."

"Miss Wilson, that is quite enough," her mother said sharply. "But as you wish, your sister will be second, and you shall be third in the procession."

Her mother handed each of her friends a large bouquet of flowers from the table and ushered them out of the room. In the vestibule, there were three gentlemen waiting to offer their arms. She recognized Mr. Fish, Mr. Schermerhorn, and Mr. McAllister. They were all very eligible and wealthy young men. She watched her friends each take an arm. Then her mother took Edith by the shoulders and steered her to a young man about the same age. His face was covered in red spots. He didn't look pleased to be touching a girl or to be taking part in Cordelia's wedding.

Once her mother had ascertained that everything and everyone was exactly as it should be, she entered the chapel. She was the last guest.

A few moments later, she heard the organ start to play and the choir begin to sing.

"Ready?" her father asked, offering his arm.

Unable to find words, Cordelia placed her hand in the crook of his elbow. Matching-height footmen opened the double doors. Edith and the spotted boy went first. Followed by Lucy, Julia, and then Alida and their escorts.

"Everything will be fine," her father whispered and patted her gloved hand with his.

They walked slowly down the aisle. New York's Grace Church's pews were filled with the elite of the *Four Hundred*. Their family was back in its place at the height of society. The chapel was decorated with more white flowers than a garden and green palms that were forty feet high.

She listened to the choir sing:

O perfect Love, all human thought transcending,
Lowly we kneel in prayer before thy throne,
That theirs may be the love which knows no ending,
Whom thou in sacred vow dost join in one.

Cordelia had to purse her lips to stop herself from laughing hysterically. "O Perfect Love" was a perfect farce.

Lord Farnham stood at the front of the chapel next to the bishop. He looked younger, slimmer, and paler than she had expected. Not at all like Stuyvesant. The lord couldn't be more than few years older than she, and he appeared to be as miserable as she was. His brown hair was slicked back and his face clean-shaven. He

53

wasn't precisely handsome, but his features weren't unattractive. As they walked closer, she could see that his eyes were the pale brown of an acorn. They raked over her face and form. He must have liked what he saw, for he offered her a thin-lipped smile. Cordelia could not return it.

What sort of man marries a stranger for money? Someone he has never seen?

A despicable one.

Her father stopped and Cordelia's heart fell to her feet. The Bishop of New York began the ceremony and his sermon on marriage. Cordelia kept glancing over her shoulder, hoping Stuyvesant had come to help her escape. But he was probably on the other side of the world and she couldn't escape from who she was. Not from this. Not without ruining her sister and her family's reputation.

A tear slipped down her cheek.

And then another.

Until a steady stream of tears fell from her eyes.

"Do you, Cordelia Violet Jones, take this man to be thy lawfully wedded husband, to have and to hold from this day forward, for better, for worse, for richer, for poorer, in sickness and in health, until death do you part?" the bishop asked.

She looked at her father, who smiled back at her, and then to her mother, who sat in the first row, her face stern. Finally to Edith, who sat beside her mother. Cordelia could do this for Edith.

"I do," she whispered.

The Bishop of New York asked the pale earl the same question.

He did not hesitate before saying, "I do."

"Forasmuch as the bride and the groom have consented together in holy matrimony, and have pledged their love and loyalty to each other, and have declared the same by the joining and the giving of rings, by the power vested in me, and as witnessed by friends and family, I now pronounce you husband and wife."

The organist began to play and the choir started to sing "Bind Us Together."

The earl lifted her veil and leaned in to kiss her briefly, dispassionately on her mouth. His lips were dry and chapped. It was not at all like the magical kisses she'd shared with Stuyvesant. But this man was not her handsome prince. He was a stranger and she was bound to him for the rest of her life.

She tried to breathe in, but there was no air in her lungs. Her corset was so tight. Dropping her bouquet of orchids as her knees buckled, she started to fall. The chapel spun into darkness. Her last thought was that she hoped her exquisite dress wouldn't get dirty when her body hit the floor.

$\mathcal{T}$homas thought that nothing could be worse than marrying a stranger. He'd been wrong. Attending a wedding reception without a wife was infinitely worse. Standing in the opulent grandeur of the Joneses' ballroom, he was forced to smile while complete strangers said, "You sly, British dog, snatching her up before she'd even come out."

He didn't know that she hadn't been *out*. That he was marrying a girl from the schoolroom or nursery, depending on whom he spoke to. He forced himself to give civil responses and shake hands. Mrs. Jones stood next to him, all smiles, seemingly unconcerned that her daughter was unwell upstairs.

His *wife*.

Cordelia Violet Jones had not been what he expected. He didn't know what he had expected, but not a beautiful, tear-stained young woman. Mrs. Jones had insisted that he not meet Cordelia before the wedding, and he was too desperate for their money to protest. He felt like a villain in a melodrama taking advantage of an innocent girl. He should have stopped the wedding, or at least paused it, and asked Cordelia what she wanted. But he hadn't. Shame burned through his soul as he forced his gaze away from her and clenched his fists until his fingernails made crescents on his palm. He made himself think of Ashdown Abbey. Of the people who needed him —of Pen.

He sacrificed himself, and this stranger, for them.

Thomas walked away from his mother-in-law and took a flute of champagne from a servant's tray. He sipped it, but it didn't calm the roiling in his stomach. He heard his new father-in-law laugh across the crowded ballroom. Neither of her parents seemed particularly concerned that their daughter had fainted and had remained unconscious for several minutes.

Thomas weaved his way out of the room and walked up the stairs. He needed to check on Cordelia and make sure she was okay. To balm his guilty conscience.

He met a maid on the stairs and blushed as he asked which room was his wife's. The maid led him up a second flight of stairs and opened the door to a room. He walked in to see that the walls were made of blue silk. The room was circular and fit for a princess. She wasn't in her bed, but the doors to the balcony were open and she was sitting on the floor, with her knees tucked against her. Her long, silky hair was loose, falling past her waist and brushing the floor. That was when he realized that she was only wearing a chemisette. He forced his eyes to look away from her, wondering why the maid had let him in when she was undressed. Then he remembered that they were married.

"I only wanted to make sure you were okay," he said quietly, the sick feeling returning to his stomach. "I didn't mean to intrude upon your privacy. I will leave, if you'd like."

"No," she said in a loud voice that caused him to jump a little.

Thomas heard her light footsteps on the marble floor. She stood in front of him, with a three-inch, steel-tipped, pointed umbrella in her hand. She brandished it like a sword. He couldn't look away. She stared at him fearlessly—audaciously. She was gorgeous, like Venus or Diana.

"If you touch me, I will kill you."

"I am not here to claim my husbandly rights. I only came to see if

57

you were feeling better," he said, his face hot, and he held his hands up. "I was worried about you."

"Why? You don't even know me," she said, and pressed the pointy end of the umbrella against a button on his black suitcoat. It made a clicking sound.

"Because you are my-my wife."

She finally blinked, as if trying to refocus her understanding of him. "What do you want from me?"

"Nothing," he said quickly, casting his eyes to the floor. They were still strangers. They needed to get to know each other first. Cordelia was clearly not sweet and compliant like Pen, who he'd known all of his life. She was a complex stranger, with her own mind and heart, whom he had only met that very day. And he'd married her. It was utter madness, but there was no going back now. He had to find some way to form a relationship with her.

"Perfect. Because *nothing* is all you are going to get from me."

He looked up at her. Behind her fierce bravado he saw a scared young woman. He felt a surge of pity for her. "I want to be your friend."

"Friend?" she said with obvious sarcasm. Her eyebrows raised, but she finally lowered her umbrella sword.

Thomas cleared his throat. "We are about to spend the rest of our lives together... I think it will be easier if we were friendly partners."

He didn't want her to be scared of him. He wanted to be her friend and someday (hopefully sooner than later) her lover and her husband.

"Lord Farnham, to be friendly partners—"

"Call me Thomas," he said, offering his hand.

She didn't take it. "Thomas, if you try to kiss my hand, I'll blacken your eye."

A laugh burst out of him. He liked her. He hadn't expected that. Nor had he planned on being attracted to his wife, but from his body's rising temperature, he undoubtedly was. "May I at least shake your hand? Americans seem to shake hands excessively."

"If we are to be friends, we must promise to always tell each other the truth," she said.

"I promise."

Cordelia at last held out her hand and squeezed his hand tightly, as if trying to hurt him. "And I promise to tell you the truth, no matter how painful."

"No matter how painful."

She released her viselike grip on his hand and he shook out his fingers. "Have you ever been in love, Thomas?"

He felt himself blushing. He thought of Penelope's beautiful face. "I am not sure if this is the best topic for our wedding day."

"You promised to always tell me the truth."

He stepped back from her intensity. From her voluptuous and scantily clad body. "There is—was—someone whom I admired greatly, but after my father died, leaving me his debts, I had no other choice but to find an..."

"Heiress," she finished for him. "There's always a choice, Thomas. Even if it is a painful one."

"Yes, there is always a choice," he admitted, feeling sheepish and half relieved that his body was cooling down. "My choice would have affected more than simply me: my family, my servants, and my tenants all depend on me—I could not fail them... Have you ever been in love, Cordelia?"

"Yes, to a young man I've known all of my life."

An impossible jealousy filled his heart. He hated this unknown man who held his wife's heart. "Does he not return your affections?"

She shrugged her bare shoulders. "He said he did, but then he left and my mother forced me to marry you."

The burden of guilt he carried seemed to double with these words, taking away the sting of his jealousy. He wanted to apologize but then realized she too had said yes at the chapel. "Like you said, there's always a choice, and our choices have been made. Can't we make the best of it?"

"Honestly, Thomas," she whispered. "I don't know if I can, but I'll do my best."

"I promise that I will do everything in my power to be a good husband to you. To be faithful to you. To be a good partner," he said. "And you'll be a countess."

"You can call me The Cash Countess," Cordelia said with a wry smile.

Her smile filled him with a spark of hope. Maybe they could be friends and their friendship would grow into something more. He returned her smile. "I'd prefer that you didn't call me The Indebted Earl."

"The Ignominious Earl?" she suggested.

He laughed softly. "Please no."

"I'll try, Thomas," she said in a voice barely above a whisper. "I can only promise you that I'll try to be your friend."

"Thank you. Do you want to go down to our wedding reception?"

"Dressed like this?"

Blast. He was staring at her again. "Most people have already seen your gold-embroidered undergarments."

She gasped.

He blushed and managed to turn his eyes away from her. "I-I-I thought you knew. All the New York papers published pictures of your trousseau, including your undergarments and diamond-studded garters."

"My mother," she said, shaking her head. "She must have leaked them to the papers. She revels in attention."

"I'll send a maid in, and I can wait in the hall for you to change," he said, still averting his gaze from temptation. "Then we could go down to the party together?"

"Together."

Thomas left her room and walked down the hall. He saw the same maid who had directed him to Cordelia's room. He asked if she would go help his wife dress. The girl blushed and nodded.

He sat on a chair. Leaning back, he tried to think of very cold things. Like ice. The artic. His wife.

Thomas couldn't help but wonder if he'd made the wrong choice after all. Ashdown Abbey was saved and he could restore the estate to its former glory, but the cost was higher than he'd reckoned with. He was now tied irrevocably to a person that he did not love and who was in love with another man. At least he was attracted to her —no, he wouldn't think about that now.

Ice.

And fire.

What a mismatched pair they were: the heiress and the fortune hunter. The old world and the new.

11

*T*hrough the frosted carriage window he could see Ashdown Abbey—home. Thomas hadn't realized how much he'd missed it or how truly beautiful it was. The month of January had decked it with a beautiful coating of snow, hiding most of its flaws. He was glad that they'd been in no rush to arrive back to England.

"Is that it?" Cordelia asked, pointing to Ashdown in the distance.

"Yes, it is."

"What a pretty prospect," she said.

But to Thomas's ears it sounded like faint praise. He wanted her to understand how incredible Ashdown truly was. That preserving the abbey was worth the sacrifices that they both had made for it.

"One hundred years ago, a famous architect named Capability Brown redirected a river to create Ashdown Pond," Thomas explained, like a tour guide. "It's L-shaped, which makes it appear endless from the house."

"How interesting," Cordelia said in a dull tone that suggested she found mud as fascinating as his home.

"I am afraid the closer we get, the less nice the house will be. But

I promise that I will do everything I can to bring it up to your standards."

She shook her head. "I'm not sure if you can."

He turned to her and saw that she was smiling—teasing him. Despite their long trip across the Atlantic Ocean, he still hadn't completely understood her sense of humor. He had to stop thinking of her mocking mouth. He hadn't kissed her since their wedding and it hadn't been much of a kiss. She kept him an arm's length away from her, but at least she hadn't skewered him with her umbrella.

Yet.

But they had become friends. Which meant that she loved to tease him and he was learning her style of humor.

"My standards are exceptionally high," Cordelia declared. "Nothing short of a seven-hundred-year-old abbey, complete with a ghost, will meet them."

"We have a monk."

"How very Catholic of you."

Thomas laughed, shaking his head. "No, no. I mean we have a ghost called the monk that is said to haunt the family rooms."

"I am shivering already," she said with another mocking smile. "Why does the monk haunt the abbey?"

Thomas leaned in and spoke in a conspiratorial whisper. "Tradition has it that the monk lived in the abbey, when King Henry VIII sold it to my ancestor. The monk refused to leave his home. He said, 'Over my dead body.' So, the king's soldiers killed him."

She wrinkled her nose. "That is rather dreadful."

"Yes, and what's worse, they never gave him a proper burial, so he wanders around the abbey without any peace."

Her eyes widened, as did her smile. "Have you ever seen the monk?"

"Can't say I have, but Pen—Miss Hutchinson used to swear she could feel his cold fingers on her shoulders."

"How delightfully horrifying," Cordelia said with a giggle. "I suppose I asked for it. Although, I should have preferred a female ghost."

Thomas wrung his hands together. "If only I had known."

"Would you have provided one for me?"

"Of course, I want to give you your money's worth."

Cordelia's laugh trilled through the carriage. Her laugh stopped abruptly when they arrived in front of the house. Thomas turned to see his entire staff in a line before them in the cold winter air. Hibbert in the front, followed by the familiar faces of Cook, Mrs. Norton, and several new servants he did not recognize. He saw his mother and then he saw her—Penelope. She was more beautiful than he remembered. She still wore black, mourning for his father, and looked paler.

"What in heaven's name are they doing outside in this weather?" Cordelia asked.

"They are lining up to meet you."

"How medieval," she said with a snort. "I hope they don't plan to pledge themselves to me."

Thomas's face flushed with heat and embarrassment. "It's a tradition."

"I am so relieved," Cordelia said, "for I left my pointy umbrella in my other trunk, and I am unable to knight anyone without it."

He gave a weak laugh. He didn't want Cordelia to think their traditions were foolish. He didn't want her to be disappointed in his home. In him.

Their carriage pulled to a stop in front of the main entrance, and Thomas did not wait for the footmen to open the door. He sprung out of the carriage and bounded toward Penelope and his mother. Before he knew it, Penelope had thrown her arms around him. If things were different, if he weren't married, he would have enjoyed the embrace. Instead, he awkwardly patted her on the back and then disentangled himself. He hugged his mother, which was not some-thing he usually did, but he didn't want Cordelia to wonder why he'd embraced his family's ward and not his own mother.

"She's just standing about, looking silk-gownified," he heard Cook whisper in a voice loud enough for everyone to hear.

Thomas turned around to see Cordelia still standing by the carriage. He hoped that Cordelia hadn't heard her. She made no sign that she had. Thomas hadn't noticed before the difference between Cordelia's clothes and Penelope's, but he did now. Cordelia's dress of iridescent black and violet shot silk looked sadly out of place in Ashdown. Such a dress belonged in Paris or at a fancy palace like his cousin's estate. His mother's and Penelope's black clothing looked cheap in comparison.

He took his mother's hand and led her to where Cordelia stood. "Mother, allow me to introduce you to my wife, Cordelia."

Cordelia executed a curtsy worthy of a Russian ballerina. She smiled and held out her gloved hand to his mother. "The pleasure is all mine, Lady Farnham."

"You have excellent manners," his mother said in an astonished voice. "I should never have thought you an American."

"She means it as a compliment," Penelope said.

"Cordelia, this is my family's ward, Miss Penelope Hutchinson," Thomas said.

They did not shake hands but bowed to each other, neither young lady looking particularly pleased with the other. Thomas realized in that moment that he did not want them to be friends—how awkward that would be. But he did not wish for them to be rivals either. To have both his wife and his first love in the same house was going to be uncomfortable, to say the least.

Thomas took Cordelia's elbow and introduced her to the butler. "Hibbert has been at Ashdown longer than I have."

Cordelia nodded. "Pleased to meet you, sir."

Hibbert bowed back and then took over the introductions to the rest of the servants. Cordelia smiled and looked each of them in the eye. She bowed to both Mrs. Norton and Cook, before Hibbert stopped in front of an older lady with a round face and body.

"Lady Farnham, this is Miss Vaughn. The dowager hired her to be your lady's maid," Hibbert said in a grave tone. "If she meets your approval?"

"I am sure we shall get along splendidly," Cordelia said, and held out her hand to Miss Vaughn.

Thomas held his breath, praying that the woman would return the gesture to his wife, but she looked from Cordelia to Hibbert in confusion.

"Servants don't shake hands with the family," the butler said in a dignified tone.

Cordelia dropped her arm and gave a tight smile. "Miss Vaughn."

Hibbert continued down the line of servants until they reached a pair of young maids, probably not more than fifteen years old. This was probably their first position. They giggled as they bobbed curtsies to Cordelia.

She gave them a warm smile and cast a glance at the butler before she curtsied absurdly low and added, "It is a great pleasure to meet you, Hattie and Millie."

Hibbert cleared his throat in obvious disapproval. Thomas felt his color rising once again. He did not want his butler to correct his wife.

"Thank you, everyone," Thomas said. "Please return to your duties."

The servants all looked at Hibbert before moving. Once he nodded, they all filed around the house to the servants' entrance. His mother followed Hibbert into the house, leaving only Thomas, Cordelia, and Penelope. He glanced from one woman to the other. They were about the same height, but their figures couldn't have been more different. Penelope was slim and straight, whereas Cordelia was all lovely curves. Penelope's face was heart-shaped, her skin pale, her hair a warm chestnut brown, and her eyes were currently cast down. Cordelia's complexion was bright, with a few errant freckles decorating her nose, and her luxuriant hair was not one color but many—a mixture of blonde, brown, and red. Her blue eyes looked directly into his—almost a challenge.

"Allow me to show you to your room, Lady Farnham," Penelope said at last.

"Thank you," she said, and gave Thomas an arched look before following her into the house.

Thomas exhaled slowly. This situation was going to be even harder than he had imagined.

12

---

*C*ordelia's heart sank when they walked into the old house. It looked as if it were crumbling to bits—a portrait of decaying grandeur. They passed an enormous room that had weapons decorating the walls. It truly looked medieval. Miss Hutchinson led her up a large staircase to an enormous room that was shockingly bare, save a few pieces of worn furniture, including an old canopy bed that looked like Shakespeare might have slept in it. The only decoration was one enormous, moth-eaten tapestry that took up an entire west wall. The carpet on the floor was threadbare and it was impossible to tell what the original pattern had once been. The entire room was cold, drafty, and out-of-date.

The ward looked at Cordelia expectantly, as if she was waiting for Cordelia to say something.

"Thank you for showing me to my room, Miss Hutchinson."

"Please call me Penelope, or Pen, as Thomas does," she said with a superior smile, as if to tell Cordelia that she'd known Thomas longer than she had.

"Penelope, you may call me Cordelia," she said with a forced smile. "We are living in the same house, after all."

There was a knock at the door.

"Come in," Cordelia called.

Miss Vaughn entered the room and curtsied so lowly to Cordelia that her nose nearly touched her knees.

"I will leave you to get settled," Penelope said, and left the room.

Miss Vaughn bowed again. "My lady."

"You don't need to curtsy to me, Miss Vaughn," Cordelia said, and held out her hand once again. "But I would still like for you to shake my hand."

Miss Vaughn beamed and eagerly took Cordelia's hand between both of hers. "We were all very sorry for you, my lady. Hibbert is a right snob, he is."

"In that moment I could have cheerfully killed him."

"Most of the lower staff would have helped you, my lady."

Cordelia tried to hold in a smile but found she couldn't. She was relieved to find one friendly face in her new home.

"The footmen will be bringing up your trunks to the wardrobe— all nineteen of them. May I ask what's inside?"

"Clothing, of course," Cordelia said. "Our wedding presents will arrive in a few months. There were so many that my father had to hire a steamer to ship them."

"I bet you have more dresses than a princess."

"I've never met a princess, so I wouldn't know. But my mother did purchase a great deal of clothing for my trousseau."

Not that Cordelia had any say in what clothing was selected. Her mother had told her that she had "no taste" and couldn't be trusted to purchase even a proper pair of gloves.

"You must be as rich as Croesus," Miss Vaughn said wonderingly.

"I don't know about that, but I have yet to visit Greece."

Her slight jest was lost on the older woman, who shook her head in agreement.

"Good thing too. Or most of us wouldn't have been hired in December," she said. "You wouldn't have believed the state of the house when I arrived. There was only the stuffed-shirt Hibbert, Mrs. Norton, Cook, and the dowager's maid, Miss Poole. The rest of the staff had left for paying positions. Well, Hibbert had us all on our hands and knees scrubbing the house from the top to the bottom. He made me scrub the old vestibule where they say the monk's ghost walks—I clutched my cross around my neck and scrubbed as quickly as I could."

"Surely you don't believe in ghosts."

Miss Vaughn tilted her head to the side. "I wasn't worried about the monk so much as the late earl, who shot himself in the ash grove near the house."

Cordelia's stomach turned unpleasantly, and she touched her chest in surprise. "Lord Farnham's father committed suicide?"

"You didn't know, my lady?" Miss Vaughn said, and she continued to ramble. "It was quite a to-do, because even though he was an earl, he couldn't have a funeral service. My old mother kept saying he ought to be buried face down at the crossroads, with a stake through his heart to keep him there."

"Why a stake if he's already dead?"

"To keep the evil spirit from wandering."

"Do you know where they did bury the late earl?"

"At the churchyard in Petersley Village, but there's not even a marker on the grave."

Cordelia released a long breath. She was absurdly grateful that the late earl was not buried at Ashdown Abbey. One ghost was quite enough; two would be entirely pretentious of any house.

"Where is my bathing room? I was hoping to have a bath. Get off some of the dirt from travelling."

"I can fill the tin hip bath for you, my lady," she said. "I'll have the cook start boiling the water in the kitchen."

"There's not plumbing in this house?"

"Not on the first floor, my lady."

Cordelia blinked in surprise. "We came up the stairs. This is the second floor."

Miss Vaughn shook her head. "In England, my lady, we call the main floor the ground floor, and the next floor the first floor, and so on."

"Thank you for letting me know. I am sure there are many things you do differently in England than we do in America. And you're welcome to bring any of them to my attention."

"I will, my lady."

Cordelia walked to the shabby chair and sat down. It was as if she had travelled back in time to a house that was more a castle than a home. And with none of the modern conveniences she'd come to expect. "Where does that door lead to?"

"Lord Farnham's room, of course," Miss Vaughn said with a little laugh. "There's a dressing room between them. I've had the footmen place your trunks in the adjacent room to this one. There's not enough space for them in your dressing room."

"Ah," Cordelia said, and summoned her best polite smile. "How clever of you. If you'll see to my bath, I'll rest until it is ready."

Miss Vaughn gave her another smile and deep curtsy before leaving the room. Cordelia took off her gloves and pulled out the hat pins before taking off her hat. She set them both on a side table before opening the door to the shared dressing room. Like the rest of the house, the furniture was worn and out-of-date. But the room was spacious. She gulped when she saw copper bowls, which she assumed were chamber pots. She'd never had to use one before and hoped that she wouldn't get anything on her clothing. And what of the smell?

Cordelia couldn't hold in a shiver of disgust.

She opened the opposite door that led to Thomas's room. Cordelia felt surprised that she was disappointed to find it empty. She'd somehow grown fond of her husband. He wasn't playful and boisterous like Stuyvesant. But there was something endearing about the slow way a smile formed on his face and how he listened when she spoke—truly listened as if he wanted to know everything she was thinking. Thomas would never be as broad or as handsome as Stuyvesant, but his narrower frame was muscular and his pale features attractive.

Thomas's room was just like hers: overlarge and sparsely furnished with shabby furniture. She also felt an identical chilly draft. She looked at the walls and could see no sign of electric lights or central heating. The entire abbey was out-of-date, inconvenient, and belonged in a museum.

Cordelia wondered where Thomas was. She needed to talk to him urgently. If they were going to be friendly partners, their first step together would be to modernize this mausoleum.

13

It took Miss Vaughn and the two giggling kitchen maids three trips to fill the hip bath to only one-third full. They placed it in front of the fireplace, which thankfully had a decent blaze. When Cordelia stepped into the basin, it was only lukewarm and didn't cover her entire body. But even if she was shivering, she was glad to be clean. Miss Vaughn handed her a towel and then her chemise.

"You really are a princess," she said admiringly. "Even your underthings are sewn with golden thread."

Cordelia smiled and put her arms through her silk robe, then tied it around her waist. Miss Vaughn helped her into her corset and pulled the strings tight. She sat down on a stool while Miss Vaughn combed out her hair. She then twisted it around into a bun on the top of her head. The door opened and Thomas stood in the doorway, his tall figure framed by the light of a candle. He was dressed in a black tuxedo that made his shoulders look broad. A shiver crawled down her spine as she reminded herself that she didn't want to find him handsome.

"I am sorry," he said, turning around. "I did not realize that you were not yet dressed."

"Please stay, Thomas," Cordelia said, feeling heat rush to her cheeks. "Miss Vaughn, will you be so kind as to fetch my celestial-blue dress?"

Miss Vaughn dipped a quick curtsy and then left the dressing room through the door that led to Cordelia's room. Cordelia stood up, conscious that she only wore a light robe. Thomas stayed, watching her with open admiration. But their bargain had been for her money, not her person.

Stuyvesant had admired her too. Yet he'd still left her all alone in her tower.

"I was hoping to speak to you about some renovations to Ashdown."

Thomas's eyes moved up from her gorgeous form to her face, his expression embarrassed. "Yes, Ashdown needs extensive renovations, and I was hoping that you would help me."

"With what?"

"As you've no doubt noticed, the walls are bare. Anything of value has long since been sold. I was hoping you would help me replace the furnishings. Pick the colors of the paint and the carpets for the floors."

Cordelia's mother's voice came into her head: "You have no taste."

"Are you sure? I don't have much experience with decorating."

"I daresay you have more than I do, and I want you to be happy here," Thomas said. "I want Ashdown Abbey to feel like your home."

"Then I will need a proper bathing room."

Thomas laughed. "Anything."

Miss Vaughn re-entered the room and their awkward tête-à-tête was at an end.

"I'll wait for you in the hall," he said, leaving the room.

Miss Vaughn carried in her arms a beautiful blue gown made by Worth. The beadwork on the bodice was a work of art—resembling flowers and vines. Cordelia couldn't help but touch it. She untied her robe and let it fall to the floor. She lifted her arms and Miss Vaughn carefully helped her into her underclothing and her corset.

Then, at last, the gown, buttoning up the back. Miss Vaughn rearranged her hair and put on her jewels—her favorite pearl necklace and matching earrings.

Cordelia picked up her long cream gloves off the table, opened the door, and pulled the gloves up past her elbows. "Shall we go down to dinner?"

Thomas offered his arm and she placed her hand inside the crook of it. They walked down together, and for the first time, she recognized the smell of his cologne—it was an American scent. A bit of tobacco, with a natural note of cedarwood. For a brief moment, she felt the warm familiarity of home. Had it been a gift? Or had he bought it for her?

They entered another large, dilapidated room. Dowager Lady Farnham and Penelope both wore somber black dresses. Standing beside them were two sober-faced, middle-aged gentlemen that Cordelia instantly recognized as clergy.

"Cordelia," Thomas said with a ready smile, "may I introduce you to our cousin and rector, Mr. Ryse?"

She held out her gloved hand and the older man bowed over it.

"My lady."

She stiffened a little. Titles were such silly things, after all. It wasn't as if she'd done anything to earn it, besides being extremely wealthy.

Mr. Ryse released her hand and pointed to the red-bearded gentleman at his side. "Lady Farnham, may I introduce you to my colleague Mr. Hudson."

Cordelia held out her hand once again. "A pleasure. And how clever of you, Mr. Ryse, to have a friend visiting so that our numbers at dinner would be even."

The rector gave her a polite smile.

Mr. Hudson kissed her hand and laughed merrily at her little joke. "Believe me, Lady Farnham, the pleasure is all mine."

The group did not wait for a pre-meal drink but headed into the adjacent dining room. It was enormous and drafty like the rest of the house, with a long table down the center.

Cordelia felt a little overdressed and overbejeweled as she sat at the end of the table. Thomas sat at the head. They were as far from each other as possible, and she missed his scent. His mother and ward sat across from each other in the middle. Mr. Ryse was seated by her mother-in-law, and Mr. Hudson by Penelope on the opposite side. Hibbert led the two footmen into the room, and they began serving the first course of white soup—it was lukewarm. Only the butler served the wine.

"I am so glad that you have returned, Thomas. America must be a dreadful place," Dowager Lady Farnham said in a loud voice. "I hear there are no servants there."

Cordelia choked on her wine.

"Mother, there are servants in America," Thomas said, his cheeks bright red as if he were embarrassed by his mother's ignorance. "It's not uncivilized there."

She continued, undeterred. "I thought Americans did not like to be servants."

"Oh, they don't," Cordelia agreed with a smile, recovering her countenance.

"Then, you have no one to wait upon you?!"

"At least no Americans," she assured them with a saucy wink. "All of our working class are English."

Mr. Hudson let out a loud guffaw and pounded the table with one fist. Cordelia almost giggled at her own wit before she realized that she had offended the rest of the party. Thomas's face looked strained, Penelope's countenance had gone three shades paler, and Mr. Ryse's permanent scowl could have been etched in stone. Her lively sense of humor could not have been worse timed.

"I am glad to hear that the English who live in America know their class and don't try to rise above their stations," Dowager Lady Farnham said with an approving smile.

"Unlike some people," Mr. Ryse said, lifting his glass of wine to drink it.

Cordelia blushed and wondered if the rector was referring to her. Her fortune was from railroads, and not from dusty old ancestors. The English aristocracy seemed to think that working was beneath their dignity. It was no wonder they were all going bankrupt.

"Ah, Cook's white soup," Thomas said, attempting to ease the tension. "How I've missed it."

Cordelia wasn't sure why, because the soup was lukewarm and the cream was separating from the broth. As if it had sat too long, waiting to be served, or the walk from the kitchen was too long.

The next course was white fish with vegetables—also cold. The portion the footman gave Cordelia was little more than two bites. She'd have no difficulty tying her corset strings at this rate. She noticed the large portions he gave the gentlemen. Even Dowager Lady Farnham and Penelope's servings were generous in comparison. Cordelia pushed the fish around on her plate with her fork. Even the servants thought that she was an interloper.

"Do you have fish in America?" the dowager asked.

Cordelia could only blink. Was her mother-in-law jesting? She looked at the woman incredulously, but there was no smile on her face. The ridiculous question had been sincere. This time she would respond more seriously. "Yes, we have many fish in America. There are two oceans and a great many lakes and rivers on the continent."

The dowager nodded and took another bite of fish before asking her next question. "Do you have potatoes in America?"

Cordelia snorted, trying to keep in her laughter. It was as if the dowager thought that she was from a different world entirely, instead of a different country.

"Potatoes are actually from the Americas, my lady," Mr. Hudson said with his friendly smile. "Sir Walter Raleigh introduced the vegetable to us."

The dowager leaned her head to one side and practically squinted across the table. "Are you sure, Mr. Hudson?"

Before he could answer, Mr. Ryse patted her hand. "Yes, indeed, Blanche. Mr. Hudson is a great historical scholar."

Her mother-in-law's name was Blanche. How funny that Cordelia had never known it before. She wondered if she would be permitted to use it, or if she would have to call the woman "my lady" for the rest of her life.

The older woman shook her head. "I would never have believed it otherwise if not for your word, Mr. Hudson."

"Mama, what sort of notion do you have of America?" Thomas said. "I have never heard such absurd questions in all my life. Everything we have here they have there."

His mother shook her head. "Oh, I can't believe that."

Cordelia had to cover her mouth with her napkin to keep in her own mirth. Mr. Hudson let out a great bark of a laugh but was given a quelling look from his colleague, Mr. Ryse.

The rest of the dinner passed quickly. The footmen continued to serve Cordelia absurdly small portions of cold food so that by the end of the dinner, she was still hungry.

After dinner, she followed the ladies out of the dining room to a drafty sitting room, where coffee was set out. Cordelia did not wait to pour herself a cup. She didn't even drink it but held it with her gloved hands, absorbing its warmth. There wasn't a room in the entire abbey that was not drafty and cold. She sat on a threadbare chaise, as far away from her mother-in-law as she could. She doubted that she could keep her countenance if the woman continued to ask such ridiculous questions about America. She wasn't sure if her mother-in-law was cunning or really as vague as she presented herself. As if Cordelia was something alien because she was from another continent.

Penelope poured a cup of coffee and delivered it to the dowager before getting her own glass. Cordelia wondered if she'd broken some sort of British protocol by obtaining her own cup. She decided she didn't care and took a sip of the hot liquid. It needed sugar.

"I have been meaning to mention something to you, Cordelia," Dowager Lady Farnham said. "There are two hundred British families whose names and titles you must memorize and always remember. We have a book of the peerage, and Penelope can assist you."

Cordelia was tempted to say that in America there are *four hundred* families in society whose names you must always remember, but she didn't. "I daresay that won't be too difficult for me, since I passed the entrance examinations to Oxford University."

"Really?!" her mother-in-law said incredulously. "Women attend university in America? How unorthodox."

Cordelia didn't point out that Oxford was in England. The college allowed ladies to study, not earn their degree.

Thomas and the other gentlemen entered the room just then. He sat down on the chaise next to Cordelia, but Penelope's eyes looked hungrily at him. Jealousy, like bile, rose in her throat. She forced herself to swallow it down and smile.

"My dearest Penelope, will you play for us?" Dowager Lady Farnham asked.

Penelope assented and sat at the antique piano, which was out of tune. She played competently without playing well. She glanced at Thomas, who seemed to make a point of *not* looking at Penelope. When her song was over, Cordelia clapped loudly, as did Mr. Hudson. She couldn't help but wish that *he* was their rector, instead of the relation, Mr. Ryse.

"What a perfect young lady you are, my dearest ward," Dowager Lady Farnham said. "Such fine accomplishments."

"And such irreproachable manners," Mr. Ryse added, looking directly at Cordelia.

"It was a very pretty song," Cordelia added politely.

"Very enjoyable," Mr. Hudson said with his infectious smile as he rubbed his beard.

"Well done," Thomas added, still not meeting Penelope's eyes that seemed to be glued to his face.

"Cordelia, would you like to play next?" her mother-in-law asked.

She would very much like to play, but she didn't want to overshadow Penelope's performance. "No, thank you."

"Do you not have pianos in America?"

"Yes, we do have pianos in America," Cordelia said, trying to keep her tone light.

"Then you were never taught to play," Dowager Lady Farnham stated more than asked. "Your governess never taught you how to play the piano? How very odd. But perhaps you didn't have a governess. Are there no governesses in America?"

Poor Mr. Hudson looked down at his hands, and Mr. Ryse gave her another glance of disapproval.

Unable to keep silent any longer, Cordelia stood up. "I was lucky enough to be taught by a music master, and I should be happy to play for you."

She walked over to the piano seat, and Penelope stole the chance to sit next to Thomas on the chaise, as if attempting to claim him. It was clear that she had feelings for Cordelia's husband. The entire situation was uncomfortable and unfortunate. Pulling off her long gloves, Cordelia set them on her lap. When she was unhappy, music was always her greatest comfort. So, she curled her fingers on the ivory keys and played the most difficult song she had memorized: Beethoven's "Piano Sonata No. 32 in C minor, Op. 111." Cordelia poured all her frustrations and disappointment into the piece. When she pressed the final keys, the tips of her fingers were tender. She felt triumphant and almost happy.

Cordelia turned in her seat to look at her audience. Mr. Hudson was already on his feet, practically yelling, "Brava!"

Mr. Ryse clapped only twice.

The dowager did not look at all abashed and gave a few half-hearted claps. "You play rather well for an American. I am sure if you had been English, your performance would have been creditable."

"Nonsense, Mama," Thomas said, standing up. "Cordelia, you're incredible. I've never heard your equal. You could be a professional."

She glanced at Penelope, who was wiping a tear from her cheek. Cordelia no longer felt triumphant but petty. She had let her love for music take over her good manners, and she'd behaved rudely.

"I think I'll retire early," Cordelia said, and pulled her gloves back on. She couldn't endure this stifling room for another minute. "I'm tired. It has been a great joy making both of your acquaintances, Mr. Hudson and Mr. Ryse."

"Good night, dear girl," the dowager said almost kindly.

Cordelia thought that perhaps all her mother-in-law's comments on America were caused by her ignorance, rather than condescension. She wished she had not tried to make a joke of them.

"Good night, Dowager Lady Farnham, Penelope, Thomas."

Her husband's eyes glanced furtively at Penelope, but he stood up and offered his hand to Cordelia. "I'll go with you."

She was tempted to say no. He was only offering out of duty, but a small jealous part of her wanted to take him away from Penelope. She placed hers into his and she stole one last glance at Penelope, whose head hung low. The pit in her stomach deepened. Had the girl really hoped to win Thomas back? He was already Cordelia's husband.

Cordelia allowed her hand to go limp inside Thomas's, but he simply held it tighter. They walked silently up the crumbling staircase to their rooms. He stopped before her door. Cordelia's heart beat faster—Thomas hadn't kissed her since the stiff kiss in the chapel. Not that she'd encouraged him. How could she, when her heart belonged to Stuyvesant, and Thomas's belonged to...

"When I asked if you've ever been in love and you said yes, did you mean your family's ward, Penelope?"

Thomas dropped her hand, as if it were too hot to hold. "Why do you think that?"

"Her eyes never leave you when you're in the same room, and you never look back," Cordelia said. "We promised that, as friends, we would not lie to each other."

"Yes," he said so quietly that she had to lean closer to hear it. "But I broke it off before I came to America, and I promise that I will not encourage her attentions. She is my family's ward, and it would cause a great deal of talk if she were to leave Ashdown."

Cordelia sighed. It appeared that her husband wouldn't *discourage* Penelope's attentions either. Had he kissed Penelope? The sting of jealousy in her heart was replaced by a dull ache.

"And your gentleman? What was his name?" Thomas asked.

"It does not matter. He's on the other side of the world," Cordelia said, opening the door to her room and closing it behind her.

She leaned against the handle, and tears slipped down her cheeks.

Stuyvesant.

14

---

*H*ibbert handed Thomas a calling card at breakfast: *Mr. Septimius Merrill, Estate Agent.*

"Mr. Merrill is in the library, my lord," the butler droned in a monotone voice. "Lord Rutledge hired him to handle your affairs whilst you were in America."

Thomas choked as he swallowed his bite of eggs. He was back in England. The blissful holiday from his financial affairs and responsibilities was now over. "Very good, Hibbert. I shall come at once."

The butler bowed and his face looked pained.

"Is there something else, Hibbert?"

The older man shook his head. "You are an earl, my lord. You should finish your breakfast. Your man of business should wait upon your pleasure."

Thomas stood up and wiped his mouth with his napkin. "I wish that were so, Hibbert, but that world, I think, is now gone. I am as much at Mr. Merrill's mercy as he is in mine."

The butler's implacable expression was back in place. "Very good, my lord."

Thomas patted the man's shoulder and then regretted it. He'd meant to show affection and gratitude, but the look on Hibbert's face was shock. Thomas had allowed the more casual manners from America to affect his behavior. He walked slowly to the library, tripping over the tears in the carpet. He and Cordelia could not update Ashdown fast enough.

Opening the door, he saw a man probably in his thirties standing by the window. His hair was black and slicked back, with hints of gray at the temples. His forehead was rather short and his dark eyes small, giving his face a pinched look.

Mr. Merrill bowed to him.

Thomas returned the motion before gesturing with his hand for the man to be seated. "Mr. Merrill, how good it is to meet you. I have heard from my mother and my staff that you have been a godsend to Ashdown."

The man smiled and his small eyes practically disappeared into his face. "I am pleased that my work has met your approval, my lord."

Thomas took a seat behind a desk, conscious of his young age. He did not know what he was supposed to do next. Drumming his fingers against the mahogany, he smiled self-consciously.

"Have all of my father's debts been paid in full?"

"Yes, my lord."

"And all the outstanding tradesmen's bills?"

Mr. Merrill laughed. "Indeed, my lord, or you would not have fresh food in the abbey. Nearly every local tradesman had not been paid in many years."

Thomas could only nod, the shame turning in his stomach. His family had eaten but not bothered to pay for their food. He hoped that others had not gone hungry because of his family's mismanagement.

"After the wedding, my father-in-law gave me some sound advice on how to make the estate more profitable."

Mr. Merrill pulled a small notebook and a pen out of his interior jacket pocket. "Yes, my lord?"

Thomas swallowed heavily. "He suggested that, with the poor harvests lately, it would be in our best interest to farm the home field with several different crops, then take on cattle in one section, and if there is a good place, plant an orchard…That way if any of our crops fail, we will have diversified our holdings and be able to weather poor years better."

"Very sound ideas, my lord," Mr. Merrill said. "Shall I have a draftsman make out a map of the estate, and then we can discuss where it would be best to locate your new projects?"

"Excellent," Thomas said, and then bit his lip. He felt like he was playing at being a grown-up. He had no idea what he was supposed to say or do.

Hibbert opened the door to the library and announced, "Lady Farnham."

It wasn't his mother but Cordelia. Thomas got to his feet as she swept into the room in shining magnificence. To use Cook's phrase, Cordelia was looking all "silk-gownified." Her dress was midnight-blue and it shimmered with every step. Her gorgeous hair was piled on top of her head and her smile dazzled. She was bright, new, and beautiful. His wife appeared out of place in his shabby abbey.

"Mr. Merrill, may I introduce my wife, Lady Farnham."

The estate manager blinked his small eyes, as if stunned by her. He recovered himself quickly and gave her a sharp bow. The man was rewarded with one of Cordelia's brilliant smiles and her outreached hand. He hesitated a moment before shaking it.

"I hope that I haven't intruded."

"Not at all," Thomas said, and he was about to pull her up a chair, when she found a perch on his desk. He sat down beside her and breathed in her intoxicating French perfume.

"I assume you were talking about the estate."

"Yes, my lady."

Cordelia clapped her gloved hands. "Excellent! There is a great deal of work to be done to the house to make it livable."

Mr. Merrill nodded. "Yes, my lady. A renovation is in order. I daresay it will take several years to complete."

She shook her head. "That is unacceptable, sir. There is no

plumbing anywhere but on the ground floor, tucked in the most inconvenient corner. This is 1894, not the Dark Ages."

Thomas felt the blood run to his face in embarrassment, but the estate agent laughed.

"I suppose England must feel like the Dark Ages to you, my lady, compared to the bright and shiny city of New York."

Cordelia inclined her head. "I don't see why we couldn't have working plumbing on all four floors of the house in a few months."

"To get the job done so quickly, we would need a dozen crews."

"Then hire them."

Mr. Merrill scoffed. "The cost would be nearly three times as much."

His wife shrugged her shoulders. "Cost is not a consideration."

The man turned to Thomas. "My lord?"

Thomas's eyes were on his wife. He could see the frustration in all her features. He couldn't imagine Mrs. Astor, Mrs. Jones, or any New York woman being questioned by their employees as if they were not competent.

He forced himself to smile. "Mr. Merrill, my wife is my partner in all things. You may safely presume that anything she says has my full support and agreement."

Cordelia gave him a glowing look and squeezed his hand.

"Then, cost is *not* a consideration?" Mr. Merrill repeated incredulously.

"Speed is our greatest concern," Cordelia continued, still holding his hand. "You will also need to hire an army of carpenters and tradesmen. Ashdown Abbey was obviously not designed for modern amenities, and it is essential to add walls and doors particularly to the first-floor family rooms and guest rooms. We will have to cannibalize many of the middle rooms to ensure that all of our guest rooms have their own private bathing room and water closets."

Thomas watched Mr. Merrill furiously scribble down notes.

"How soon would you want the crews to arrive, my lady?"

"As soon as tomorrow if possible," Cordelia said, cool and confident. "I was up rather early because of the cold and made a full map of the house. I will see that it is in your hands by tomorrow. It will show where I want bathing rooms installed, walls and doors added, and others removed."

Mr. Merrill wrote down a few more lines before closing his notebook, restoring it to his interior pocket, and standing up. "I shall work on getting plumbers and carpenter crews scheduled as soon as possible."

"Very good," Cordelia said with another smile. "Good day, Mr. Merrill."

"Yes, thank you and good day," Thomas added.

The estate manager gave them one last bow before taking himself out the door.

Cordelia squeezed Thomas's hand once again and, to his surprise, lifted it up to her delicate lips and kissed it.

"You said that we would be friends," she said, grinning down at him. "And part of me didn't believe you, but you were telling the truth, and I am so very grateful to be your partner."

Thomas wished he could have sealed their partnership with a real kiss, but Cordelia had already let go of his hand.

"I hope I wasn't too domineering," she said, kicking her small, booted feet. "I promise not to change anything that you don't want me to."

He thought of the large holes in the carpet and truthfully said, "You can change everything with my good graces."

Cordelia giggled again. He loved that sound.

"I was hoping that we could divide the work between us," she said.

"Of course."

"I shall handle the inside of the house: new plaster, painting, furniture, curtains, plumbing, and reupholstering. If you wouldn't mind heading up having electric lights and central heating installed, reinforcing the crumbling exterior, and replacing the roof."

Thomas felt his lips twitch before he smiled. His American wife was certainly efficient. "You have a deal, partner."

She hopped off the desk. "I shall speak to your mother first and ensure that any pieces of furniture that have a particular sentimentality will be kept."

"That is very considerate of you."

Cordelia beamed at him. "Then I shall show Hibbert and Mrs. Norton which pieces of furniture are to be donated or burned, and which ones are to be kept... I shall probably have to travel to London soon to purchase new furniture. I daresay nothing in the countryside would be quite up to our standard."

He felt a surprising pang in his chest. She'd only been at Ashdown for one day, and she was already planning to leave it. Not that he blamed her; it was a hovel compared to her home in New York.

Thomas cleared his throat. "I don't know if you heard your father, but he purchased us a fully furnished house in London."

His wife had refused to speak to either of her parents after the wedding. Again, he could not blame her. They had used her disgracefully to restore their own standing in the community, without any consideration of her feelings or ambitions.

Cordelia stiffened and the smile fell from her mocking lips. "I don't think that I will stay there... I shouldn't wish to put out the servants for only three or four days. Miss Vaughn and I shall be snug at the Savoy Hotel."

Thomas didn't speak. He was holding his breath, waiting for her to include him in the invitation.

She clapped her hands again. "I shall go today. There is so much to do before I catch the afternoon train. I don't have time to dawdle."

His wife swept out of the room, with the same sparkle and energy that she had entered it. Every aspect of the space appeared more dilapidated without her.

88

15

She found her mother-in-law in a small sitting room on the ground floor. Both she and Penelope were sewing.

"There you are, Lady Farnham," Cordelia said.

The older woman smiled. "You are Lady Farnham now too, and I am the dowager. Perhaps it would be less confusing, Cordelia, if you called me Blanche."

"I should like that."

Blanche lifted up the handkerchief she was working on. "Would you care to join us?"

"You are so kind," Cordelia said, and actually meant it. "I was hoping that I could discuss with you which pieces of furniture you want preserved or reupholstered, and which ones I can simply replace."

Blanche's whole face lit up. "New furniture! How lovely. I daresay in America everything is new."

"Many things are."

"How wonderful," she said. "I haven't had any new furniture since my wedding, nearly twenty-three years ago. My parents gave me the formal dining table and chairs as a part of my dowry."

Cordelia sat on the edge of a chair and folded her hands in her lap. "Then we must keep them."

Blanche sighed and shook her head. "It has become so shabby like the rest of the house."

"I daresay the table only needs a good polishing, and the chairs can be reupholstered in a dark velvet."

"Do they have velvet in America?"

Her mother-in-law's questions had annoyed her last night, but this morning she realized that the poor woman's world was so small. She had only ever lived in England, and, therefore, Cordelia could patiently answer every question. "Happily, we do. Penelope, are there any particular pieces you would like kept?"

Penelope glanced up from her sewing, her pretty mouth pinched. "I have no right to have an opinion."

Cordelia couldn't have agreed more, but she attempted a conciliatory smile. "You are a member of our household and therefore anything you say will have weight in our decision-making."

"I should like my room untouched," she said, before leaning back over the handkerchief and sewing with great speed and determination.

Shuffling to her feet, Cordelia bid both ladies adieu.

She closed the door behind her and walked into every room on the ground floor. Including the unfortunately placed and rather smelly water closets. Her second time around, she realized why every course at dinner last night had been cold. The large formal dining room was on the opposite side of the house from the kitchen.

It simply would not do.

The main hall, with all the armor, was right next to the kitchen and more than large enough to hold Blanche's table and fifty matching chairs. The walls were wood-paneled and the floors were a dramatic checkerboard pattern of black and white. Of all the rooms in the house, it was nearly perfect as it already was. All it needed was proper lighting.

She walked into the kitchen and saw the butler.

"Hibbert, just the person I was hoping to see. Would you mind coming on a walk with me?"

"A walk, my lady?"

Cordelia felt the eyes of every servant in the room on her face. She forced herself to smile. "Yes, I should like to have a few pieces of furniture moved."

"Very good, my lady."

Hibbert held out his right hand for Cordelia to go first. They entered the main hall. Their footsteps echoed against the marble tiles.

"I am excessively fond of this room."

The butler gave her a curt nod.

Praise didn't seem to sway him. Cordelia attempted another smile. "I should like for the formal dining room table and chairs to be moved here and for the main hall to become the formal dining room."

"The other room has served as the dining room of the Ashby family for over three hundred years."

"How pleasant," she said, nodding. "I cannot wait to hear more about my husband's family, and I am sure no one knows more about Ashdown Abbey than you."

She was pouring on her sweetness rather thick, but nothing seemed to breach his implacable reserve.

"There is no need to change the traditions of this house or this family," he droned in a monotone voice.

"Be that as it may," she said, no longer smiling, "I am now the mistress of this house, and I want the table and chairs moved—today. Before dinner."

Hibbert stiffened. "Very good, my lady."

"Thank you, Hibbert," Cordelia said. "Would you please send Mrs. Norton to speak to me? And please have her bring a notebook. There is much to be replaced."

Cordelia waited in the empty main hall for the housekeeper to arrive. Mrs. Norton was already scowling before they even walked up the stairs. The housekeeper was an older, heavy-set woman, with a rough-hewn face as if she'd been carved from wood. Her long arms hung limply at her side, and her gray hair had been scraped back from her face in an unforgiving and unattractive bun. Cordelia politely told her that one third of the bedchambers were going to be split in half and made into private bathing rooms and water closets for the bedchambers immediately adjacent on both sides.

"But what of the furniture in those rooms?" Mrs. Norton asked gruffly, without even bothering with the honorific "my lady."

"I wandered through them this morning and the rooms have a layer of dust on the floor. Most of the furniture appeared to be in poor condition. All the mattresses and linens and draperies need to be replaced."

"We have not had the staff to keep up with the house until very recently."

Cordelia held up her hands. "I am not accusing you, Mrs. Norton, I am merely explaining that there is a great deal of furniture that is not in excellent condition. I should like for it to be given away to our tenants if it is still serviceable. If it is not, please have the pieces burned. The remaining furniture will be refinished and redistributed to the remaining bedchambers."

If the woman pursed her mouth any tighter, the small line of her lips would entirely disappear. Cordelia must be handling it all wrong. She was trying to improve the lives of their servants, not to offend them.

"And I should also like to replace the mattresses and linens in the servants' quarters, both the attic and basement. Would you be so good as to provide me with an accurate count?"

"Yes, my lady."

Cordelia tried another smile. "I appreciate all that you do, Mrs. Norton. Would you be so good as to find the best locations in the attic and basement for the addition of bathing rooms and water closets? Thomas and I wish for our staff to have the best accommodations possible."

"Yes, my lady."

"Could you make sure to give an accurate count of the needed textiles and linens to Miss Vaughn before we leave for the four o'clock train to London?"

"Yes, my lady." The housekeeper repeated the same three words, but her sharp features looked mutinous. She clearly didn't approve of an American outsider coming in and changing the abbey. Cordelia could only hope that once Mrs. Norton experienced the joy of hot water in abundance, the housekeeper would forgive her.

For not being the dowager.

Or the beautiful and compliant Penelope.

16

Cordelia said that she would be gone for three or four days in London.

Tomorrow, it would be four weeks to the day since she'd left Ashdown Abbey. It was now February. Thomas hadn't realized how much he would miss her company and her sharp wit. Every day felt like winter without her: cold and dark. His mother, bless her, was not the most intelligent conversationalist. Penelope was beautiful to look at but painful to talk to. She took everything he said literally and never once argued a different opinion. No one told jokes or offered false opinions for humor, as Cordelia was so fond of doing in her most deadpan voice. Only her dancing eyes gave her away.

He would have assumed that she'd left him if dozens of crates didn't arrive every day but Sunday. The day after she'd left for London, they'd received forty claw-foot tubs, followed by fifty-five water closets and sinks.

After a week, a shipment of Italian marble arrived—just in time for the builders to lay it into the newly created bathing rooms and water closets—followed by seventy-two mattresses and enough new linens for Buckingham Palace. Every single bed in the abbey had a new, soft, top-of-the-line mattress.

The third week, a team of upholsters arrived to refresh the dining room chairs. He'd also received over one hundred pieces of furniture to replace every single piece on the main floor, except his mother's prized dining room table. They were followed by an endless stream of painters and wallpaperers.

This week, new windows for the entire abbey arrived, with one hundred and three men to install them. Ten other crews were handing draperies in the rooms. Every item was carefully marked and assigned in Cordelia's perfect script precisely where it was to go. He was impressed by her memory and her organizational abilities.

All that was left to replace were the threadbare carpets and decorations for the freshly painted but blank walls. His father had long ago sold any painting of value.

He glanced out the window and saw a caravan of wagons arriving in front of his home. Pulling out his pocket watch, he looked at the time: four o'clock. It was late in the day for crates to arrive. He wandered out of the library and to the back of the house where packages were delivered.

Hibbert was already out there to meet them.

Thomas counted twenty-eight wagons, all of which appeared to be full to the brink.

"I wonder what her ladyship is sending to us today."

The driver of the first wagon jumped out of his seat and handed a paper to Thomas. The packages weren't from his wife—they were wedding presents from America. He let out a low whistle.

"Where shall I have the men put them, my lord?"

He had no idea what to do with all of them. "Um—how about the ballroom. It's the only space large enough to store them until we can open them all."

"Very good, my lord."

Thomas was about to return to the library, when he noticed that a carriage was pulling to the front of the house. Without thinking, he jogged to meet it. He opened the door and Cordelia jumped out.

"I am so sorry, Thomas!" she said, shaking his hands and giving him a smile that warmed him to the core. "Everything took so much longer than I expected... I was able to find the most incredible woman to restore the abbey's tapestries, but none of the art in London quite took my fancy, so I was forced to spend a few days in Paris. The paintings I bought should be arriving in a few weeks."

He held on to her hands. He'd forgotten how stunning she was. How vibrant. "I am glad your trip was a success. I missed you."

"You did?" she said with a smile. She slipped her hands from his, then linked arms with him. "How is the work progressing?"

Thomas's body temperature rose as he led her to the main doors. "You will not believe what we have accomplished in your absence. The bathing rooms and water closets are nearly done, and the electric lights are installed. The workers for a central heating system have begun, but it will probably take a few more months before it is completed. I've had workers reinforce all the brickwork on the façade, and they'll be starting on the roof in the next fortnight."

"You have been a busy bee."

He couldn't help but smile. He'd missed her banter. "As have you. The entire abbey is practically new, except for the carpets."

"Oh dear," she said, talking from one side of her mouth. "I'd forgotten about them. Are they more holey than ever?"

"Well, Ashdown was once an abbey."

She let out a trill of laughter and his heart lightened as he joined in with her. "Shall we pick the new carpets together next month, when the builders are finished with the alterations to the house?"

"I should like that very much," Cordelia said, squeezing his arm.

They passed by a side table that had a basket with a stack of mail from America. It was where Hibbert put the family correspondence.

"Oh, I forgot," he said, handing her letters to her. "These arrived for you, but I didn't know when you were coming home, so I didn't send them on."

Her large eyes widened at the sight, and she eagerly took them from his hands. Flipping through them one by one, the light in her eyes seemed to dim with each name and then died out entirely. She handed him back two of the letters. One from her father, and the other from her mother.

"Please have these returned to the sender," she said, her voice on the edge of tears. "I am a little done in from travelling, and if you do not mind, I shall have my dinner in my room."

"As you wish," he said, cursing himself that he hadn't waited until the morning to give her the letters so that they might have spent more time together.

He watched her lovely figure walk slowly, with a definite droop, up the stairs.

17

The new mattress was like heaven, but she hadn't slept well at all the night before. There had been no fire in the hearth, even though it was February. Miss Vaughn brought her breakfast tray, which consisted of gruel thick enough that it might have been useful in cement work. Clearly, the servants had not forgiven her for making changes to the abbey yet. Although, how anyone would like to go down two flights of stairs to use the water closet, she would never know. Or why they would prefer sleeping on lumpy mattresses, with unknown bugs in them, instead of the new down-feather ones.

If the renovations were not the problem, it must be she.

She felt like an alien entirely in another world at Ashdown. She had almost not come back. Even in January, London had been lovely; but Paris was like visiting home. She'd visited the city so many times before and she knew several people there, Parisians and Americans, all of which were happy to see her and were most welcoming. She had not eaten even one meal alone. Everything was warm and beautiful, and she felt as if she'd belonged.

Thomas must have worried that she wasn't coming back, for the relief was visible in his face when she returned after four weeks. It had taken her that long to run out of excuses to stay away.

From her husband.

From the woman he loved.

What a tangled mess Thomas's debts and her mother's ambitions had made. And now all three of them had to live with it. She could no longer hide at the Savoy, sipping cocktails, purchasing more textiles, and dreaming about kissing Stuyvesant. This was her life and there was no escaping it.

Glancing at the letters on her side table, a new wave of tears fell down her face. Edith's letter had been the shortest and probably the most honest. Her sister was happy, now that everyone wanted to be her friend again because Cordelia was a countess. She wrote merrily of new dresses and her upcoming visit to Newport. Cordelia read the letter so many times the night before that she knew all the words by heart.

The next letter in the stack was from Alida, who cheerfully offered to murder Thomas for her, followed by a letter from her twin, Julia, who had sent it separately so that Cordelia could enjoy opening more mail. Julia was always so thoughtful. The last letter was from Lucy, who seemed to be as miserable as she was and nearly as friendless without her.

Cordelia sniffed and laughed out loud. Of course Stuyvesant hadn't written. Why would he? He had already proven that he did not care enough to save her from a marriage not of her choosing.

She did not have even *one* friend in England. Not one soul who wished to spend time in her company. Except possibly Thomas. But her feelings for *him* were as complicated as his were for *her*. Thomas genuinely seemed to enjoy her company and often gazed at her with admiration; but then his eyes would flicker toward Penelope. It appeared that she still held his heart as Stuyvesant did hers, even though Cordelia knew her former friend no longer returned her sentiments. Love was not rational or practical.

Tugging on the cord, she waited for Miss Vaughn to come and dress her. At least, *she* seemed to like her. Cordelia thanked the woman and wandered down the stairs until she reached the old dining room, where the grand piano her father had sent as a wedding present had been placed. She opened the lid and began to play Bach.

Music had always been her greatest companion.

Her love.

She poured her loneliness, her foreignness, and her frustration into the notes as they soared into the air—lilting and lovely. Cordelia played until her fingers were sore. She should be opening the mountains of wedding gifts in the ballroom. But she didn't want to because they reminded her of home.

Leaning against the piano, she heard discordant notes and remembered the old instrument that she'd played on the first night. It was no equal to the grand piano and would need to be donated somewhere. Perhaps to the village school that she'd passed on her way there. She would go right now and ask the teacher. Any excuse to leave the dreary abbey.

She called for her carriage but did not ask for Miss Vaughn to accompany her on the trip. There was no need for a companion if she was only travelling a couple of miles to the village.

Cordelia arrived at lunchtime. She saw the children eating from their pails outside of the school in the cold air. She opened the door. There was a prim woman in her late twenties, with a small pair of spectacles and dark brown hair, pulled severely back. She sat at a desk at the front of the room by the chalkboard.

"Lunchtime is not over yet," she said, without looking up.

"I am afraid that I did not bring my lunch."

At the sound of Cordelia's voice, the woman's head popped up from the papers that she was grading. She knocked a pencil off her desk as she rushed to stand up and curtsy. "My lady."

For half a second, Cordelia wondered how the schoolmarm knew who she was, but then, how many American countesses lived near the school?

"I am sorry to interrupt you, ma'am," Cordelia said. "But I was wondering if you would like a piano for your school?"

The schoolmarm blinked behind her spectacles. "A piano?"

"Yes, for music lessons for your students," Cordelia said. "Or perhaps a school choir. Music is an integral part of an education."

The schoolmarm shook her head. "That is a generous suggestion, my lady, but I do not know how to play the piano, and neither do any of my students."

"Oh, that is unfortunate." Sometimes Cordelia forgot how privileged her life had been, despite all the difficulties. "Perhaps if you had a free half hour one morning in the week, I could come before school starts and give you a lesson. I could even stay and teach the children music, if that was agreeable with you."

"You want to teach me how to play the piano?"

Cordelia smiled as she pretended to be offended. "I can assure you that I am most qualified to be a music teacher. I have been taught by a master, and I have practiced daily for nearly thirteen years."

"But-but you are a countess."

"I prefer being called Cordelia," she said, offering her hand.

The schoolmarm extended hers. "Miss Agnes Walker."

Cordelia smiled as she shook the woman's hand. "I don't wish to pressure you, Miss Walker, but if you would like to learn, I would be privileged to teach you. And your students too. Music is a gift that can be enjoyed forever."

Miss Walker pushed her spectacles up the bridge of her nose. "I've always wanted to learn the piano, and my Friday mornings are open. Is 8:30 too early? School starts at nine o'clock."

"I shall be there," Cordelia said. "May I call you Agnes?"

The schoolmarm nodded vigorously.

"And you'll call me Cordelia?"

"If that is what you wish."

"It is indeed," she said. "I shall have the piano delivered tomorrow and tuned before our first appointment on Friday."

"Thank you, Cordelia."

"Thank *you*, Agnes."

She had made her first friend in England.

18

Cordelia woke up shivering again. She pulled the coverlet close around her face, but her teeth still chattered. She could hardly wait for the central heating system to be completed. She could see her breath in the air. Were all old English estates this drafty? Or did she somehow end up with the worst one? Cordelia pulled her coverlet over her head and curled into a ball for warmth. She'd not known what cold was before coming to England. The New York winters had nothing on the chill of England that seemed to travel right through your skin and into the marrow of your bones.

Miss Vaughn brought in her breakfast a half hour later. Cordelia peeked her head out from her covers and opened the lid to her tray. There was a half a slice of burnt toast, almost completely black, and an egg that appeared to be made of rubber. The only thing that looked remotely edible was the cup of chocolate. She picked it up and sipped.

Gah!

She nearly spit it back out. The chocolate was not sweet at all but bitter. Almost like drinking brown mud.

"Miss Vaughn," Cordelia said, placing the cup back on the tray.

"Would you mind taking my breakfast back to the kitchen and bringing me something else? I'm not feeling quite like toast, eggs, or chocolate."

Miss Vaughn tutted as she picked up the tray.

"I don't mean to offend."

"I'm not tutting at you, my lady," Miss Vaughn said sternly. "I'm tutting at that rascal Cook, who should know better than to send up such rubbish. I doubt even a starving hog would eat it."

"And whilst you are in the kitchen, would you mind asking for someone to light my fire?"

"Yes, my lady," she said, and bowed before leaving the room.

"Thank you."

A few minutes later, Hattie arrived to light the fire, and Miss Vaughn brought in another breakfast tray. Cordelia was famished and opened the lid expectantly. On the plate there were two pieces of burnt bacon, something that might have once been a sausage, and a squat muffin. She picked up the muffin and it was as hard as a baseball. The only thing that looked edible was the glass of orange juice. Cordelia picked it up and took a drink. It was so sour that she could barely swallow it.

She picked up the brittle, burnt piece of bacon. "Well, Miss Vaughn, I think I may have found your starving hog."

Miss Vaughn shook her head, but Hattie laughed. Cordelia glanced at the young maid—they were probably the same age. Hattie sobered and lowered her eyes.

"I am sorry, my lady. I didn't mean to laugh."

"Don't be sorry, Hattie," Cordelia said. "I'm glad that someone laughed at my joke. Was your breakfast burned as well?"

"No, my lady," Hattie said. "But I ate two hours ago."

"I think my slices of bacon might have been fresh then," Cordelia said. "Miss Vaughn, I feel awful asking you again, but would you please take the tray back to the kitchen and get me a cup of tea or coffee and a biscuit?"

Miss Vaughn slammed the lid down on the tray. "I will get your food myself this time, my lady, after I shove this sausage down Cook's throat."

Hattie laughed again and covered her mouth.

"I suppose I'll have to talk to Hibbert about it," Cordelia said.

"Not the butler," Miss Vaughn said, shaking her head. "Cook and the rest of the females on the staff report to Mrs. Norton. She's the one you need to have a word with."

Cordelia didn't look forward to speaking to the old battle-axe but nodded. "Very well."

"Come, Hattie, you've got coal to fetch."

Hattie bobbed a curtsy to Cordelia and followed Miss Vaughn out.

Miss Vaughn returned a third time with the breakfast tray and although meager, it was at least edible. There were three small jam tarts and a pot of tea with a teacup. Cordelia thanked Miss Vaughn and quickly devoured the jam tarts and sipped two cups of tea until her insides finally felt warm.

Meanwhile, Miss Vaughn filled her claw-foot tub full of hot water in the new bathing room. Cordelia half sighed, half sobbed as she sank down beneath the bubbles. At last, she was warm. But inside, she still felt cold, unwelcome, and unloved at Ashdown.

In the countryside.

In England.

19

ordelia sat alone in the carriage with a basket of tins. Mrs.
Norton explained that it was her responsibility to ladle the
leftovers from lunch and bring them to the less fortunate in Petersley Village. The housekeeper gave her a few tins, but Cordelia had
asked for more so she could separate the vegetables from the meats
and the sweets.

"The previous Lady Farnham never separated the food," she said.
"The hungry do not care."

"But I do," Cordelia had countered. "Why not give them the very
best I can? So, please get me more containers, and I will separate the
different dishes into them."

Mrs. Norton did bring more tins but with an air of one who had
been grossly injured. Cordelia ignored the housekeeper's airs and
made the packages as nice as she could.

"Ma'am, I am sure you are not aware that my breakfast trays
have been inedible," Cordelia began. "I believe that Cook is your
subordinate, and I would like you to talk to her."

"To reprimand her."

Cordelia cleared her throat. "Remind her, perhaps. I should hate
to have to dismiss any of my husband's loyal staff, but I am the

mistress of Ashdown Abbey now and I will not brook insubordination. Nor incompetence."

Mrs. Norton bared her yellow teeth like an angry dog. "I understand, my lady."

"Thank you," she said, and carried out her basket full of tins to the carriage.

The driver drove past dilapidated cottages whose roofs were in much need of repair before reaching the village of Petersley. The driver stopped at a narrow, shabby home. Cordelia introduced herself to the occupants and gave them several tins of food. Mrs. Brooks gratefully received it and asked her inside. She was a trim lady, with large eyes and a prominent nose. Cordelia looked around in shock. The cottage was clean, but there were no modern amenities—no running water, plumbing, heating, or electricity. It was as if she'd stepped into another world entirely—one from a hundred years ago.

Poverty.

She knew the word, but she'd never seen it in real life.

"We've missed the tins of food from the great house," Mrs. Brooks said. "Times have been scarce but better since Lord Farnham's hired the local tradesmen to work at Ashdown."

"Is your husband working there?"

"My husband is dead."

"I am sorry to hear that."

A waif of a girl bounded into the house. "Nancy, where are your manners? Bow to Lady Farnham."

The thin girl had a face pinched with hunger and was probably no more than twelve or thirteen. The same age as her sister, Edith. She bowed to Cordelia.

Cordelia had thought she'd known hard times, but she'd never starved. She'd never not had the conveniences and privileges of money. She'd never stopped to think about how everyone else lived. About the poor people who didn't live in mansions on Fifth Avenue. About the servants in her own house. She now understood why Mabel disliked her. Why she thought that Cordelia was spoiled. In

Mabel's eyes, Cordelia had everything, and she'd only ever thought of herself. What she wanted, not what others needed. It was time for her to grow up and to do better.

Cordelia smiled at the girl and held out her hand. "It is a pleasure to meet you, Miss Brooks."

The girl looked at Cordelia's gloved hand wonderingly.

"Nancy, shake the countess's hand, girl," her mother snapped.

The daughter briefly touched Cordelia's hand before letting go. Her eyes focused on the floor.

"Is Nancy in school?"

"She's looking for paying work," Mrs. Brooks explained, "but the inn in town wants a maid with experience."

"If Nancy would like a job as a maid, I would be happy to hire her at Ashdown Abbey," Cordelia said. "Mrs. Norton would be in charge of her, and there would be pay as well as room and board."

"Really?" Nancy piped up, hope transforming her pinched features to prettiness.

"If your mother approves, of course."

"May I, Mother?"

"We could use the money," Mrs. Brooks said bluntly. "She can walk over this afternoon, if you'd like."

"Oh no, she doesn't need to walk, unless she wants to," Cordelia said. "It's so cold outside. She can ride with me in the carriage."

Both women's mouths hung open. She supposed village girls didn't typically ride in the same carriage as a countess.

"If you don't mind waiting while I make a few more stops," Cordelia said. "In fact, why don't I come back for you when I'm finished with my deliveries so you have a little time to pack your things."

Mrs. Brooks agreed, with many thanks.

Cordelia brought tins to more houses. She was humbled by the graciousness and stunned by their poverty. She felt chastened. Changed. She had no idea that another world existed so closely to hers but was entirely different. Some of the tiny houses were immaculately clean, while others were so covered in grime it made her skin crawl. But what haunted her was the hollow faces of the children. She saw the hunger in their eyes and wished she had more to offer them than leftover food in a tin.

When she returned to the Brooks' house, Nancy was waiting outside, with a small worn bag in her hand. The footman opened the door to the carriage for her and she was wide-eyed. Nancy sat on the seat across from Cordelia and folded her arms primly.

When they arrived at Ashdown, Cordelia led Nancy into the house through the main entrance. She saw Mrs. Norton in the sitting room and ushered Nancy in to meet her.

"Mrs. Norton," Cordelia said with a smile. "I have a new house-maid for you."

"I don't need another housemaid," she said stiffly.

Nancy whimpered.

Cordelia squeezed the girl's bony shoulder in reassurance and then walked to the windowsill and ran her white glove over it. She showed the now dusty finger of the glove to Mrs. Norton.

"I do believe we could use at least one more housemaid," Cordelia said. "Please have Millie and Hattie show her the ropes. I would like her to receive the same wage as them as well. I'll let you see Nancy to her new room. Thank you, Mrs. Norton."

The housekeeper scowled at Cordelia but led Nancy out of the room. Nancy looked over her shoulder back at Cordelia, who gave her a warm smile of reassurance. Nancy grinned back and Cordelia's own heart lightened.

If she couldn't be happy in England, perhaps she could help others be happier and healthier.

20

*I*t had been two months since Thomas had admitted to Cordelia that he loved Penelope. Cordelia had not mentioned it again, but it felt like she'd removed herself further from him. It was as if the entire Atlantic Ocean lay between them.

Cordelia had lived at Ashdown for as long as she'd been gone in London, but he rarely saw her. But he did hear her all morning—not her words but her music, and it was haunting. She made the grand piano make sounds he had not realized were possible from the instrument. She could play for hours on end. Misery had never sounded so beautiful.

Sometimes he saw her at luncheon, where she was always painstakingly polite to him. Most afternoons, she went through the endless crates of wedding presents from America with Mrs. Norton and the new girl she hired named Nancy. Cordelia used the gifts to make every room in Ashdown feel less drafty and more homelike.

Overlooking the renovations took up most of his day and gave him something to do. The sound of the workers sometimes drowned out the eerie melody of her music. In fact, he hadn't heard her playing all morning. The only sound he could hear was the steady pounding of hammers on the roof. Unconsciously, he walked toward the old dining room, where Cordelia played the piano. He opened the door, and the woman sitting there was not his wife—but Penelope. He'd avoided her like his wife avoided him. It was uncomfortable being in the same room as her.

Penelope still wore the same oppressive black dress, reminding him of his father's death. She stood up and smiled at him.

"Thomas, can I help you with something?" Her voice sounded eager.

He couldn't meet her eyes. "I was only looking for my-my wife."

"Cordelia teaches a music class to the children at the village school on Friday mornings," she said, the tone of her voice shifting from eager to resigned.

"Ah, that explains why there hasn't been any music this morning."

"I could play for you."

"Thank you for offering, but I need to check with the foreman about the progress of the roof. It ought to have been done by now," Thomas said, and turned to go.

"You don't have to avoid me."

He finally looked at her. "I'm not avoiding you. I'm just very busy right now with the renovations. I did wish to speak to you about something."

Hope shone on her face, and he felt another pang of guilt.

"Anything," she said.

"I am aware that my father, as your guardian and trustee, unlawfully used your inheritance to pay his own debts. I have made arrangements for the missing monies to be replaced."

"With her money?"

Thomas blushed. What other money was there? "Yes."

"Then I don't want it and I won't take it."

"Why not?"

"How can I accept anything from *her*, when she has taken everything from me?"

Thomas almost touched Penelope's arm to comfort and reason

with her, but he flinched before contact. "It's not Cordelia's fault. If you wish to blame anyone, blame me."

"I could never blame you," she said with such earnestness, such sweetness. So different from Cordelia's playful archness.

"You don't have to. I blame myself," he said, and went back to the library, which he'd made into his office. He went over the central heating plans, but he couldn't concentrate. He tried to blame the pounding of the hammers, but it was really the lack of music that he missed. Thomas blinked and tried to reapply himself to the blueprints. After a few minutes, he stood up and opened the door as Mrs. Norton was passing.

"Is my wife back?"

"Not yet, my lord," she said, and bobbed a curtsy before giving him a wide, familiar smile. He'd often thought that the housekeeper loved him more than his mother did. She'd certainly spent more time with him when he was little. She was like a surrogate grandmother.

"It's nearly luncheon. Shouldn't she be back by now?"

"I expected her over an hour ago," she said in a clipped tone. "But her American ways are quite different than ours."

"Yes, they are. Thank you, Mrs. Norton," Thomas said, and instead of going back to the library, he left the house and walked to the stables. He asked the new head groom, Mr. Rowell, to saddle his horse, and he rode into the village.

As his chestnut mare galloped through the fields, he couldn't help but remember his visit to the village for the burial of his father. He supposed he ought to feel some remorse or regret, but he'd barely known the man. His father had never shown any interest in him or bothered to hold a conversation with his son. The late earl had been away from home as much as possible and only returned when he was out of funds.

How Thomas hated him. He hated his father for shooting himself and leaving Thomas to clean up the mess of his debts. He hated him for defrauding Penelope out of her inheritance. He hated his father almost as much as he hated himself for taking Cordelia's money and making her miserable. But how could he atone? He'd saved his home and his family, but he'd lost his self-respect, and his wife avoided him.

He despised himself.

Thomas didn't have difficulty spotting the new carriage with his coat of arms on the panels in front of the schoolhouse. He swung out of his saddle and tied the reins of his horse to the fence. Peering through the door, he saw that the schoolroom was vacant. He walked back out to the street and looked around, but the only person he saw was Thayne walking toward him, carrying a parcel.

"Thayne, have you seen Lady Farnham—my wife?"

"I believe her ladyship is playing with the children," Thayne said, his disapproval evident in his face.

Thomas turned to see Cordelia in a large muddy field, dressed impeccably in an emerald silk gown, standing by a wicket surrounded by school-age children. She was holding a cricket bat, and her hatless honey-brown hair shone in the sunlight. The bowler pitched the ball and Cordelia swung the cricket bat. She hit the ball high over the players and into the bushes.

"What do I do now?" she cried.

"Run to the opposite wicket," a boy called.

She lifted her skirts and ran to the opposite wicket. He could see her silk stockings and fashionable high-heel boots.

"Now go back," the boy called again.

"Right!" Cordelia said, and ran back to the first wicket.

"Keep going," the boy said.

Cordelia nodded and ran again to the opposite wicket and on her way back, she was tagged with the ball by a little girl. She clutched her side with one ungloved hand and let out a loud sigh. "Did you just get me out?"

"Yes, ma'am," the little girl said, her face red.

"Oh, thank you. This game is exhausting," Cordelia said with a laugh.

"Can I play too?" Thomas asked.

Cordelia smiled and looked into the eyes of the little girl who'd gotten her out. "Do you think we should allow Lord Farnham to play?"

"Yes, but only if he's on my team."

"Right," Cordelia said. "Lord Farnham, you are on the fielding team."

Thomas pulled off his gloves and stuffed them into his jacket pocket. He hadn't played cricket since school, and he'd forgotten how much he loved the game. He chased after the ball, threw it to the children, and finally took his turn at bat. The bowler pitched the ball, and he swung as hard as he could. The ball soared over the farmer's fence.

"Is that a home run?" Cordelia asked.

He laughed. "There are no home runs in cricket, but if you hit it out of the field, it's worth six points."

"Six points!" she exclaimed. "That's highway robbery."

He laughed again and noticed the bright color of her complexion and the difference sunshine made to her face. She wasn't classically beautiful like Penelope. She was radiant—glowing with a happiness he had never seen before. The children surrounded her with their smiles.

"Did we lose?" Cordelia asked.

"'Fraid so, your ladyship," the little boy who'd coached her said.

"Oh dear, I don't think we should have allowed Lord Farnham to play," she said. "Has he lost your ball? I promise I'll make him get you a new one."

"Jenny'll find it," the boy said.

Cordelia exhaled loudly. "I'm afraid it is time for me to go, but thank you ever so much for letting me play cricket with you. And don't forget to practice the song at home before our lesson next Friday."

She then held out her ungloved hand and proceeded to shake the hand of every child present. Thomas stood at the end of the line and held out his own hand. Cordelia looked at his hand and then to his eyes, not taking his hand. He knew he ought to drop it, but he couldn't somehow. She'd shaken every other dirty little hand; she could shake his too. At last, she placed her hand in his and shook it. Her touch was like electricity. It was the first time he'd ever felt her skin.

"Good game, Lord Farnham."

"It was, Lady Farnham," he said, holding her hand. "May I escort you home?"

"I suppose so. It's your family name on the side of the carriage, after all."

"Our name," he said quietly.

They walked to the edge of the field where her hat and gloves were on the ground. Thomas scooped them both up and offered them to her. He was absurdly relieved when she didn't put them on but carried them underneath one arm. When they arrived at the carriage, he touched her hand once more to help her inside. He asked the driver to tie his horse to the back of the carriage and climbed inside.

He sat next to her as he had so often before, but this time it felt different. Charged with some unknown energy. Cordelia's face was so close to his—close enough to kiss. The last time he'd kissed her, the day of their wedding, she'd fainted. That kiss had been passionless, a formal courtesy from a stranger. But he wasn't a stranger anymore, was he? They were husband and wife, after all.

She was leaning toward him, her eyes on his lips as she licked her own. The tension between them was palpable in the air. He wondered how her warm lips would feel against his and he longed to learn the shape of her mouth. He tipped his head down and she instantly moved back against the seat, creating more distance between them. Sitting back, he felt foolish. He had completely misread the situation.

"I didn't know that you were an avid sportswoman," he managed to say after a few minutes of driving in silence.

Cordelia smiled, her color still high from cricket or from the almost kiss. "I used to play baseball with my little sister and our neighbors, when we went to Newport for the summer."

"You have an excellent swing."

The carriage pulled up in front of the house. He waved off the footman and helped his wife out of the carriage again, absurdly grateful that she had still not put on her gloves. One last chance to touch her soft hand with his own. Again, he held her hand longer than he should have, reluctant to lose the only connection they'd made. She pulled her hand back again.

"I suppose I'll see you at dinner?" Thomas said.

"I suppose you will. I'm fond of food," she said, and then turned to walk away from him into the house.

Thomas stood stupidly, trying to sort out his own jumble of feelings, the attraction he felt for two women who lived in his house. He glanced at Cordelia's retreating figure, when he saw roof tiles falling right above her. He didn't stop to think but ran to her and tackled her out of the way. The tiles fell at their feet and shattered on the pavement. He breathed in and out, realizing that he was lying on top of her. Common civility said that he ought to remove himself immediately, but their bodies aligned so agreeably.

"Are you all right?" he asked, touching her face with his hands.

"I'm fine," she whispered. "I would be better if you were to get off me so I could breathe."

Thomas rolled to his feet, then he helped Cordelia stand.

"That was close," she said, glancing down at the shattered tiles.

"Too close," Thomas said, anger overcoming his fear. "I will go and speak to the workers at once."

"Thank you," she said, and then disappeared inside of the house.

Thomas walked around the house to the servants' entrance. He took the back staircase up the three flights of stairs to the roof, but when he arrived to give the workers a piece of his mind, no one was there. Not one of the two dozen roofers. He walked around and found stacks of roof tiles in crates, but they were far from the main entrance. Slowly he walked down each stair until he reached the kitchen. Hibbert was speaking with Cook, but they both stopped and bowed to him.

"Hibbert, have all the roofers gone home for the day?"

"Yes, my lord," he said. "They left before lunch. They told Mrs.

Norton that they'd run out of mortar and left to make more. They said they'd be back around three o'clock."

"Very good," Thomas said. "Hibbert, I would like a full inspection of the house. Every room. I want to know if anyone is here that shouldn't be."

"Right now, my lord?"

"Yes."

Hibbert bowed once again and began telling different members of the staff to check certain rooms. Cook fed Thomas strawberry tarts and tea in the kitchen while he waited for over a half hour. Hibbert arrived back and bowed again. "Everything is in order, my lord. Nothing is missing and no one is here that shouldn't be."

"Very good, Hibbert. Thank you."

"Will there be anything else, my lord?" Hibbert asked, but Thomas could tell that the man wanted an explanation of his request.

"Nothing at all," Thomas said, and walked back to the empty library. He sat down at his desk, with the central heating blueprints, trying to sort out what had happened. A worker had probably been careless and left a stack of tiles precariously near the edge and they fell. He would have a word with the foreman to make sure no such accidents happened in the future. Particularly near his wife.

He had not known her long, but if Cordelia died, she would take with her all the music in his life. She was like a haunting melody that was working its way into his heart. The more he heard her, saw her, spoke with her, the more he wanted to be in her company. To touch her. She was like a spot of sunshine in an otherwise cold climate, and he longed to be near her warmth.

21

The sound of footsteps startled Cordelia awake. She sat up in bed and looked around her dark room. No one was there. She clutched her hand to her heart that was beating erratically. Perhaps it was only a bad dream—she'd nearly been killed by roof tiles yesterday. Cordelia slowly exhaled. She'd had a nightmare, that was all. Yet it had felt as if someone had been standing over her, watching her while she slept.

It was not quite morning, but Cordelia didn't try to go back to sleep. She was too awake for that. She got out of bed, her feet cold on the floor of her drafty room, and walked over to the curtains, which she pulled open. The sun had not yet risen but was already giving out a faint light. She glanced at her door—it was wide open.

Cordelia swallowed. Her door had been closed before she went to sleep last night. Miss Vaughn had helped her undress and then she'd left through it, closing it so loudly that Cordelia had jumped. Her nerves had been on edge last night after the incident. They were still on edge this morning, but she was relieved on some level to know that she wasn't going mad. She had heard footsteps, and whoever was in her room had left her door ajar.

For one insane moment, she remembered the ghost called the

monk, who was supposed to haunt Ashdown. But ghosts didn't open doors because there was no such thing as ghosts. She almost smiled thinking about what her old French governess would have said if Cordelia had told her she'd seen a specter. Madame Raubier would have given her a tirade and then forced her to copy down lines. Thinking of Madame Raubier helped calm Cordelia's over-wrought nerves.

She sat on the window's ledge to watch the sunrise. Her body felt sore and stiff. She wondered if it was from the game of cricket or from being tackled by Thomas. A small smile formed on her lips. Thomas hadn't hesitated. He'd risked his own life to save hers—the wife he didn't want.

Wife.

The smile that had started to form fell back into her usual frown. It felt like she'd exchanged one prison room for another.

Cordelia pulled her knees against her chest, holding on to her cold toes. The sun was starting to rise, and its rays reflected onto Ashdown Pond. She untied her hair and let it fall loosely around her shoulders and down her back. She felt like Rapunzel again, but Stuyvesant wasn't there to play Romeo. The familiar, dull ache in her chest returned for her beloved childhood friend.

He hadn't come.

He never rescued her from her tower.

He didn't really love her after all.

Thomas admired her—but he didn't love her. And that wasn't enough for Cordelia. She didn't want his kisses if Penelope still held his heart.

Miss Vaughn walked through the open door and set down the tray of food on the table. Cordelia thanked her automatically but didn't bother opening it. She knew that inside, there would be one small muffin and enough oatmeal to fill a thimble. The first week she'd sent her plate back to the kitchen three or four times every morning to get enough food, but she was tired of fighting with the upper staff. Clearly, Mrs. Norton and the cook didn't approve of her. She didn't know if it was because she was an American or because she was not an inbred English aristocrat. Part of her wished to complain to Thomas, but it felt like tattling and admitting that she wasn't competent enough to run her own house.

"Aren't you hungry, my lady?"

Cordelia shook her head, then stood up. "Would you please help me dress?"

"Of course, my lady," Miss Vaughn said, then curtsied.

"You don't have to curtsy every time you see me," Cordelia reminded her.

"I have to, my lady. Mrs. Norton would sack me if I didn't."

Cordelia didn't know what to say as Miss Vaughn fetched her an organza dress. She found it perfectly ridiculous that the upper servants wielded so much power in the house. In America, her mother had reigned supreme. The thought of a servant telling her what to do or how to behave appropriately was laughable. Her mother would never have stood for it. Cordelia needed to assert herself. She was the only reason why Ashdown Abbey hadn't been sold—her money.

She sat motionless at the dressing room vanity while Miss Vaughn arranged her hair. The electric lights around her mirror felt bright and harsh. Shivering, she could hardly wait for the new central heating system to be completed next month. The cold draft seeped through her clothes into her skin.

Cordelia finished her toilette and then went down to the sitting room. It was the only place that she found any solace in her sadness. The only place where she didn't have to pretend to be someone else. To be happy.

She sat down on the piano bench and lovingly stroked her fingers over the ivory keys. She would start this morning with Chopin's preludes. Cordelia began playing slowly, softly, with the gentle melancholy required of the piece. Her fingers began to speed up, louder, faster, harder, flying over the keys. She closed her eyes and lost herself in the music—her only escape. She played the notes into a crescendo, then lifted her fingers just above the keys, breathing in and out.

She placed her fingers back on the keys and played another melancholy prelude, moving from heart-wrenching despair to wistful nostalgia. It wasn't until she was at the end of the third piece that she realized that Penelope was in the room watching her.

Cordelia's hands fell from the piano. "I am sorry. I didn't realize you were here."

Penelope nodded. She still wore a ghastly black dress, but her face was beautiful enough that it didn't matter. A brief and surprising pang of jealousy pressed against Cordelia's heart. Thomas loved the beautiful Penelope and not her. She shook her head for that thought to go away. She didn't want or need Thomas's love. Theirs was a marriage of convenience. A partnership. And it wouldn't ever be anything more. Her heart was already given.

"You play very well."

"Thank you," Cordelia said, and attempted a sort of smile. "My piano master, Mr. Phelps, insisted I practice for four to five hours every day. I used to begrudge the time, but now I find it is my favorite part of the morning."

A little color stole into Penelope's cheeks. "My governess taught me how to play, but not like this. Not like you play."

"I am sure you used your hours on important things."

"Not really," Penelope said. "I learned to read and write, but not much else."

"Didn't you read the classics?"

"A little Horace."

"That's all?" Cordelia said, trying not to show the surprise on her face. Her mother had insisted on scores of governesses. She'd learn to speak, read, and write fluently in English, French, and German.

Penelope shook her head. "An English girl's education is not very extensive. We are not considered as important as sons, for they are the ones who inherit the estates and serve in parliament."

"I planned to go to Oxford University," Cordelia burst out. "I'd already passed the entrance exams."

"Really?" Penelope said, stepping closer to her.

"But my mother had different plans for me."

Penelope reddened, and Cordelia felt herself blush.

"You didn't want to be a countess?"

Cordelia shook her head. "No, I am an American. Titles do not matter to me. I do not think that some people are better simply because of their last name. Nor that aristocrats deserve any special privileges because of their birth."

"America must be a strange place."

"England is a strange place to me," Cordelia said. "Your ways are strange to me. I feel like I am constantly out of tune with how I am supposed to behave, but I was not raised for this life. I do not know what is expected of me."

"Not to play cricket with village children or teach them a music class."

Cordelia laughed. "Is that so very bad of me?"

"Shocking—beyond the pale," Penelope said with a shy smile.

"English ladies are hedged around with what seem to me boring restrictions," Cordelia said. "Why can't I play cricket if I wish to? And I thought that women were supposed to be charitable. What is more charitable than giving one's time to teach children music?"

"Our country is older than yours. We are less prone to change. A countess does not interact with grubby school children of a lower class."

"Change is the only constant in life," Cordelia countered. Her time volunteering at the local school was her only joy the last few weeks.

"If you wish to be successful here, you will need to change."

"How so?"

Penelope swallowed. "You are the lady of the house. You set the example for everyone around you."

"I'll try harder," Cordelia said. "I will not give up teaching music to the village children, but perhaps you could give me some other suggestions?"

Penelope shook her head, her sorrowful expression returning. "I do not think that we can be friends."

"Because you love my husband."

121

"No, because *you* don't."

"Why should I?" Cordelia countered. "Our marriage is a bargain. Cash for a coronet. And I have upheld my end of the bargain. The new roof. The new bathing rooms. The new windows. The newly painted walls. The new furniture. All from my money."

"But you're unhappy, and it makes Thomas unhappy."

Cordelia raised one eyebrow. "And you want Thomas to be happy with someone else?"

"I only want Thomas to be happy," she said in a voice barely above a whisper. "He of all people deserves some joy."

"Why?"

Penelope blinked her big eyes, as if the answer was obvious. "Be-because he is the kindest person I have ever met. He always puts his needs last."

She watched Penelope leave the room and couldn't help but think that Thomas *did* deserve to be happy.

But how could Cordelia make Thomas happy, when she wasn't herself?

22

"What do you think of this carpet?" Thomas asked Cordelia as they stood together in an Ipswich shop.

She looked drawn and forlorn after the near accident yesterday. He wondered how much sleep she'd gotten the night before. From the black circles underneath her eyes, very little. Her expression looked unimpressed as she ran her hand over the thick dark weave. "For the servants' rooms, or for the family rooms?"

"Which one do you think it would be best for?"

One side of her mouth quirked up in an almost half smile. "Clever answer. I think it would be better suited for the servants' quarters. I would prefer something prettier and less serviceable for the ground floor and the first floor."

"Very good," he said, giving her a wide smile, hoping to coax one from her.

She took his arm and guided him across the shop to an ornate burgundy carpet, with a pattern of interlinking golden rings. "What do you think of this one?"

"For the family rooms?"

"Yes."

Thomas touched the elegant carpet, with its thick weave and

fine material. "I like it. What carpet would you like for the ground floor?"

"Over here," she said, and touched a lush thick carpet.

Thomas followed her and ran his fingers over it. The carpet was softer than a down-feather pillow. It would be like walking on clouds. "It's perfect. I'll talk to the clerk about purchasing all three and arrange for them to be installed."

She folded her arms across her chest and walked to the window. Her face grew paler. His eyes kept darting back to where she stood while he spoke to the clerk who promised to send a man to measure the areas by tomorrow. Thomas thanked the clerk and saw Cordelia closing her eyes. He stepped quickly to her and placed a hand on her waist. She flinched and stepped forward, away from his touch.

"What are you doing?" she demanded, turning to look at him.

Thomas felt his face color. "I thought you were going to faint. I was only preparing to catch you."

"Why did you think I would faint?"

Her expression was suspicious. If she had been carrying her pointy umbrella, it would have been impaled into his heart. She had not been lying when she told him not to touch her.

"You closed your eyes and looked rather pale," he explained hurriedly. "The same way you looked at our wedding right before you fainted and I caught you."

"*You* caught me?"

"Who did you think caught you?" Thomas said with a humorless laugh. "The Bishop of New York? He's over seventy years old and quite portly; he would never have gotten to you before you hit the stone floor."

Cordelia rubbed her arms with her hands. "I didn't realize... I suppose I should have thought of it before... What happened after I fainted?"

Thomas exhaled. "I carried you out of the chapel to the carriage."

"*You* carried me?" she asked in an incredulous voice, as if she didn't think he had sufficient strength.

"Yes," he said between clenched teeth. "It wasn't that difficult, except the blasted long train of your dress kept getting underfoot."

"Did you ride with me in the carriage?"

"No. Your mother did, and she was crying."

"My mother was crying?" she said, eyeing him suspiciously. "I don't believe it. She's not the sentimental sort."

Thomas ought to have kept his mouth shut, but he wanted all truth between them. "When I asked your mother if she was all right, she said that they were tears of relief."

"Of course they were," she said. "I suppose she wasn't sure until the last moment whether or not I would go through with it."

Her face was even paler than before. Thomas felt ashamed. "Then I rode to your house in a carriage with your little sister."

"Edith?" she said, her face brightening momentarily before flickering out.

"Yes," Thomas said. "She gave me quite the talking-to. She told me that I'd better take good care of her sister or that she would come after me with her baseball bat."

"I miss playing baseball with her... I miss my sister."

"Perhaps you could invite her to come for a visit to Ashdown," Thomas suggested. "I've never played baseball, but I could show her how to play cricket."

She shook her head. "I can't."

"I mean it, Cordelia. You are my wife. My partner. Ashdown Abbey is just as much your home as mine now."

"That's not it." Her expression of misery was more marked than before.

"What's the problem?"

"I would have to invite my mother as well and I can't. I will never forgive her, and I'm not sure that I can forgive my father either. I begged him to stop the wedding and he wouldn't. So, no. I can't invite any member of my family to Ashdown."

"I'm sorry," he said. "What about one of your friends? Your three attendants were all terribly worried about you."

She nodded. "Thank you. That is kind of you. I will write and ask Lucy if she is able to visit. She has also had a difficult time of late."

Thomas smiled at her. "I'm sure a visitor from home will brighten your spirits, and if she comes, it will be just in time for the start of the London Season next month. It will be nice for us to stay in our new home in the city. And I am sure you will enjoy making friends and going to parties... I know that city life is much more to your taste than the country."

Cordelia bit her lip. "It is. But I am sorry for being so prickly today. Sometimes it is hard to pretend that everything is well and that I am happy. But I am trying to make the best of it. Truly."

Thomas was speechless. He too was tired of pretending, but what else could they do? It was too late. They were married. He'd saved his family home and now he had to deal with the aftermath. He knew he should remain quiet, but he couldn't. "Do you think this is the life that *I* wanted? To be shackled to an estate when I'm only one and twenty? To have the responsibility of providing livelihoods for over a hundred people? To be married to a woman who can't bear to let me touch her?"

"There's always Penelope," she said coldly.

"This isn't about Penelope," Thomas said. "This is about you and me. We can't run away from our marriage. You can't leave for London for weeks on end, without so much as a word to me, and then come home and avoid me for over a month. We have to communicate. We have to be partners. We have to try to make our marriage work, for both of our sakes."

The one side of Cordelia's mouth quirked all the way up to a half smile and she held out her hand.

"All right, partner," she said with a thick Southern accent. "I won't avoid you anymore nor will I runaway again—at least not without you."

"That's all I ask," he said, enfolding her hand between both of his.

23

On Cordelia's way home from delivering tins to the poor, she passed the village school. She saw the schoolmarm carrying a stack of tattered readers and trying to lock the door. Cordelia asked the driver to stop and got out of the carriage to help her.

"Allow me, Agnes," she said, and reached for the books.

"You're too kind, my lady—Cordelia," she said as she pushed up her wire-rimmed spectacles. "I was just taking the readers home to try and rebind them. They're falling apart."

Cordelia picked up the top book; the cover was no longer attached to the pages. "It looks as if you could use some new books."

"There's no money for them," Agnes said. "There's never enough books to go around to all the children, and the ones we own have been here since I was a student."

"Why don't you make me a list of what you need and I'll send for them at once. And some new sheet music too. We have a spring concert to prepare for, after all."

"The children are so excited. They love your singing time on Fridays. They look forward to it all week."

"As do I." Cordelia leaned forward conspiratorially. "I like the

children much better than any of the adults I've met in England—
save yourself, of course."

Agnes giggled—a sound that Cordelia didn't know the proper
schoolmarm could make. It was charming. "I am glad. I have practiced the piano every morning this week before school and after."

"I also look forward to our lesson," Cordelia said, and then got
back into her own carriage.

She shivered as she wrapped her arms around herself. When she
arrived at Ashdown, she went straight to the sitting room. There
were logs in the fireplace, but the fire wasn't lit. She could go to
another room, but she knew that her mother-in-law and Penelope
would be in the parlor, and she'd rather freeze than answer a dozen
questions about living in America.

At least Blanche meant well. She was thoughtlessly kind.
Nothing about her own mother was thoughtless. Everything she did
was planned and executed with emotionless precision.

Cordelia pulled the cord to call for a servant and waited. The
door opened and Hibbert entered, bowing.

"Ah, Hibbert," she said. "Would you please light the fire?"

He blinked. "I will pass your request on to a footman."

Lighting fires must be beneath an English butler's dignity, Cordelia
thought with a sigh. "Never mind, I'll do it myself."

Hibbert gave her a stiff bow and left the room.

Shedding the gloves that pinched her fingers, she knelt down
in front of the fireplace. She picked up the tinder and flint,
striking them together to form sparks until the wood caught
flame. Cordelia blew softly on the sparks to spread them, and
soon the logs were covered in warm orange-and-blue flames. She
was close enough to feel the warmth of the fire spread through
her cold fingers and onto her arms. She knew she ought to stand
up and go sit on the sofa, but she didn't want to leave the warmth
of the fire.

Would she ever be truly warm in this cold climate?

She heard the door open but didn't turn from her position near
the fire. It was probably the footman coming to light it.

"There you are!" Thomas said, his voice concerned. "I was about to come looking for you."

"Were you afraid that I was playing cricket again without you?"

Thomas instantly smiled, but the concern was still in his eyes. "I was afraid that something might have happened to you. I see now that I was being fanciful."

"I got a chill while visiting the poor of Petersley and delivering tins," she said, getting up. "And I passed several of your tenants' cottages."

"Our tenants," he corrected.

"Our tenants' cottages, and they are in terrible disrepair. And I have never seen anything like the conditions that those poor people in Petersley live in. We ought to do something to improve their living conditions. Provide some sort of work for the women. Perhaps a factory or two, where we can give good wages? It would also help make the estate more profitable."

Thomas shook his head, and for a moment, she thought he was going to disagree. "I am ashamed I didn't think of it before. Of course we must see that our tenants' cottages are repaired and in good order. And we can speak to Mr. Ryse about helping the poor in Petersley. Would you help me with the plans? I see that you are already full of ideas."

"I should like that," Cordelia said. "If we don't find a way for Ashdown to be self-sufficient, it will be an albatross on our children's and their children's necks."

He slowly smiled.

She blinked. "What?"

"You said children."

Cordelia felt her color rising. "So I did."

"*Our* children," he said, grinning again like the Cheshire cat.

She smiled reluctantly and allowed Thomas to lead her into the library, which boasted only empty shelves. He used the room as an office.

"Our library was once one of the greatest in the country," Thomas said, gesturing to the barren bookshelves. "It held over

18,000 volumes, but it was sold like everything else of value in the house. I mean to replace them. A home is not complete without a library."

Cordelia smiled. "Books are the very best companions."

"People can be too," Thomas said, and held out his hand to her.

This time Cordelia didn't hesitate before shaking it. This time she was determined to hold up her end of the agreement. She would help make both their marriage and their home profitable.

---

homas sat in the empty library long after Cordelia left it, his heart still pounding. She'd been gone for hours and he'd been so worried that something had happened to her. He leaned back in his chair and closed his eyes. The foreman had sworn up and down that he had checked the entire roof before leaving, and no tiles had been left near the edge. Even if they had, he was sure the man would not have admitted it. But why would anyone place the tiles there? All the other tiles were still neatly stacked in their crates.

If the roof tiles had not fallen on their own, then someone must have pushed them. There were no strangers in the house, which meant that whoever had tried to scare or injure his wife lived there. This thought brought him absolutely no comfort.

He leisurely walked upstairs and past Cordelia's door to his own room. Thayne was waiting, with Thomas's dinner clothes in impeccable condition.

"How was your day, my lord?"

"Fine, Thayne. Thank you for asking."

Thomas stood while Thayne assisted him out of his day dress

and into his evening clothes. Thayne knelt at his feet and shined his leather dovetail shoes.

"You seem a little distracted, my lord," Thayne said.

"I was thinking about the accident the day before yesterday," Thomas said, raking his fingers through his hair. "Is there anyone in the staff who is unhappy with—with my wife?"

Thayne cleared his throat.

"You can speak frankly with me," Thomas said. "We've known each other since we were boys; I promise I don't mean to make any trouble for you."

"Thom—my lord," Thayne said, and instead of looking Thomas in the eye, continued to polish his shoes. "I don't wish to get anyone into trouble."

"Of course not, but I trust you, and the staff is often franker with each other than they are with their employers."

Thayne sighed. "I've heard that Lady Farnham sends back her breakfast several times a day and that it infuriates Cook."

"Why does she send back the breakfast?"

"From what Miss Vaughn says, there's not enough food on Lady Farnham's breakfast tray to feed a small bird, and what's there isn't edible."

Thomas clenched his fists. "You think Cook is purposely provoking my wife?"

"Can't say, my lord. That's just what Miss Vaughn has been whispering to the maids. The lower staff is very fond of your wife, but the upper staff feels that she doesn't know her place."

Thomas exhaled and unclenched his fists. "What do you mean she doesn't know her place?"

Thayne turned his back to Thomas and put away the day clothes. "Lady Farnham asked Hibbert to light a fire for her today. He informed her that he'd call a footman to do it, and she said that she could do it herself and she did."

"Butlers don't light fires, do they?"

"No, my lord, it would be beneath his position."

Thomas sighed. "I understand. "

"Mrs. Norton is also upset with her ladyship."

"Her too?"

"Lady Farnham hired a young girl from the village without consulting her. Mrs. Norton said she didn't need another maid, and her ladyship ran her white gloves over a dusty frame and said that she could use another maid."

"Is the village girl settling in all right?"

"Nancy seems eager to please and eats like she's never had proper meal, which she probably hasn't," Thayne explained. "But she's never been taught to be a housemaid and doesn't know how to do the job properly. Mrs. Norton and the other maids have had to teach her and sometimes clean up after her mistakes."

Thomas nodded. "And do the footmen have any complaints against my wife?"

"No, she is an excellent tipper...but—"

"But?"

"They also feel like she doesn't know her place. A countess should not teach music to school children or shake hands with the lower classes."

Thomas waved his hand. "Shaking hands is very common in America."

"We're not in America, my lord, and such behaviors lower her in the eyes of the staff and the villagers."

Thomas bit his lip.

"I am sorry, my lord, I shouldn't have said anything," Thayne said, and bowed to Thomas obsequiously.

Thomas could not imagine an American servant doing the same. Yet he'd never thought of it before. He'd merely accepted it as a normal part of life, but in this moment, he realized how grating it was. He was a young man, barely one and twenty. He'd done nothing in his life worthy of being worshiped or shown excessive devotion.

He placed his hand on Thayne's arm. "Thank you, Thayne. I appreciate your candor."

Thomas went down to dinner, distracted. His mother and Penelope were somber in black gowns, but Cordelia dazzled in a breezy gown of light blue tulle and organza. She seemed weightless in it, and for the first time in weeks, she greeted him with a smile. She was so striking when she was happy. The weight that constantly pressed against his chest felt a bit lighter. As if it'd been lifted, if only for a moment.

Cordelia sat on the opposite end of the long dining table, which he realized was ridiculous. They weren't entertaining a large party. The table was enormous for just the four of them.

"Hibbert."

"My lord?"

"Please move my wife's plate to my right side."

"But that is the dowager's place."

"Move her down one chair."

"But my lord, it is not her proper place."

"Proper be hanged, Hibbert," Thomas said, and gave a small smile to placate the butler. "This table is really too large for such a small party. Perhaps we ought to eat in the breakfast room."

Hibbert visually shivered at the thought of such a social solecism of eating dinner in the breakfast room. Thomas would have laughed if he hadn't realized it would offend his butler, and he didn't wish to injure the man's sensibilities further. The butler moved Cordelia's place setting next to Thomas's and took out his measuring stick to make sure that the glass was the correct distance from the plate. Once Hibbert was finished, Thomas pulled back the chair and held it for Cordelia. She sat down and he pushed her in.

The starting course was served and for the first time, Thomas realized how little the footmen put in her bowl. The second course was the same. He cursed himself for not noticing it before. She'd sat on the opposite end of the table, but that was no excuse for him not to realize how poorly his wife was being treated in their own home.

Cordelia picked up her fork.

"Shall we exchange plates, Cordelia?" Thomas asked.

He thought he saw a smile play on her red lips. "Are you sure?"

"Yes," he said, and passed his generously full plate over to

Cordelia and accepted her meager one. He took absurd pleasure in placing it farther away from his glass than it should have been.

"This chicken is excellent and hot," Penelope said. "Hibbert, please give my compliments to Cook."

"Very good, Miss Penelope."

"Do they have chicken in America?" his mother asked.

Thomas sighed.

"Yes," Cordelia answered patiently. "We do have chickens, ducks, pigeons, and turkeys as well that we eat on Thanksgiving Day."

His mother smiled and nodded. "Is that the day when you celebrate the war ending between North and South America?"

"Mother, there wasn't a war between North and South America."

"Of course there was. It started in the 1860s."

Cordelia coughed and beat against her chest. "Pardon me."

"Tell him, Cordelia," his mother prompted. "Tell Thomas I was right."

"The war between the Northern states and the Southern states happened between 1861 and 1865," Cordelia said.

"Exactly what I said."

Cordelia picked up her wine glass and sipped it, trying to hide her smile. Thomas caught her eye, and she raised her eyebrows. He found himself returning her smile. Hibbert and the footmen removed their plates and served the next course. He was pleased to see that Cordelia received the same size of portions served to his mother and Penelope. Penelope—he'd almost forgotten that she was there. Although, how that could be, he did not know. She was still as beautiful as ever, but she didn't fill the room with her presence like Cordelia did. She was more subdued.

They played cards following dinner, and Thomas excused himself after an hour and walked to the kitchen. Cook, Mrs. Norton, and the rest of the staff were drinking coffee. Everyone stood when he entered, and he felt guilty for interrupting their evening time.

"Cook, I was wondering if I might have a private word with you."

"Of course, Master Thomas, I mean, your lordship," she said, and wiped her large hands on her white apron and followed him out of the kitchen and into the servants' lounge.

"I want you to know how much I appreciate all that you have done for me and for my family. You stayed when most didn't. Most people wouldn't have. You worked even when you weren't getting paid."

"You have paid me back for that time, my lord."

"But nothing could pay back that kind of loyalty, and I want you to know how sincerely I appreciate all that you do."

"Thank you, my lord. The chicken was most excellent tonight if I do say so myself."

"It was perfectly succulent," he agreed. "But I would like to speak to you about Lady Farnham's meals—my wife's breakfasts."

The stout woman looked down at her large hands.

"Lady Farnham is now the mistress of this house, and anything that she says should be considered absolute. If she would like changes made, I want them made immediately. I also want her breakfast tray to be so plentiful that half the food is wasted."

"Yes, my lord."

"Thank you, Cook. I don't know what we would do without you."

"Take some strawberry tarts before you go," she said, and offered him a plate laden with them. He took it.

"No one makes strawberry tarts as well as you," he said, and gave her a smile, hoping to ease the reprimand he'd just given her.

Thomas slowly made his way up the stairs to the first floor, passing Cordelia's room. He paused in front of it. What would she do if he came inside? Would she welcome him or ask him to leave? He wondered what it would be like to kiss her. *Wonderful*, he thought. She did nothing in halves. If her music was anything to judge by, she would be passionate.

Thayne opened the door to the adjoining room.

"I was coming to look for you, my lord," he said. "Is anything amiss?"

"No. I am sorry if I've kept you up."

Thomas followed Thayne to his room and handed his valet his dinner clothes and got into his night shirt. Another new thought hit him. He was a grown man. Did he really need someone to dress him? Thayne did more than that, he knew. He kept Thomas's clothing in impeccable order, and he'd earned his position as a valet just like Cook had earned hers with her loyalty. He climbed into his large, empty bed and closed his eyes.

25

He heard a high scream. Thomas bolted from his bed and threw open the door to the dressing room. He sprinted across the dark room, hitting his shin on a stool. Wishing he would have turned on the electric lights first, he stumbled forward and opened the door to Cordelia's room. The light was dim, but he could see her. She was alive. She was sitting up in her bed.

"Are you all right?"

"I thought there was someone in my room, standing over me," Cordelia said.

"Why don't you turn on your lights and I'll look around."

He saw her shadow move and a few seconds later she flipped on the electric switch. The bright lights illuminated Cordelia's beautiful shoulders and neck, which her delicate nightgown generously displayed.

"Is something the matter?"

Thomas swallowed. "Nothing."

He glanced around the room. Everything seemed to be in order, except there was no fire in the fireplace. He shivered as he felt a cold draft.

"Did your fire go out?"

"The servants haven't lit a fire in my bedchamber at night since I returned from London."

Thomas bit his lip in anger. He was frustrated with his staff. He was frustrated with himself. Why had he not noticed before how awful they were treating his wife? It was unpardonable. No wonder she had been so unhappy. He shook his head as he walked to the door and turned the knob. It opened. He shut it again.

"Did you lock your door before bed?" he asked as he turned back to see her. Cordelia had gathered her coverlet up and covered her neck and shoulders. He wondered if it was because of the cold air or his gawking. Both possibilities irked him.

"Yes," she said softly. "I thought someone had been in my room before. I've found my door open in the morning. So last night, after Miss Vaughn left, I locked it."

Thomas opened the door again and peered down the hall. He couldn't see or hear anyone. He closed and locked it this time. Although, what good locking it would do if someone clearly had the key, he didn't know, but he needed to do something.

"Right," he said. "Why don't I sleep on your chaise tonight. That way I am here if anyone were to come into your room."

He flipped off the electric lights and sat down. He lifted his legs on the chaise and laid down his head, trying to find a comfortable position. It was not an easy task, for he was much too tall, and he was cold. He turned again.

"You can come get into bed with me, if you'd like to," Cordelia said.

Thomas bolted upright.

"Are you sure? I mean I won't be a nuisance or anything."

In the dim light he saw her move the coverlet open for him. "As long as you promise not to snore."

"I don't think I snore," he said as he climbed eagerly underneath the coverlet and like Cordelia, pulled it up to his chin. The bed was large enough that they were not touching at all. He closed his eyes and willed his body to go to sleep and not to think about

Cordelia next to him. It was an impossible task. He shivered again.

He felt Cordelia slide over to his side of the bed and lean her head against his shoulder. She smelled divine, like a flower garden—probably because she took so many baths.

"It is cold tonight."

"I am sorry there's no fire in your room. There should have been. There will be tomorrow and every other night after."

"You believe me that someone was in the room, then?"

Thomas nodded but realized that she couldn't see his face. "Yes, of course I believe you."

"Who has a key to my room?"

"I shouldn't think anyone besides you and the housekeeper," he said. "But I don't know. In a house as old as this one, it is possible that there are more keys. We can have the lock replaced."

"I should sleep easier with a new lock."

"Would it be terribly inconvenient if I put my arm around your shoulders?"

He felt her smiling against him before she said, "Not at all. It would certainly be warmer."

Thomas gently put his arm underneath her head, and she nuzzled her head into his chest—he couldn't breathe. He didn't need to. Didn't want to. She placed one arm on his chest and his heart beat so quickly that he thought that he was having a heart attack. He rested his hand on her hair. At last, indulging in his desire to touch it. Cordelia's hair was softer than he'd ever imagined. Unconsciously he began to stroke it, feeling the silk strands through his fingers.

"I am glad I'm not alone," she whispered against his chest.

"You never have to be alone again," he promised, and stroked her hair until her breathing became steady and she fell asleep holding him. Thomas thought that it was impossible for him to fall asleep in Cordelia's arms, in her bed, touching her hair. But eventually his eyelids grew heavy, and sleep took him.

26

*C*ordelia awoke feeling warmer than she'd felt since coming to this cold country. Her eyes flickered open and she realized it was because Thomas's arms were around her. His body, larger than her own, seemed to radiate heat. His frame wasn't bulky but leanly muscular. His face was less serious in sleep. There was a calmness in his features that she'd never seen during the day or night. His hair, which was always slicked back in proper order, was in repose, wild and untamed. He looked so much younger, so much less an earl and more a man that could have been her friend like Stuyvesant.

Stuyvesant. Even thinking about him still hurt. His indifference cut her to the very core. The memory of his kisses was no longer sweet but tainted with his betrayal. Cordelia glanced at Thomas's lips that were so close to her own. He was no longer a stranger. The unknown English lord who would take her away from everything she knew and loved. He was her partner and her only friend in this horrible old house.

As if sensing her scrutiny, his body shifted and his arm that was around her shoulders fell to her waist. Cordelia felt curiously warmer. Something in her stomach tightened, not unpleasantly— quite the reverse. She longed to be closer to him.

Cordelia's door opened and Miss Vaughn came in with the breakfast tray. Cordelia sat up self-consciously, Thomas's hand still resting on her waist. Miss Vaughn set it on the table before noticing Thomas's presence. The good woman's wrinkled face went beet red. "Forgive me, my lady, I should have knocked. I-I-I will come back later to help you dress."

Miss Vaughn then bowed her way out of the room, closing the door behind her. Cordelia glanced down at Thomas. His eyes were scrunched closed, as if he was trying to block out the morning light. She brushed his brown hair from his eyes and his face relaxed, but his eyes still didn't open. On impulse, she leaned down and brushed a kiss against his forehead. Thomas's eye opened wide.

"It worked," she said with a laugh. "At least one fairytale is true. You can awake someone with a kiss."

"Are you saying I look like a sleeping princess?"

"I was thinking more along the lines of a sleeping prince."

"Not a knight in shining armor?"

"There's plenty of armor hanging in the great hall, if you'd like to try it on," she offered. "And swords and axes, should you like to run someone through after you dance with them."

"It'd be more likely that I would wish to run someone through who danced with you."

"I never thought you'd be a jealous husband."

"Nor did I," he admitted, and the look he gave her caused the tightening in her stomach to intensify.

If Cordelia stayed still, he would kiss her. And she certainly no longer hated him, but she wasn't sure if she cared for him either. Her heart still felt bruised by Stuyvesant.

She flung off her covers and opened the breakfast tray, expecting the usual meager offering only to find the tray laden with biscuits, muffins, bacon, sausages, and eggs. What caused this change? Did the servants know that he was in her room?

No, Miss Vaughn had not been expecting him.

Cordelia picked up the tray and set it on the bed between them. "There's enough for two."

Thomas sat up. If he was disappointed, his face didn't show it. He picked up a piece of bacon with his fingers and took a bite. Cordelia relaxed and picked up her fork and speared a piece of egg, bringing it to her mouth. For the first time, her food wasn't cold—wasn't inedible. Thomas snagged his second piece of bacon.

Cordelia pointed her fork at him. "Don't steal all of the bacon."

He popped the rest of the piece in his mouth and raised his eyebrows. Cordelia laughed. She'd never seen Thomas behave silly before. It was surprisingly endearing. She stabbed the last piece of bacon ruthlessly with her fork and he laughed. Unlike the forced sound he made when he was in company, this laugh sounded joyful. She couldn't help but respond with her own laughter. They ate the rest of their breakfast together in comfortable companionship.

Thomas got out of bed. She could see the bottom of his muscular legs and his bare feet. "I'd best get dressed. The workers will be here soon. When you're done practicing the piano, would you mind helping me with the plans for the tenants' cottages?"

"I should like that very much."

He shifted from one foot to the other, as if unsure of what to do. Cordelia looked down at her hands, feeling like a little girl playing at being a grown woman.

"I will see you later, then," he said, and left her room through their dressing room, closing the door behind him.

Cordelia walked to her favorite seat at the window. The sunlight crested over the hills and warm light surrounded all the ash trees and bushes. The estate no longer looked cold and desolate. Signs of spring were everywhere, from the small buds on the trees to the green sprouts poking out of the ground. England no longer seemed like a cold, austere country, but one on the cusp of change. Like her marriage. Maybe it could be as warm and loving. Thomas was a good man and a handsome one.

She pulled the cord for Miss Vaughn and smiled even when the woman tightened her corset strings. She selected a white gown and sat extra still while Miss Vaughn arranged her curls on top of her head.

Cordelia felt lighter as she walked down the stairs and even found a fire going in the sitting room. Today was going to be a good day after all. She ran her fingers lightly over the piano keys and decided that today was a day for Mozart. Light, lilting, and lovely Mozart. She and Mozart spent several delightful hours together before she joined Blanche, Penelope, and Thomas for luncheon. She noticed that Thomas's eyes no longer avoided Penelope because they were already focused on herself. Laughing at her wit. Hanging on to her words.

Could it be that he was growing fond of her?

How strange.

After luncheon, he offered her his arm and they began to walk together to the library, when Hibbert opened the main door and two fashionable people came into the grand entry. The couple looked to be in their early thirties. The gentleman had the sallow skin so often seen in an Englishman and a large mustache that curled at the ends. He was dressed impeccably in a suit that could only have been tailored in Paris. The woman was startlingly beautiful, with an abundance of dark hair and a stylish gown that showed all of her ample curves. There was a sort of sensuous, animal magnetism about her—she inevitably drew every eye in the room.

Except for Thomas's. He let go of her hand and bounded toward the man, his hands outstretched. "Oliver, I didn't expect you! I'm afraid Ashdown is all covered in dust. We are not getting carpeting installed until tomorrow, and it will take at least a fortnight."

"I didn't come to see Ashdown Abbey but your wife," the man said with a sophisticated accent. "Please introduce us."

Thomas smiled and held out his hand to Cordelia, and she placed her own inside of his. "Cordelia, may I introduce you to Lord and Lady Rutledge, better known as my favorite cousin, Oliver, and his wife, Lois."

"It is an honor to meet you both," Cordelia said, and carefully curtsied the way her mother had taught her. By the time she looked back up, Lois was at her side.

"I can't tell you how pleased I am to hear your American voice," she said in an American accent of her own, with a slight Southern lilt. "We American girls must stick together."

"It's true," Oliver cut in. "She made us leave Constantinople a week early so that we could come back and meet you."

Cordelia blushed and grinned. "Thank you. I am so happy to meet you as well."

Lois gave a smile that was part kitten and part tiger. She took Cordelia by the arm and said, "Cordelia and I are going to have a cozy chat without you. Ladies can never say what they really mean when gentlemen are present. And I want to know all the details from your wedding to this very morning."

Cordelia led Lois to her favorite sitting room and offered to call for tea. She was glad that all the furniture was new and stylish.

"Oh no, tea in the afternoon always makes my insides feel uncomfortable. I much prefer brandy and a cigar, but I don't suppose you have either of those," Lois said. "Now, you were formerly a Jones, yes?"

Cordelia nodded.

"As in the family from 'Keeping up with the Joneses'?"

"I believe so."

"I'm afraid your family, and all the other old knickerbocker families, would have nothing to do with mine before my marriage," Lois said bluntly.

"I am sorry."

"Don't be, darling," she said with another tigerish smile. "I am to be a duchess one day, and now all the old American crows who wouldn't invite my family to their parties because we were *new money* are now begging to make my acquaintance."

"Do you like it here in England?" Cordelia asked. "It's not quite like home."

Lois scooted closer to her on the sofa and took one of Cordelia's hands. "My poor, dear child. Tell me everything. Are your servants positively fiends?"

"Yes!" Cordelia said. "Whenever you ask them to do something, they act as if you have insulted their dignity."

"English servants are malignant and stupid and make life barely worth living," Lois said. "And I should like to hang a few and burn the rest at the stake."

A laugh bubbled up inside of Cordelia and it felt like relief to let it out. "They're impossible."

Lois nodded wisely. "I know, it was the same way when I arrived here five years ago."

"Does it get any better?"

"It took me a little time to learn all the ins and outs of life in my beloved household. And I realized that none of the servants had ever really grown up; they are like children. They have always done things the same way. And I found it is easier to indulge them and work around their silly little rules."

"I don't understand half of their rules," Cordelia said.

"You will," Lois said, patting her hand. "It has only been a few months."

"It feels like an eternity."

"I know. Oh, how I know. I was not created for a life living in a dreary country estate. Once the London Season starts in a couple of months, you'll not have two minutes in your day left for pining."

"Is it as lovely as Parisian parties?"

"The London Season is not quite as gay as Paris, but the events are sparkling and full of snap. But watch out for the Prince of Wales," she said. "Tum-Tum's fond of pretty American girls, but his flirtations are mostly harmless. All of his lovers are married women who are much older than you."

Cordelia reddened and wondered if Lois was one of his lovers.

"Oh, Cordelia, I forgot how young you are," Lois said with another laugh. "Are you already in the family way?"

"No. Not yet," she said, feeling a blush form on her cheeks. She was still a virgin.

"Don't let it worry you. It took me over two years before I had our darling little Duff, and then his sister arrived not twelve months later."

"Do you have more children?"

"Only the two," Lois said. "The prerequisite heir and a spare. Once I'd done my duty, I was finished having children. It was so uncomfortable, and I got quite fat."

Still blushing, Cordelia managed to give a wan smile. "I look forward to the London Season and making new friends."

"You'll find plenty of American women among the elite," Lois assured her. "You can always tell an American."

"By their accent?"

"No! By their *clothes!*" Lois said with another tigerish smile. "I could tell at once that you were American. Is your dress from Worth?"

"Yes."

"No one makes clothes as well as Charles Worth. He's worth a visit to Paris anytime of the year."

"He made my entire trousseau," Cordelia said, hoping to steer the conversation to less-murky waters. "All ninety gowns."

"I cannot wait to see them all!" Lois exclaimed. "You know, you should throw a weekend party with a ball before the London Season. That way you can make some acquaintances before you are surrounded by a thousand people you do not know."

"A weekend party, here?"

"And a fancy-dress ball would be perfect in this setting," Lois continued, as if Cordelia hadn't spoken. "There is such a haunting atmosphere about this old abbey. It quite gives me the shivers every time we visit. I've never stayed a night under the roof."

"We have a ghost…a murdered monk."

"Excellent," Lois said, and clapped her hands. "I know just the costume I will wear. I picked it up while I was in Egypt in December. It's the most gorgeous Egyptian dress and the jewelry is to die for. Tell me you'll throw a party so I can wear it? Your house party would be the perfect start to the London Season."

"I suppose so," Cordelia said. "But I've never been to a fancy-dress party."

Lois grinned. "They're ever so much fun."

"I've always wanted to go to a masquerade."

"Then make your ball a fancy-dress masquerade," Lois said. "I'm sure Blanche will help you with the invitation list, but I promise to bring a prince. You should probably oversee the preparations for the party yourself."

Cordelia thought of her absent-minded mother-in-law, who seemed unable to grasp that America was not another planet. "Good idea."

Lois waved her hands excitedly. "I promise you that you'll never lack for friends again."

"Thank you so very much."

"I must leave, or we'll miss the last train," Lois said, and hugged her. She released Cordelia and then put her hand underneath Cornelia's chin and raised it. "Chin up, you're going to be a marvelous countess."

Cordelia opened the door and Lois swept out of the room. Cordelia sat back down. Somehow just being in the presence of Lois was physically draining. She radiated so much energy and charm and seemed to be so happy with her British husband. Cordelia hoped that she could be half as happy with Thomas.

27

"*Y*ou can't imagine all the dust, but at least I no longer have to fear the ceiling will fall on anyone's head," Thomas apologized as he gave his cousin a tour of the newly renovated areas of the house.

Oliver laughed. "I can't fathom the transformation. Ashdown was a complete wreck when I last visited. I take it that your wife's family was generous?"

Thomas blushed. "Very."

"She seems like a charming young thing; pretty too," Oliver said dispassionately. "Are you now grateful for my advice?"

He felt his face go redder. "I am...thank you... I can repay the money you gave me now."

Oliver waved his hand. "No, no. I said it was a gift. I am just so pleased how well it has all turned out."

"From a financial standpoint, things could not have gone better, but from a personal standpoint..."

"Trouble in the nest already, eh? Still pining for the fair Penelope?"

Thomas instinctively said, "No" and realized that he meant it. Whatever feelings he thought he might have felt for Pen had faded quickly. He wondered if he'd ever really cared for her at all. Or if he'd only imagined himself in love.

How he felt for Cordelia was entirely different. It was a level of passion and intensity that he'd previously not known existed. He thought of confiding to Oliver about the oddity with the roof tiles but feared it would come across as silly or overreacting. He'd never seen anyone in her room, and the roof tiles could have been an accident. He had no proof of any malicious intent.

"No. It's only that Cordelia is having a difficult time with the staff. Things are done so differently in America."

Oliver waved this aside too. "Lois had the same problem when she first arrived. She used to say that our butler was a positive fiend; but eventually they got used to her ways and she got used to theirs. I wouldn't lose sleep over it, Thomas."

"I worry that Cordelia isn't happy here."

"She will be, once the London Season starts," Oliver assured him. "American girls aren't used to living in the country. Once you're in town and going to parties every night, you'll see her perk up."

"You're right. I hadn't thought of that."

"Is she with child? Lois was often quite melancholic when she was expecting."

"Not yet."

"You're both very young. I expect you'll have an heir in the next year or two," Oliver said.

Thomas nodded and managed a sort of smile before leading Oliver to see where the new electric lights had been installed and the places for the new central heating system.

"Now that your structural renovations appear to be completed," Oliver said, "you really ought to try and replace some of the art that was lost."

"Cordelia ordered several paintings from Paris," Thomas said. "They are still in crates in the ballroom. We plan on hanging them when the carpet has been laid."

His cousin nodded. "You should also hire a painter to come do a portrait of your wife. Nothing pleases Lois more than posing for a portrait."

"That's an excellent idea."

Oliver patted Thomas on the back. "Marriage takes time to get used to, for both men and women; just give it a little more time."

Thomas agreed and was relieved to see Lois walking toward them.

"We'd best get going, Ollie, or we'll miss our train," she said, and placed her hand on her husband's arm. Oliver patted her hand.

"Goodbye, Thomas," he said with his jaunty smile. "We'll see you soon in London."

"Sooner," Lois said. "I've convinced Cordelia to throw a masquerade ball before the start of the Season."

"Please say that you don't want me to dress up like a pirate or something equally ridiculous," Oliver said.

"Of course not, darling. You'll be going as a sphinx."

Oliver rolled his eyes and his wife laughed. Hibbert brought their hats and wraps, and Thomas walked them out to their carriage. Instead of returning inside, he strolled along the river that ran by his house. He appreciated Oliver's praise and advice, but all he could think of was how much he cared for Cordelia. He didn't care if she bore him an heir or not. She was more than enough for him.

I'm in love with my wife.

He loved her and he wanted Cordelia to love him and not whoever that American bloke was. But how did one tell their wife that they loved her? Especially if they married her for her money?

Thomas realized that he'd never courted Cordelia. Never attempted to win her favor. He would have to show her how much he cared and then tell her the feelings of his heart.

28

$\mathcal{A}$fter dinner, Thomas escorted Cordelia to her room. He
stood awkwardly in front of her door, with its newly
replaced handle and lock.

"Thank you for the new lock," she said, and pulled a key out of
her pocket. "I feel much safer knowing that I am the only one with a
key to my room."

"If-if you need any-anything, I'm only a room away," he said,
absurdly hoping that she would ask him into her bed again. Only to
be near her. To talk to her without anyone else being present.

"Thank you," she said, and then went into her room, closing the
door behind her.

Thomas sighed and opened his own door. Thayne was waiting
for him.

"Did you have a good evening, my lord?"

"Yes, thank you."

Thayne efficiently went about his duties and Thomas climbed into
his bed. It was cold and empty. He put his hands behind his head and
tried to fall asleep. But all he could think of was Cordelia and how grad-
ually he'd fallen in love with her. He'd always assumed that love was an

instantaneous attraction, a sort of "love at first sight." The first time he'd seen Cordelia he'd felt only relief mixed with a little guilt. Relief that she was pretty, and guilty when he saw her face, her eyes red and swollen by tears. He knew he should have called the wedding off then. But he didn't. He had steadfastly looked forward and thought of Ashdown.

Ashdown Abbey. He'd been willing to sacrifice everything for it only to realize that he now would willingly sacrifice Ashdown for Cordelia. She meant more to him than family, tradition, and responsibility.

"THOMAS! THOMAS!"

He jumped out of bed and raced through the dressing room, this time avoiding the stool that he'd tripped on before. A fire burned in the fireplace, so he could see Cordelia standing on her bed, gripping her steel-tipped umbrella like a weapon. He glanced around the room. No one else was there and the door was closed. He walked to the door and turned the knob, but it was locked.

"The woman didn't come through the door, but she came through the wall there," Cordelia said, and pointed to the west wall that had wooden paneling from the floor to the ceiling.

"It was a woman? Are you sure?"

"Yes, I could see the outline of her shape from the fire."

"Did you see her face?"

"No," Cordelia said, jumping off of her bed and putting on her robe. She came closer to him, still holding her umbrella, but this time like a baseball bat. He breathed in her beautiful, flowery scent. She pointed again to the paneling with the umbrella. "She was wearing white and just stood over me. Looking at me. Then I screamed, and the woman walked to the wall and disappeared inside of it."

"She disappeared in the wall?"

"There must be some way through," Cordelia said, her voice

raising higher. "I am not mad. She must know of a secret door or passageway into the room."

"Good idea," Thomas said. He gently knocked on the paneling every few inches until he heard a hollow sound. He knocked on the wall just adjacent to it and there was a muffled thud, then again in the place where he'd heard the hollow sound—there was something behind that section of the wall.

"I think it must be this panel," he said, his hands pressing against the wall, trying to find the spring to open it. He pushed it with his shoulder, but it didn't even budge.

"May I try?"

"Of course," Thomas said, moving out of the way.

She didn't touch the hollow part of the wall but looked at it intently, her eyes taking in every carving and detail. Then her gaze raked over the entire wall. Thomas almost believed that he could see her thoughts turning behind her eyes. Cordelia pointed to a carving of an ash tree—the symbol of the Ashby family. It was emblazoned on their coat of arms. Cordelia's mother had even had it embroidered on Cordelia's underclothing.

"Try pressing it," Thomas urged.

Cordelia kneeled down and touched the trunk of the ash tree.

Nothing happened.

Thomas sighed in annoyance and leaned against the paneling. It suddenly swung forward, revealing a dark corridor. He swayed and almost toppled over, but Cordelia caught his arm and steadied him. Thomas leaned his head into the secret passage, but it was completely black inside.

"Should we see where it leads?" Cordelia asked.

"I can't see anything."

"We'll need a candle," she said.

He watched her take an ornamental candle off her mantle and light it in the embers of the fire. She held it out before her as she walked toward him.

"Aren't you frightened?"

Cordelia shook her head. "Not anymore. I'm not at all frightened when we are together."

"You're very brave," Thomas said. "I don't know if I am terrified for you or for me, but I am definitely frightened."

"I'll hold your hand if that helps."

Thomas intertwined his fingers with hers. "It does, thank you."

Holding the candle in front of them, they walked down the dark pathway to the stairs. They climbed the narrow spiral staircase, up and up, until they reached a wall.

"I suppose we need to press something again," Thomas muttered. "Another ash tree, do you suppose?"

"There." Cordelia pointed to the wall where a singular leaf was carved. She pressed her fingers against it and then pushed the wall with her other hand. Again, there was a secret door carved right within the wall. They walked through the opening onto a carpeted floor, in a room with a lower ceiling.

"Where are we?" Thomas asked aloud, more to himself than to Cordelia.

"Somewhere in the female servants' quarters," she answered.

"How can you tell?"

"The carpet," Cordelia said softly. "You picked it out for the entire second floor."

Thomas tried to orient himself. He hadn't spent much time on the second floor. He'd always respected his servants' privacy and stayed clear of it. He walked onto the carpet, taking the candle and holding it high in the air. They were in the middle of the second floor between the two wings—the original abbey and the addition his great-great-grandfather had added. This corridor separated them, which meant that the stairs were only around the corner. He walked quickly and shined the light down the stairs—he saw no one.

"I suppose we've lost whoever it was," Cordelia said from behind him.

"They're probably back in their bed," Thomas agreed. "Would

you like to go back down the stairs or through the secret passageway?"

"The secret passageway."

They retraced their steps to the door in the wall, which was still ajar. This time Cordelia took the lead and stepped inside. Thomas followed after her and pressed the ash-leaf carving. The secret door closed. They carefully went down the spiral staircase and back to the outside of her room, where they started. Cordelia didn't go inside but kept walking down the opposite way of the narrow corridor.

"Where are you going?"

"I want to see where this other side leads to."

"All right," Thomas said, and followed behind her.

They turned a sharp corner, and then it seemed as if the pathway ended in a stone wall. Cordelia touched the wall with her hands.

"Solid?" he asked.

"Solid," she said. "May I hold the candle?"

Thomas handed it over, and again, Cordelia meticulously examined the walls on both sides of the dead end. But as far as Thomas could see, there were no carvings of ash trees or anything else. The stones looked as if they belonged to the original structure. They were thick and uneven.

"Just a dead end," he said, and leaned back against the left side of the wall. He let his elbow swing back and he bumped his funny bone against a rock that jutted out farther than the rest. He jumped when he heard scraping. Turning around, he saw a small chamber, no bigger than a closet, with an old trunk covered in what looked like centuries of dust.

"What do you think this room is?"

"The old lock up," Thomas said. "It was common in old homes to have the valuables stored in a secure location to protect against thieves or marauders. Particularly during the English Civil War."

"Wasn't the English Civil War in the 1640s? Do you think this trunk is over two hundred and fifty years old?"

"We won't know until we open it."

He dropped to his knees and brushed off a layer of dust as thick as a quilt. He unlatched the small trunk and gasped at its contents. There was a handful of golden coins. He picked up one and turned it over in his hand—it was a Tudor sovereign.

"Is it real gold?" Cordelia asked.

Thomas handed her the coin. "Look on the back. It's King Henry VII. This coin is probably closer to four hundred years old."

He heard her sharp intake of breath and was pleased to have impressed her. "How many do you think are in the trunk?"

"Ten."

"I feel like a pirate who has just found buried treasure," Cordelia said, smiling and grabbing her cheeks. "But from the age of the coins, these must be from before his son King Henry VIII dissolved the monasteries."

"It was probably the bishop's or whoever the senior member of the abbey's personal fortune was," Thomas agreed. "I wonder why he didn't take it with him."

"Because he never left," she said, and shined the light to the corner of the small chamber, where there were bones and what was left of a robe. "I think we found the body of our ghost, the monk."

Thomas stood up and stepped away. For a moment, he thought he might be sick. Cordelia, suffering from no such impediment, moved farther into the small stone chamber and carefully examined the remains.

"We ought to have a proper burial for the poor fellow," she said. "Perhaps it will end his haunting of the abbey."

"You don't really believe—" Thomas started, but a second look at what remained of the corpse made him clutch his stomach once again.

"No, I don't," Cordelia said. "But either way, I don't want a dead body ten feet from my bedroom."

Thomas could only nod. He managed to get a hold of himself enough to pick up the small trunk and carry it back to her room. He set it on her bedside table.

"Shall we split our treasure evenly?" he suggested.

Cordelia laughed. "But we found the trunk in *your* house."

"Our house, partner."

Cordelia smiled and nodded her head. "I suppose you'd better stay and help guard the trunk until morning. But don't eat all the bacon at breakfast."

"I won't," Thomas promised, placing a hand on his heart. "Only half of the bacon, partner."

29

---

ordelia woke up before Thomas and stole out of the bed. She opened the curtains to let light into the room. Thomas groaned and turned over onto his stomach. Cordelia unlatched the trunk and picked up a large golden coin in her hands, examining it. One side bore the Tudor coat of arms, surrounded by what looked like leaves, with a crown on the top. There were words around the edges, but she couldn't quite make them out. On the other side, there was a king on an elaborate throne, holding a scepter in one hand and an orb in the other.

"Absconding with our treasure?" Thomas asked with a yawn.

"Examining it," Cordelia said, and sat on the edge of the bed. She handed him the coin and he turned it over. "What do you think they're worth?"

"No idea," Thomas admitted. "But they should be pretty close to solid gold. The coin's value was in the metal, not in the currency itself."

Thomas flipped her the coin and she caught it between her hands. "Who do you think was in my room last night?"

"Let's narrow it down, then," Thomas said. "You said that you were certain it was a woman. Was she large or thin?"

"Thin."

"That rules out Cook, Mrs. Norton," he said, "and possibly Miss Vaughn."

"It couldn't be Miss Vaughn," Cordelia stated. "She is my greatest defender in the household."

Thomas looked down at his hands. "I am sorry that you've needed to be defended."

"They haven't attacked me with steel-tipped umbrellas or anything," Cordelia said, trying to make him laugh.

His lips quirked, but his eyes remained serious. "Only with no fires, cold water, poor food, and incompetent service."

"You knew?"

"Thayne recently told me that you were having a rough time with the staff," Thomas said, looking at her with his pale acorn-brown eyes. "I talked to Cook, and if you have any other difficulties with Mrs. Norton or Hibbert, please let me know."

"I can take care of myself."

"I don't doubt that," he said, and bit his bottom lip.

Cordelia imagined what it would be like to bite that lip herself and blushed. "Perhaps it is time for Hibbert and Mrs. Norton to retire," she suggested hopefully. Thomas's face fell, so she added, "With a large pension, of course, in deference to their many years of excellent service."

Then she could hire her *own* staff.

He shook his head. "I offered to let them retire, when we returned from New York, but both insisted that Ashdown was their home and that they didn't wish to leave it... And I don't think they have anywhere else to go."

"What of their families?"

"Hibbert never married, and Mrs. Norton's husband died when my father was a boy. He was the assistant to the games master. Poor Mrs. Norton didn't even have a surname until she married. She was simply another 'Mary' from the workhouse. She has no other home or family but Ashdown. She's lived here for over forty years and worked for the last few for an irregular salary. I couldn't possibly ask either of them to leave after their loyalty."

Cordelia clenched her teeth to keep in all the words she shouldn't say. She knew all too well how much it hurt when others criticized people you loved. Thomas clearly cared about these people. Still, Hibbert was constantly correcting her, which was beyond the pale from a servant. Mrs. Norton never did what Cordelia asked the first time, and when she finally did it, the deed was only accomplished with a great deal of grumbling. And she would love nothing more than to replace the irascible cook with a French chef or two.

"Could you tell if the woman last night was short or tall?" he asked.

She leaned back against the pillows and lifted her knees to her chest. "It's hard to say. They were leaning over me, watching me sleep. I would think they were of average height."

"Which leaves one of the ten housemaids."

"And Penelope and your mother," Cordelia said.

Thomas blinked and she could see his jaw tighten. He obviously didn't like that she was accusing his family. Despite her earlier resolution to keep her mouth shut, she'd still managed to offend him.

"I don't mean to point a finger at anybody," she said quickly. "But such a secret passage would most likely be known only to the family."

"I didn't know about it."

"Your mother and Penelope will be eager to know where we found this trunk. We can casually ask them if they knew about the passage."

"I really don't think that's necessary."

Cordelia felt herself stiffen. Thomas didn't want to hear any criticism of the perfect and proper Penelope. She couldn't help but think about how Thomas always gave Penelope a special smile that seemed to be reserved just for her. It seemed to reference a lifetime of memories and inside jests. Whenever he looked at her, Penelope lit up like an electric light, her beauty brighter and more sparkling.

Cordelia felt cold all over and hugged herself. She may be Thomas's wife and partner—maybe even his friend, but she still wasn't the woman he loved. "All right."

She heard a knock and sprung to her feet, pulling on her robe and tying it. "I'm coming, Miss Vaughn."

Her maid stood in the hall, her brown hair pulled tightly back and the same stern look on her face. She was holding the breakfast tray.

"Please come in."

Miss Vaughn placed the tray on the table, carefully avoiding any looks in Thomas's direction. She set down the tray and bowed to Cordelia before leaving the room. Thomas picked up the tray and placed it on the bed between them.

He opened the lid and picked up a piece of bacon and held it out to her. "A peace offering."

Cordelia took the bacon and bit it. "I didn't mean to upset you."

"I know."

"And I shouldn't have accused your mother."

Thomas lips quirked into a charming smile, and he mimicked Blanche, "Do they have bacon in America?"

Cordelia felt a bubble of laughter form inside of her chest and force itself out. "I must admit that she hasn't asked me that particular question yet."

"Give it time. Give it time."

She couldn't help but think that those words applied to all aspects of her life. She needed to give her marriage, Ashdown Abbey, and these people time to get to know her. And she ought to make a greater effort to get to know them.

They finished the breakfast tray, and Thomas dropped a kiss on her brow before leaving the room with the trunk. She didn't know what to make of that slight affection. Or why she felt tingly afterward. And how she missed him when he left. She pushed down these confusing emotions while Vaughn dressed her.

Cordelia went on her morning walk through the ash grove. She loved how the morning sunshine streamed through the canopy of leaves, creating rays of light. Standing underneath her favorite tree, she watched the sun rise over Ashdown Abbey. The ancient building's reflection in the rectangular pond—it was too beautiful for words. Maybe she could be happy here.

When she returned from her walk, she didn't go to the sitting room but opened door after door until she found Penelope and Blanche in a parlor. They were both working on needlework, and her mother-in-law set down her materials and smiled. Penelope's usually pale face was red, and she didn't make eye contact with Cordelia.

"Cordelia, how are you this morning?"

"Very good, Blanche."

"Would you like to stitch with us?" she asked. "We are making clothes for the needy. That is, if you know how to sew. Do you have sewing needles in America?"

"We do have sewing needles in America, and I would be happy to help, but I—Lois suggested we throw a party before the London Season starts. I was wondering if you would make us a list of whom to invite, Blanche. And perhaps Penelope could help me write the invitations. We only have three weeks until the last weekend of March."

"A party!" Blanche exclaimed. "It has been so long since we've had a house party at Ashdown. What fun!"

"Lois suggested a fancy-dress party if that's agreeable."

"Must it be a fancy-dress ball?" Penelope asked, her eyes still focused on her hands.

"Lois seemed quite set on it," Cordelia said apologetically.

Blanche clapped her hands. "Oh, I remember my first fancy-dress ball. I wore a tiara that the Empress of Josephine once owned. It was all diamonds and belonged to my grandmother. Do you have tiaras in America?"

"There's no royalty in America," Cordelia said patiently. "But my mother has a rather pretty tiara and diamond bracelets that belonged to Marie Antoinette. She often wore them to parties."

"You must miss your mother greatly, poor girl."

Cordelia almost said yes, but the truth was far more complicated than a simple yes or no. She'd longed for her mother's love and approval her whole life. Cordelia was never pretty enough or polished enough for her mother. Every time she'd eaten dinner or even had tea with her mother, it was always a test of her manners, her posture, and her mastery of languages. Perhaps now that she was a countess, she'd finally have her mother's elusive approval. But Cordelia no longer wanted her mother's affections or approbation. She wanted nothing to do with the woman who bartered her own daughter for social advancement.

"I miss my home," she said at last. "And my friends. But I am eager to make new friends here. Lois thought that a small party before the Season would be easier for me to meet people. She even promised to bring a prince!"

"A prince; how wonderful," Blanche agreed. "I recall meeting the Prince of Wales when I was a debutante."

"What about you, Penelope?" Cordelia asked, trying to include her in the conversation.

"I've never had a London Season."

"Oh," Cordelia said, and swallowed. "Well then, this party will be an excellent opportunity for us both to make new friends before it starts."

"I don't have any dresses."

"We can go shopping."

"There is no need," Penelope said stiffly. "I'll get the paper for the invitations."

30

---

*C*ordelia changed out of her morning dress to a more elaborate dress required for luncheon. She sometimes felt that the majority of her day was spent changing her clothes. The ostentatiousness of it made her uncomfortable. Every time she visited the poor in Petersley with her tins of food, she wore a new glamorous dress, while the ladies she visited wore their same home-spun clothes.

The disparity between her life and theirs struck her forcibly each time. She didn't ascribe to the British aristocracy's belief that by their noble birth they deserved the finer things of life. The American way of earning status based on work and success didn't seem to apply here at all. She didn't know their husbands, but she knew that these women worked very hard taking care of their homes, gardens, children, and often elderly relatives. But it seemed like they were stuck in the same slot they had been born into. There wasn't the same chance for upward mobility as in America. At least, not without innovation or inventions. And a bit of luck.

Cordelia sat through a very boring lunch without Thomas. She couldn't help but wonder where he was. The ladies weren't entirely without masculine company. Mr. Ryse, the rector of Petersley, was there. He gave fulsome smiles to Blanche and she giggled in return. Cordelia wouldn't have called him her beau, for she didn't think that her mother-in-law had any intentions of marrying the minister. She would lose her rank and position if she did. But Blanche did seem pleased when he came to dine with them, which was altogether too frequently for Cordelia's taste.

"Lady Farnham," he said sycophantically. "Miss Walker has shown me the new books you purchased for the school. They are as fine as you'll find anywhere but a bit extravagant for a village school."

"I am glad to hear it," Cordelia said with a polite smile. "The children in the village deserve the best education they can get."

"A basic education is good enough for any common child," Mr. Ryse said. "Reading, writing, and arithmetic. Music and the arts should be reserved for the upper classes whose minds are naturally more receptive to their teachings."

Agnes must have also told the rector about Cordelia's music classes on Fridays.

"My paternal grandfather left home with only fifteen cents in his pocket and no formal education at all, but he managed to acquire a fortune of over fifteen million dollars from hard work and ingenuity. One's station in life does not equal one's intelligence or possibility for advancement."

"In the Bible, it talks about casting pearls before swine."

"And are you suggesting that the village children are swine and books are pearls?"

"Oh! Are we talking about books?" Blanche asked. "We used to have a lovely library at Ashdown, so many beautiful books. But they are all gone now. Like so many of the pretty things in this house —gone."

Penelope placed a hand on Blanche's arm.

"Cordelia has brought many fine things from America," Blanche said. "It's a fascinating place from all accounts. Did you know many Indians, Cordelia?"

Startled by the question, Cordelia was embarrassed to admit that she hadn't. "I am afraid not."

"Did you know any cowboys?"

"I believe there are more cowboys in the western parts of America," Cordelia explained. "New York is like any European city."

Blanche shook her head. "New York is too young to be like Paris or London."

"I should like to see New York," Penelope said. "I hear that there are people from all over the world there."

"Yes, there are. It's quite a melting pot of cultures."

"How very irregular and highly uncomfortable," Blanche said.

Cordelia smiled slightly before taking a bite of her food. Penelope skillfully led the rest of the meal conversation away from controversial topics. After luncheon, Cordelia went down to the kitchen to collect the tins for the tenants. She asked for fresh fruit and vegetables as well to be put in baskets. Cook clearly resented the waste of the food but did as she was asked.

The poverty in Petersley no longer shocked Cordelia. The people were not unknowns but acquaintances, with names and stories. Despite their diminished circumstances, they had been kind to her. She gladly stopped to chat with each of them in their kitchens and asked about their families. Visiting the village was becoming one of her favorite things to do. It felt as if she was doing something truly meaningful with her life, besides changing her clothes every couple of hours.

Thomas stepped onto the road in front of the carriage. The driver pulled the landau to a stop. He was wearing a hat and a tweed coat, carrying a shotgun, with a shot bag slung over his shoulder.

"Hello!" he called.

"Would you like a ride home?" Cordelia asked.

Thomas's smile widened when she said "home," but he shook his head. "It's a lovely spring day, so I'd rather walk."

"Ah," Cordelia said, and looked away to hide her disappointment.

"Would you like to join me?" Thomas asked.

167

She glanced down at the empty baskets and her umbrella. She picked up her umbrella and said, "Yes."

Thomas offered her a hand out of the carriage and told the driver to continue to Ashdown. They walked side by side for a few minutes in silence until they reached the field of ash trees that surrounded the west side of the abbey.

"Do you like to go shooting?" he asked.

"I've never shot a gun before."

"I could teach you," he offered. "Most weekend parties will include some shooting. It's a good skill to have."

"What am I supposed to shoot?"

"Birds," Thomas explained.

Unable to resist, Cordelia asked innocently, "Oh, do you have birds in England?"

Without missing a beat, Thomas responded, "Yes, and we have fish too."

"How extraordinary!" she said in a perfect imitation of his mother.

He threw back his head and laughed. Cordelia laughed so hard that she tripped on a rock and fell forward onto her gloved hands. Before she could feel embarrassed, she heard a shot. Instinctively, she kept her head down. Thomas dropped to his knees beside her.

"What the devil?"

"Did you accidently shoot your gun?" Cordelia asked.

"No. I would never be so careless near you," Thomas said. "But I could swear I heard a shot nearby. Whoever it is, they shouldn't be here. These trees are a part of the estate."

Thomas helped Cordelia to her feet and switched sides of the road with her. He kept looking around and over his shoulder as if he was trying to locate whoever shot their gun. She took off her dirty gloves and unpinned her hat. If she hadn't laughed, she wouldn't have tripped over the rock. She held her hat in her hands and they walked the remaining quarter of a mile to Ashdown Abbey. Thomas put a hand on her elbow and continually looked around them.

He insisted on walking her up to her room and Cordelia was glad for the support. She was shaken by her fall and the sound of the shot.

"Shall I take your hat?" he asked when they reached her door.

She handed it over to him. They walked into her room, and she set her umbrella on the side table.

"What the blazes?!" he exclaimed, and she saw his finger pointing through a round hole on the edge of her hat. A bullet hole had burned through the hat's fabric. "A stray bullet, perhaps? But no one should have been shooting on our property."

Cordelia felt the blood drain from her face. She touched the cameo on her neck collar and nodded jerkily. "Yes. I am sure it was only an accident."

Thomas cleared his throat. "I don't want to alarm you, but when I spoke to the foreman to reprimand him about the roof tiles, he swore that his men would never leave them on a ledge. And when I examined the roof myself, I saw that all the other tiles were neatly stacked in the crates."

She sat down on the edge of her bed because it was the closest piece of furniture. "You think someone is deliberately trying to hurt me?"

He nodded, his expression grave. "I hope not, but I do think it would be wise for us both to be on our guards."

She turned to look him in the eye and something caught her attention: there was a single piece of paper on her pillow. She leaned over, picked it up, and unfolded it. Inside, there was only one handwritten sentence in all capital letters: *IF YOU VALUE YOUR LIFE, YOU WILL GO BACK TO AMERICA.*

Cordelia dropped the note like it was on fire. Panic seized her heart and she felt hysterical. "Someone is threatening *me*... Someone tried to kill me. Why would they want to kill me? What have I done? Is teaching children how to sing and giving them new books to read so very bad?"

Thomas stooped down and picked up the paper. She saw him clench his jaw as he read the contents before folding it back up and

169

pocketing it. He sat down beside her on the bed and put his arm around her shoulders. "Nothing. No, you've done the opposite. You've done everything. You've made Ashdown Abbey into a home again. You've helped the village and improved our tenants' homes. You've even helped the local school."

"Nobody likes me here," she said, watching her hands shake as she admitted the unpleasant truth. "Nobody wants me here."

"That's not true," Thomas said. "I want you here. I like you... I more than like you. I—I need you, partner."

She felt so numb, removed from everything around her. She didn't want to be liked or needed; she wanted to be loved. She'd tried so hard to please her mother and now the people of Ashdown and Petersley, but it never was enough. She never was enough. Someone had shot at her from the ash grove, her favorite trees and the place where she loved to think.

"We should leave," Thomas said suddenly. "We could go to London tonight."

"But we sent out the invitations yesterday for a party at Ashdown that is in less than a fortnight. Can you imagine what kind of gossip there would be if we weren't here for our first party?"

"I don't mind the gossip as long as you are safe."

"And how do we know that we won't be bringing the person who is trying to hurt me with us to London?"

"You think it is one of the servants?"

She shook her head. She was too hysterical to think. To reason. "I-I-I don't know. I'm not sure that I would feel any safer in London than I do here. There are so many strangers there. So many places and nooks for people to lurk."

"We'll stay at Ashdown until the party is over. Until then, don't go anywhere by yourself," Thomas said, standing up. "I'll go and speak to the local constable at once and have him come over and investigate. If I need to, I'll even call in Scotland Yard."

Cordelia did not trust her voice, so she nodded.

Thomas pressed a gentle kiss to her cheek. "Be safe, my darling."

He went back out her door and Cordelia pressed a hand to her cheek. He'd called her *his darling*.

Somehow that was more shocking than being threatened and shot at.

31

A week later, a gentleman named Mr. Holden from Scotland Yard, with a long brown beard and only one eye, met with Thomas.

"Mr. Holden at your service, my lord," the inspector said with a curt bow, raising his bowler hat off his head.

"Thank you for coming." Thomas led Mr. Holden to his closed carriage. He didn't dare ride about in the open-air landau anymore.

"Tell me more about your wife, Lady Farnham."

"My wife is from New York. She is the daughter of Mr. and Mrs. Jones."

"The railroad family?"

"Yes," Thomas said, and paused before adding, "and I fear that someone is trying to kill her."

"Why do you believe that, my lord?"

"Someone shot a hole through her hat last week, and if she hadn't tripped, it would have been through her heart. And before that, roof tiles nearly fell on my wife, and if I hadn't pushed her out of the way..."

"Might these incidents have been accidents?" the inspector suggested. "And your wife's presence only a coincidence?"

Thomas cleared his throat. "I would have agreed with you if we had not found a threatening note in her room."

Mr. Holden raised one eyebrow. "A note?"

"It said, 'If you value your life, you will go back to America.'"

"Did you recognize the handwriting?"

He shook his head and pulled the folded note from his breast pocket and handed it to the inspector.

Mr. Holden held it close to his left eye and then extended his arm for a farther view before placing it into his briefcase. "Do you have any suspicions of who would want to hurt your new wife?"

"She's having a rather difficult time with the upper staff, but I don't think they'd shoot her over it."

Mr. Holden gave a wry smile. "Who else resides at Ashdown Abbey?"

"My mother, Dowager Lady Farnham, and my family's ward, Miss Penelope Hutchinson."

"Do they often go shooting? I'm aware that many upper-class ladies enjoy the sport."

"Both my mother and Penelope are proficient with a gun, but Hibbert, our butler, assured me that no one had used the gun room that day. He keeps the keys."

"And there's no one else?"

"Mr. Ryse, the local rector, is a sort of relation. The position at Petersley Church is paid for by the estate, and he always gives short sermons on Sundays. He is a great friend of the family and often eats his meals at Ashdown Abbey."

"Does Mr. Ryse approve of your choice of wife?"

"I believe so. Without Cordelia's money, he would have been out of a position, as would everyone on the staff. Ashdown would have been sold, and it's not easy for a man of his years to find a new position."

"Or one where so little is required."

"I couldn't say," Thomas said. "I don't know the duties of a rector."

They fell into an uncomfortable silence. Thomas couldn't bear it if anything were to happen to Cordelia, but he also couldn't endure the thought that someone he cared for might try to hurt his wife. Surely, if they had issues, they'd come and speak to him instead.

Mr. Ryse was the one who had taught him how to ride a bicycle and skip a rock. His father's brief visits never allowed for such things nor would he have bothered to spend time with his only son. Hibbert was the one who patched up Thomas's childhood scrapes and listened to his adventures. Edwin Thayne, his valet, had been his childhood friend and had stood by him when others would not have. Cook and Mrs. Norton had both been warm and loving, when his mother had been neither. She never could be bothered with dirty boys. Although, she'd always seemed fond enough of Penelope, but perhaps it was because she was a girl.

The carriage stopped in front of the abbey. Thomas got out first and Mr. Holden slowly stepped out behind him. He whistled again as he looked at the historical building.

"Quite an ancestral pile you've got here. Has it been in the family for generations?"

"Since King Henry VIII sold it to my ancestor," Thomas said, and led the way into the house.

Mr. Holden seemed to notice every detail of the house, from the new electric lights to the newly acquired paintings from France.

"If I may be so bold, what was your wife's dowry?"

Thomas debated not telling the man, but he didn't want to keep anything to himself that could protect Cordelia. "Two million dollars."

Whistling again, the inspector raised his eyebrows. "If you weren't so eager to protect your wife, you would be my principal suspect."

"There's something else."

"Yes?"

"Someone dressed in white has been entering my wife's room and watching her sleep," Thomas said quickly. "We put a new lock on the door, but they entered through a secret passage that I recently discovered."

"I should like to see your wife's room and the secret passage."

"This way," Thomas said, and led the inspector up the grand staircase to the wing of family rooms. He knocked on Cordelia's door. Miss Vaughn answered it.

"Is Lady Farnham in her room? The inspector from Scotland Yard would like to see it."

"Come in, Thomas," Cordelia called from behind Miss Vaughn.

Miss Vaughn swung open the door further and Cordelia stood dressed in a peach chiffon tea gown, with a V-neck and elbow-length sleeves. She was stunning and the one-eyed inspector looked at her appreciatively.

"Cordelia, allow me to introduce Mr. Holden, from Scotland Yard," he said, pride in his voice. "My wife, Lady Farnham."

Cordelia offered her hand and Mr. Holden bowed over it. "I suppose you're here to see the secret passageway."

"I am, my lady."

"Thomas will show you; I think Miss Vaughn would have my hide if I ruined this dress."

Mr. Holden smiled at her.

"We won't be long, Cordelia," Thomas said.

He showed the inspector how to press on the ash tree to open the secret door in the wall. He then led the inspector down the corridor and up the spiral stairs, which led to the second floor, where the staff's rooms were. Again, he showed the inspector where the carved leaf was that opened the passageway. Mr. Holden had a small black notebook, where he took feverish notes. Thomas also showed him the priest's hole, where they had found the skeleton (since buried and blessed by Mr. Ryse). Then Thomas took the inspector back to Cordelia's room, where she stood waiting for them next to Miss Vaughn.

"Lord Farnham, I presume that this was your mother's room before it was your wife's?"

"Yes."

Mr. Holden scribbled something into his notebook. "Lady Farnham, what do you recall of your nightly visitor?"

"A slight person who appeared female in form and smelled pleasant—like they were wearing some sort of perfume."

"Did they ever touch you, my lady?"

"No," Cordelia said firmly. "They simply stood over me and watched me sleep."

The inspector raised one eyebrow and gave her a penetrating gaze. "Did you recognize the handwriting on the note?"

Her face grew paler. "No, sir."

Mr. Holden nodded and wrote some more in his little black book. "I should like to speak to the rest of the family now."

"Very good."

"My lady," he said, and tipped his hat to Cordelia. "I look forward to seeing you again."

Cordelia curtsied gracefully to him. *A princess couldn't have been more poised*, Thomas thought. She was the perfect countess.

He led Mr. Holden back down the stairs to the parlor his mother preferred. It was the only room that hadn't been renovated or redecorated. She and Penelope were sitting and sewing. They stood when Thomas entered the room.

"Mr. Holden, allow me to introduce you to my mother, Dowager Lady Farnham, and my family's ward, Miss Penelope Hutchinson."

"A pleasure," Mr. Holden said with a bow.

His mother merely nodded in response.

"Nice to meet you, sir," Penelope said.

"Won't you sit down?" his mother said with a smile.

Mr. Holden took a seat in a sedan chair, and Thomas sat next to Penelope on the sofa. He saw her sweet blush and instantly regretted sitting by her when he saw Mr. Holden observing it.

"Miss Hutchinson, I know that this is an impertinent question, but I need to ask it all the same," Mr. Holden said. "The constable informed me that before Lord Farnham married the current Lady Farnham, it was generally assumed in the village that he was going to marry you. Is that true?"

Penelope's gentle blush deepened to a fiery red. "There was nothing formal. It was a sort of family expectation is all."

"Do you consider yourself jilted?"

"No, it wasn't Thomas's fault."

"Whose fault was it?" Mr. Holden asked.

"His father's, of course. If the late earl hadn't left so many debts, Thomas would not have been responsible for discharging them."

Mr. Holden wrote down a few more sentences in his notebook.

"Dowager Lady Farnham, were you aware that there is a secret passageway that leads from the servants' floor to your old room?"

"Yes, my old room once belonged to the Bishop of Suffolk," she said.

"Did you ever tell your son or his wife about this extra entrance?"

His mother smiled her polite, blank smile. "Oh dear. It quite slipped my mind."

"Does anyone on the staff know about it?"

"Hibbert does, I believe. He's been at Ashdown longer than any of us. Mrs. Norton might, but I am not sure. I don't entirely recall. It hasn't been used in many years, of course."

"Have you entered your daughter-in-law's room at night and watched her while she sleeps?" Mr. Holden asked softly.

His mother tried to smile but couldn't quite manage it. Thomas held his own breath waiting for her answer.

"No."

"Do you like your daughter-in-law?"

"She's not a bad sort of girl, even if she is an American," his mother said, as if that explained everything about Cordelia.

"Are you sorry to lose your place as the mistress of the house? Your room? Your precedence?"

"Yes," she said. "When Mrs. Norton called me Dowager Countess of Farnham, I almost wished my husband wasn't dead, but it really is so much better for everyone that he is. Even if Thomas didn't marry Penelope and Cordelia is an American."

Thomas did not know what to say. He felt sympathy for his mother but realized that she was as much a stranger to him as his father. He'd been allowed to see her for an hour before dinner growing up, when he wasn't at school. But he had no idea who his mother was or what she thought. Or how she'd felt about his father's death, his marriage, or the changes to her longtime home. He should have talked to her about all of these things, but he had no experience doing that. His family had never confided in each other. Perhaps that was why he wanted a different relationship with his wife—one with open communication.

"I should like to speak to the servants now," Mr. Holden said.

Thomas stood up and opened the door. He left the room without glancing back at his mother or Penelope.

32

"You've got your wish, my lady," Miss Vaughn said, as she helped Cordelia into her mauve evening gown, with a scooped neck and extravagant puffed sleeves trimmed with lace.

"What wish?"

"The uppity Hibbert's been taken into custody for questioning."

"What!?" Cordelia gasped in surprise.

Even Miss Vaughn's wrinkles seemed to smile as she explained, "He is the only member of the staff with access to the guns, and the inspector found the weapon that was used in Ashdown's gun room. But the clincher was the paper from that horrible note matched the stationary in his office."

"Good heavens," Cordelia exclaimed.

"Not that I ever gossip, my lady," Miss Vaughn said primly.

"Of course not."

"But if I were to gossip—"

"Yes, Miss Vaughn?" Cordelia prompted.

"I'd tell you that Thayne is pleased as punch to be a butler at his young age. It's practically indecent, it is. He's not even twenty-five."

"Neither is Lord Farnham."

Miss Vaughn tutted. "But he was born to his position, my lady, not given it."

"Isn't being born into something the same as being given it? He didn't do anything to receive his title."

The older lady shook her head. "Our traditions make us who we are, and if we were to lose our traditions, we would have nothing left."

Cordelia felt somber during dinner; she always did when Mr. Ryse dined with them. Thayne poured the wine, and the footmen served the courses. The food tasted blander than usual. She had no appetite. All she could think about was Hibbert and that his obsession with traditions and estates caused him to attempt murder. It seemed incredulous to her. But as she'd been told so many times in the last few months, she wasn't English.

After dinner, she didn't join the card game. She wasn't in the mood. Blanche and Mr. Ryse competed against Thomas and Penelope. She felt a flash of annoyance at the puppy eyes Penelope always gave Thomas and the smile he responded with. She tried to read but could not concentrate. Penelope kept giggling and reminiscing.

"Oh, Thomas," she said, "do you remember when we climbed the giant ash tree and got stuck for hours? We screamed for help until we were hoarse."

Cordelia glanced up in time to see Thomas's face light up as he laughed. He looked younger, carefree, and happy. Penelope made him happy, whereas Cordelia could not.

"And we would be up there still if it weren't for the goodness of Mr. Ryse," he said, clapping the older man on the shoulder. "You climbed up and carried us down one at a time."

Mr. Ryse nodded, but there was a light in his eyes. "Aye, and a rare lecture I gave you both once all of our feet were on the ground."

Penelope glowed brighter than any light bulb. "Yes, and Thomas bravely took all the blame. Although, I do recall that it was my idea to climb that particular tree."

"I was your knight, after all."

She clapped her hands. "Yes, I'd forgotten. I was your princess."

Thomas guffawed.

Cordelia snapped her book closed. She wasn't reading it anyway, and her life was anything but a fairytale. Hibbert had tried to kill her, and they were chatting like nothing had happened. If anything, Thomas seemed to be trying too hard to be cheery and laughing loudly at the weakest of jokes. She bit down on the insides of her cheeks to hold in her frustration. Setting down the book, she walked to the door. Jealousy mixed with anger coursed through her body like hot blood. She couldn't endure another half hour of their tender memories or shared happiness.

"Leaving already?" Blanche called.

"I'm a bit tired."

"I'll accompany you," Thomas said, springing to his feet, casting a quick glance of apology to Penelope.

"But what of our game?" Mr. Ryse protested.

"Yes, Thomas, you can't leave Penelope without a partner," Blanche said.

"I'm sure Pen can handle herself very well without me," he said, and took Cordelia's elbow and escorted her out of the room. Her pulse quickened, as did her temper. Still, she took his offered arm and smelled his American cologne; she felt the same sort of odd tingling in her stomach that she'd felt when they were alone in her room. She couldn't help but wish that he loved her and not Penelope.

They walked together until they reached the door to her room.

An errant lock of hair fell across her face, and before she could brush it out of the way, Thomas gently picked up the curl and tucked it behind her ear. "May I kiss you?"

She opened her mouth, but no words came out, so she nodded.

His hand moved to her cheek and he softly cupped it before kissing her. His warm lips brushed gently against hers, yet she felt the kiss all the way to her toes. Thomas wrapped his arms around her waist and held her tightly against him. She felt warm and safe and wonderful. Not even Stuyvesant's kisses had made her feel this way. He deepened the kiss and Cordelia's entire body tingled; she knew that she would never be the same.

Someone cleared their throat. Cordelia instinctively stepped back. Behind Thomas, Thayne stood waiting patiently.

Thomas's jaw tightened and he looked annoyed, but he asked civilly, "Do you need anything, Thayne?"

"There's a gentleman and two ladies at the door, my lord."

"At this hour?" Thomas said. "Tell them to come back in the morning."

"They're American, my lord," Thayne said, glancing at her when he added, "and the gentleman refuses to leave the premises until he sees Lady Farnham."

"What name did he give?"

Thayne held up a card. "Mr. Stuyvesant Bradley, my lady."

Cordelia touched her throat and felt a rush of adrenaline surge through her body at the very sound of his name.

Before she realized what she was doing, Cordelia walked forward and grabbed the card out of Thayne's hands. Her breathing was fast and erratic as she read the words again: *Mr. Stuyvesant Bradley*. Her heart was beating wildly, and she could not wait another moment to see him. Picking up her skirts, she started quickly down the stairs to the main entrance. She heard Thomas's footfalls behind her, but she didn't stop. Couldn't stop. She rounded the corner and there he was, hat in hand, standing by the first footman who was eyeing him askance. He was so handsome! The pounding in her chest doubled in speed.

"Cordy!" Stuyvesant called, and easily pushed past the smaller footman and grasped her by her arms, which was good, for she was strangely light-headed and would not have been able to stand much longer on her own. "Cordy, I've been so worried about you. Your mother's servants always said that you weren't home, and you never answered my letters."

Her lips parted and she gasped in surprise. "You-you wrote to me?"

"Dozens of letters."

"I never received even one letter from you," Cordelia said, momentarily forgetting everyone else in the room. "My mother must have kept them from me."

"Why didn't you wait for me?" he asked gruffly, his grip on her arms tightening. It pained her a little but helped to ground her as the room seem to be closing in on her. "I would have married you instantly if I'd known. I learned of your marriage through an old paper of the *New York Times* I came across in Gibraltar. Some such rot about an American fairytale wedding."

She shook her head and moistened her lips. "My mother locked me in my room, and I sent a letter to you, begging for your help. I even bribed a maid with my diamond earrings to send it."

"I never received it," he said, looking her directly in the eye. Into her soul.

Cordelia believed his sincerity. Her best friend hadn't abandoned her. He *did* love her! Mabel, her maid, had lied to her. She'd taken the earrings and never delivered the letter. Mabel had always seemed resentful of her, and Cordelia had been a fool, a desperate fool, to have trusted her at all. Exhaling, she looked up and saw bright red hair under the most fashionable hat. Reluctantly, she pulled away from Stuyvesant and threw her arms around her dearest friend.

"Oh, Lucy, you came!" she said, squeezing her tightly. "I've missed you so much."

"And I you," Lucy said softly. "I should have written and given you warning that we arrived in England, but I ran into Mr. Bradley on the ship across the Atlantic and he kindly offered to escort me and my chaperone, Mrs. Stewart, to your home. We should have sent a telegram first. We didn't mean to arrive so late or so unexpected. I am sure we can find some rooms at a local inn."

Cordelia saw an older woman standing a few steps away, eyeing the reunion with interest. The footman Tim watched their scene stoically and Thayne incredulously—gossip would be rampant in the servants' quarters tonight. Her smile wavered and her chest felt impossibly tight.

"You could never be unwelcome," Cordelia said, wrapping her arms around herself, rubbing the place on her skin where Stuyvesant had touched her. "We have plenty of rooms, and I have missed you all so much."

"Cordelia," Thomas said from behind her, "would you be so kind as to introduce me to your friends?"

Thomas.

Her husband.

She tried to smile. To act naturally.

"Thomas," she said in a strained voice, "allow me to introduce you to my dearest friend Miss Lucy Miller, her chaperone, Mrs. Stewart, and Mr. Stuyvesant Bradley; he was my next-door neighbor in New York. I am pleased to introduce you all to my husband, Lord Farnham."

Thomas gave a tight smile and bent over Lucy's outstretched hand and then Mrs. Stewart's. He held out his hand to Stuyvesant. "Mr. Bradley."

Her old love made no attempt to be pleasant but took Thomas's hand and gripped it tightly. "Lord Farnham."

Like two cats, they tried to stare each other down, gripping the other's hand as tightly as possible. Cordelia rocked back and forth on her feet, unable to look away. Unable to speak. She wanted to cry. To laugh. To scream. To do something. To say something to ease the growing tension in the room and in her heart. Her hands longed to touch them both. To comfort and soothe them. To receive comfort. But she didn't. She couldn't.

"Welcome to Ashdown Abbey," Thomas said.

"It is certainly a beautiful old building," Mrs. Stewart said in a whispery, sweet voice. "I have quite a fondness for antiquities, do I not, Lucy?"

"Yes-yes," her friend stumbled on her words, her eyes on Cordelia, full of pleading. "I long to see it in the light of day."

Her words pulled Cordelia out of her stupor. "And you will tomorrow." She turned to the first footman. "Tim, please have Mrs.

Norton prepare the guest rooms twenty-eight through thirty for our guests."

"Yes, my lady."

"Thayne, if you would be so kind as to ask Cook to prepare some tea for my guests and have it sent to their rooms. Also, please send some men to fetch their trunks."

"Very good, ma'am."

Thomas and Stuyvesant still held each other's hands in a death grip. She didn't want either of them to be hurt, but somehow she knew that they all would be. Cordelia walked over and gently took Thomas's arm and tucked her hand inside the bend of his elbow. He instantly let go of Stuyvesant's hand. Thomas's gentle touch strengthened her and sent shockwaves of adrenaline through her body.

"You've all come at the perfect time," she said in a breathless voice that did not sound like her own. "We are having a large party joining us tomorrow for the weekend, and there will be a fancy-dress ball on Saturday. Stuyvesant, you've always enjoyed dressing up."

"I have no costume."

"I'm sure we can find something for you," Thomas said.

They led the way farther into the house and her American friends followed them. Her grip on Thomas's arm tightened. She hoped Thomas wouldn't take them to meet his mother and Penelope yet. She wasn't quite ready for that ordeal.

"It'll be a masquerade," Cordelia rattled on, desperate to fill the awkward silence. "Thomas's aunt, the Duchess of Oxenbury is coming with her husband, the duke, and Lord and Lady Esher, Lord and Lady Rutledge, the Earl and Countess of Gresham, Baron and Baroness Whitby, the Marquess and Marchioness of Grimsby, Viscount Brinkley, Mr. and Mrs. Hawkins, and Mr. and Mrs. Bracken. We even have a prince coming—Queen Victoria's grandson."

"You English folk sure like your meaningless titles," Stuyvesant said, shaking his head.

She felt Thomas's arm stiffen underneath her touch. "Our country is built on tradition."

"I can hardly wait to meet a real prince," Lucy piped up.

Cordelia knew that her friend was trying to ease the awkward situation and was grateful to her. If only she could ease Cordelia's racing mind and beating heart.

"America is built on hard work and industry," Stuyvesant retorted. "Something I don't think any English aristocrat could understand. You sit in your old castles collecting rents like your ancestor's did."

"It is actually an abbey."

"Yes," Cordelia cut in breathlessly. "Ashdown Abbey is a fascinating historic structure. I look forward to giving you all a tour of it tomorrow, and we can talk then, but it is getting late. Ah, Thayne, you are back. Would you please lead Mr. Bradley to room thirty and give him any assistance that he needs?"

"This way, Mr. Bradley," Thayne said, pointing down the hall.

Stuyvesant gave her one more searing look before following him. Cordelia clutched Thomas's arm tighter for support. This evening was both a dream and a nightmare.

"I had the rooms numbered for easiness, but sometimes it feels a bit like a hotel," Cordelia said with a fake laugh. "Lucy, if you and Mrs. Stewart will come with me, I'll take you to your rooms. Hopefully, the tea will have already arrived."

She pulled her arm free from Thomas's and linked it with Lucy's. "I have completely redone your rooms, so feel free to admire anything and everything."

Cordelia was still pretending in front of her friend because of her chaperone. Lucy must have realized it, for she squeezed Cordelia's hand. "There is so much to admire."

Rattling on about unimportant things, Cordelia managed to get both ladies into their correct room. The fires were lighted and the bed covers turned down. At least her staff's war with her did not extend to her guests.

Mrs. Stewart stayed close to Lucy as they waited for their trunks to be brought up. There was no chance for a private word, so Cordelia excused herself.

Thomas was already in her bed when she arrived in the room.

Miss Vaughn was waiting in the dressing room. She helped Cordelia undress and put on her nightgown before leaving. Cordelia slipped under the covers.

Thomas turned on his side to face her. "When you said you loved someone before we married, did you mean Mr. Bradley?"

There was no anger or resentment in his tone. No accusation. But she felt as if her heart was under attack. "Yes."

Thomas nodded once and, without another word, faced the opposite direction.

She stayed awake for over an hour, her mind reeling. Stuyvesant was here and he still loved her. But she was already married to Thomas, the man at her side, the man her heart ached for.

33

*S*he woke up alone in her bed. Thomas was not sprawled about, waiting to eat all of her bacon. Trying to organize the chaos of her thoughts, she squeezed her eyes shut. It was as if her two separate worlds were colliding. Stuyvesant, the familiarity of home and shared values, coming up hard against her new home, Thomas, and century-old traditions. She felt herself being torn in both directions, not wanting to let go of either.

Miss Vaughn knocked. Cordelia pulled on her robe and unlocked her bedroom door. It was probably foolish to keep locking it, after Hibbert had been incarcerated, but she still found herself uneasy. He had not been the one entering her room. She was certain of it. He was too large, too masculine, and he didn't wear perfume.

"Here you are, my lady," Miss Vaughn said, placing the tray on the bedside table. If she noticed the absence of Thomas, she made no sign of it.

"Thank you, Miss Vaughn," Cordelia said, climbing back under the covers. "Would you please run me a hot bath?"

"Of course, my lady."

Miss Vaughn left the room. Cordelia lifted the lid to her tray and her heart felt heavy when she saw enough food for two. Thomas would be eating breakfast with Stuyvesant, Lucy, and Mrs. Stewart in the breakfast room, along with Penelope. She wondered how Thomas would explain Stuyvesant's presence. Penelope would know that he wasn't on the guest list. Cordelia had told her that Lucy was coming for a visit, at least, but she hadn't expected her to arrive before their move to London for the Season.

Stuyvesant, Lucy, and Mrs. Stewart weren't in their table-setting plans for thirty people either. There were now thirty-three guests, and she was short one male. It was such a silly thing, but her house party could be ruined before it started. Cordelia sighed. She would have to redo the place settings, even though they'd already taken her days to get just right because of their precedence. Where people sat depended on their rank and titles, rather than their personalities. As such, Lucy would have to sit far away from her, for she had no title. And she would need to find another man—Mr. Ryse, perhaps?

She picked up a piece of bacon with her fingers and chewed it into nothing. She toyed with her food.

Cordelia couldn't stay in bed all day waiting to find out.

She felt better after her bath, less low. And there was something about a lovely morning frock to give her a bit of confidence. Confidence she desperately needed to meet both Thomas and her guests. She walked toward the sitting room and saw Thayne coming her way.

"Thayne," she said. "Have you seen Lord Farnham this morning?"

"Yes, my lady," he said, executing a bow. "Lord Farnham took Mr. Bradley out shooting."

"Ah," Cordelia said, both regretful and relieved. "Then you and I can work on the table placements. Hibbert... I worked on them before, but we need to adjust things for our additional guests, and I was wondering if you could have someone deliver an invitation to Mr. Ryse."

"I should be happy to assist you, my lady."

"Thank you, Thayne," she said. "I should also like to visit every room and make sure they are ready for our guests."

"I am sure the housekeeper would be happy to accompany you."

Cordelia swallowed. Mrs. Norton seemed to be offended by everything Cordelia asked her to do. Like Hibbert, she fought against any change in tradition. "That would be perfect. I was also going to mention that I would like dinner to last only an hour, Mr. Hibb—please ensure that the footmen bring the courses quickly."

"Of course, my lady."

She found Lucy, Penelope, Mrs. Stewart, and Blanche in the blue sitting room.

"Blanche, would you mind if I stole Lucy for a little while?" Cordelia asked from the doorway.

"Not at all," Blanche said with her usual bovine smile. "Mrs. Stewart was just telling me about these fascinating vegetables called avocados that they have in America."

Lucy linked arms with Cordelia and they closed the door behind them.

"Did my mother-in-law ask you the most ridiculous questions about America?"

Her best friend giggled. "She was very kind though."

"I am so sorry that I have been the worst hostess to you, but I still need to go through all the rooms to make sure they are ready for my other guests. Would you mind coming with me? It'll be a dull job."

"Nonsense!" Lucy said, smiling. "I can't wait to see the fruition of all your efforts. My own bathing room is positively a work of art. I thought I was in Italy whilst in the tub."

They found Mrs. Norton, who was less enthusiastic at the prospect. But after a not-so-subtle hint from Cordelia that if she did not, she would lose her position, she accompanied them. It was a good thing that the housekeeper didn't know that Thomas would never let his wife dismiss her. Still, Cordelia felt a pang of guilt for threatening the older woman. She wished they had a better relationship, but Mrs. Norton only seemed to respond to threats, rather than requests.

Cordelia pointed out to Lucy the white bear hearthrugs, shaded lamps, and silk tapestries that she'd received as wedding gifts.

"Yet you love her."

"I do," Thomas said. "And I will do everything in my power to make her want to stay."

"Then, you won't force her to stay?"

"I am not her mother. I would never ask her to do something against her own will or conscience."

Stuyvesant shouldered his gun. "I think if we'd met under different circumstances, Thomas, we might have been friends. But I will not lie to you. I am going to ask Cordelia to come back to America with me, where she belongs."

"I think Cordelia can decide for herself where she belongs."

They heard a crack and the falling of a bough.

"What was that?" Stuyvesant said, gripping his gun, ready to fire.

"A branch fell off a tree," Thomas said, picking up his shot bag, his nerves suddenly on edge. "In Sussex, the villagers call the ash tree "widow makers" because the large boughs can fall without warning."

"Nothing out of the ordinary, then?"

"No. But I should like to go see. There have been strange accidents of late," Thomas said, and pointed to the path that led back toward Ashdown through the grove.

They walked together in uncomfortable but honest silence. They reached a clearing right before the house when he spotted the large tree bough. His heart stopped—mingled in the branches was a scrap of dress material and two squashed hats. He stooped down to pick up the first hat and he recognized it as Cordelia's. His heart began to plummet against his chest. He bent down and touched the ground around the tree; there was no blood. If she were grievously injured, there would be blood. He could see shoe imprints from two different people—women. The tracks led back to Ashdown.

"This branch didn't fall down of its own accord," Stuyvesant said from behind him, standing at the edge of the trunk. "Look, it's been sawed half through and pulled off by a rope."

"We need to go back to the abbey," Thomas said, and began jogging without a glance to Stuyvesant. Cordelia was still in danger.

"What's your hurry?" he said as he ran up to meet Thomas.

Thomas debated a polite lie but decided for Cordelia's safety to tell the truth. "There have been a series of accidents since Cordelia's arrival."

"Accidents?"

"I don't think that any of them were accidents," Thomas admitted. "Someone on the estate is trying to harm Cordelia, and I don't know who it is."

"Why would someone want to hurt her?"

"Your guess is as good as mine," he said with a frustrated sigh. "It's not the villagers, of that I am certain. Cordelia volunteers at the local school and has provided good-paying work for the men. Which narrows it down to one of the twenty-eight people who live at Ashdown."

"This only strengthens my resolve to take her away from this place."

"I offered to take her away and she wanted to stay at the abbey," Thomas said through clenched teeth. "She's not a bag or an item you can pick up and do whatever you'd like with. She's an intelligent person, who can make up her own mind."

"I'm going to keep my eye on her."

"I never thought that I would say this, but I hope you do," Thomas said. "I want her to be safe...and I want her to be happy."

He didn't wait for the man to reply but strode into the house. He handed his gun and shot bag to Thayne before dashing up the back stairs. He ran to her door and opened it without knocking. Cordelia was standing in her shift and corset, her diamond-studded gold garters holding up her muddy stockings. He rushed to embrace her in relief but checked himself before he touched her—her American suitor was now here. The one she said she loved.

Standing just inches away, he breathed heavily as he asked, "Are you injured at all?"

"I'm fine."

"I was so worried."

"I don't think it was Hibbert trying to hurt me."

Unable to resist touching her, Thomas placed a reassuring hand on her bare arm. "I don't think so either... Are you sure you don't want to go to London immediately? Stuyvesant could escort you, Lucy, and Mrs. Stewart. Then my mother could host our guests."

"You want me to leave with Stuyvesant?"

"No!" Thomas gasped, his heart falling to his stomach. "But I want you to be safe. I have failed you so many times, Cordelia. From our wedding to this morning...I don't want to fail you anymore."

"You've never failed me," she whispered.

"Cordelia, I—I lo—"

The sound of a carriage on the gravel caused her to turn her head away from him just as he was bearing his heart to her. His eyes followed hers to the window and he realized that their first guests' carriage had arrived.

"Someone must meet them," Cordelia said quickly.

Thomas glanced down at his muddy trousers and gunpowder-stained tweed coat. "Do you want me to go like this?"

"No," she said, and pointed to the dress hanging on her wardrobe. "Help me dress."

He focused on the tiny little buttons in the back of the dress that started at the dip of her waist and went all the way up her luscious, long neck.

"There," he said when he buttoned the last button.

Cordelia didn't bother changing her soiled stockings but pulled on a pair of house slippers and dashed to the door. She turned as she touched the handle. "Do I look presentable?"

"You look lovely."

He thought he saw her smile as she left the room. Thomas walked through their shared dressing room to his own bedroom. Thayne was not there. He was probably performing the duties of butler. Thomas took off his own boots and soiled tweeds. He stacked the clothes carefully, knowing the efforts that Thayne went through to keep his togs in good shape. Thomas dressed himself in a velvet smoking suit and combed his own hair.

Thomas went down to meet his guests. Cordelia was escorting

Lord and Lady Esher into the house, when his cousin Oliver and his wife, Lois, arrived in a carriage. Thayne opened the door and Oliver and Lois stepped out. Oliver took a cigar out of his mouth and passed it to Lois, who smoked it. She placed her clawlike hand on her husband's arm.

"Oliver, Lois, so good to see you," Thomas said. "Thayne will show you to your bedchambers, and then we'll have tea in the sitting room."

"Has Cook made my jam tarts?" Oliver asked.

"With Devonshire cream," Thomas assured him.

"Come, Lois," he said jovially. "There's not a moment to lose."

Lois took another puff of the cigar and followed her husband inside the house. Cordelia walked back out at the same time. Lois tossed the cigar on the stone steps and hugged Cordelia. Thomas could tell that it took all of Thayne's self-control not to pick the cigar stub up. Cordelia stepped out of the embrace, beaming, and Thomas would have forgiven Lois a dozen cigar stubs on his front steps. Once his cousin was inside, he signaled to a footman who picked up the cigar stub.

Cordelia smiled and stood by him. "Four down, two dozen more guests to go."

Thomas impulsively squeezed her hand. "We've got this, partner."

"You'd better believe it, partner," she said, and squeezed his hand back before letting go to welcome his uncle and aunt, the Marquess and Marchioness of Grimsby. His mother's brother stepped out of the carriage. Lord Grimsby wore the same vague expression that his mother often did. He had gray hair and a large forehead. He was slender like Thomas but not as tall. His wife stepped out of the carriage next. She had a small aristocratic head, with a big beak of a nose and a massive bosom. Her brown curls looked like corkscrews around her wrinkled face, and her mouth wore a sour expression. Why did his mother invite them? There wasn't a more tedious pair among all the English nobility.

"Uncle, Aunt," Thomas said, "allow me to introduce my wife, Cordelia."

She curtsied with a grace of a dancer.

"Well, well," Lord Grimsby spoke as if Cordelia wasn't present. "I would never have supposed she was an American. Quite refined. Quite pretty too."

Thomas blushed for his uncle's bad manners, but the ordeal was far from over.

"I've never attended a party hosted by an American before," Lady Grimsby said haughtily. "Consider yourself fortunate, Thomas, that I was able, for your mother's sake, to overlook my scruples."

He swallowed. "We are glad that you are here. Please allow Thayne to show you to your rooms."

"I daresay I know where to go," Lady Grimsby stated, and took her husband's arm and walked inside the house in a regal manner.

Thomas leaned in to whisper in Cordelia's ear. "Please tell me that you have embarrassing relatives. Lots of embarrassing relatives that you are going to introduce me to in America the next time that we visit."

"Yes, but they don't have such fancy titles," she said with a saucy smile.

Her face was close enough to kiss. All he needed to do was lean a few more inches, but he heard the sound of another carriage approaching and straightened back up. Whether it was guests or their servants, he couldn't be caught kissing his wife.

35

*C*ordelia was ready for a nap after welcoming all their
noble guests. Her mind was still reeling over Stuyvesant's
unexpected arrival and the tree branch almost hitting her and
Lucy. But she did not have time to process either experience. She
was the hostess. Miss Vaughn helped her dress into a lovely
evening gown of blue satin, with an elegantly embroidered
peacock on the bodice and a square-cut neckline. Her long gloves
and dancing slippers were tinted the exact same blue as her dress—
and sable scarf, for a touch of drama. Cordelia usually didn't wear
jewels at dinner, for she didn't want to emphasize the disparity
between her own circumstances and those of Penelope's. But
tonight she wore a diamond dog collar that elongated her neck,
several studded bracelets, and her wedding ring. She touched her
ears that felt conspicuous without the matching earrings—the
diamond earrings she'd bartered away for the simple delivery of a
letter.

How different her life might have been if Mabel had delivered it
like she'd promised to. She shook her head, her curls lightly
bouncing around her face. Cordelia was not going to think about
past mistakes, or even her future life. This was her first time hosting

a dinner party, and she wanted to get everything just right. She put in her pearl drop earrings.

There was a knock on the door to the dressing room.

"Come in, Thomas," she called.

Thomas opened the door and she caught her breath. He'd never looked so handsome before than he did now in his black dinner suit, with his hair swept back. He took her hand and kissed it lightly. "You sparkle brighter than any gem."

She clutched her diamond bracelets. "Am I wearing too many jewels?"

"Nonsense," he said, and kissed her gloved hand once more. "May I escort you to the party?"

"Afraid I'll lose my way?"

"I am more afraid that I'll lose you." His words were lightly spoken, but she sensed the sincerity behind them. She had tried to forget the tree branch from early that day, but she couldn't.

Not knowing what to say, or even how she felt, Cordelia placed her shaking hand on his arm. He grinned at her, and he looked very much like himself and ever so much less refined. When they entered the sitting room, there were already many guests present, including Lois in a stunning champagne-colored gown, with enormous puffed sleeves and a neckline that showed plenty of décolleté. She waved and smiled but continued talking to the handsome young prince. Prince Albert Louis had dark brown hair that curled and had bright blue eyes. The clipped mustache over his full red lips gave him a French look.

Cordelia's hand tightened on Thomas's arm. She'd never been "out" before, and she felt nervous to be at her first adult party. She wished she was back in New York among her friends that were her own age, instead of this older, more sophisticated crowd. Thomas stopped to talk to his other aunt and uncle, Oliver's parents, the Duke and Duchess of Oxenbury.

She felt a touch on her shoulder. She turned to see Stuyvesant standing behind her. It was comforting to see a familiar face and he was dressed just as smartly as any present in his dark coat with tails.

"Cordy, may I have a word?"

She pulled at the earring that was pinching her right ear. "Of course," she said, and let go of Thomas's arm and slowly followed Stuyvesant to stand by the grand piano. Her body felt strangely heavy, and it had nothing to do with the weight of her many jewels.

"I've never seen you look more beautiful," he whispered.

She felt herself go pink with pleasure. "Thank you."

"I have travelled halfway around the world for you. And I would go to the ends of the earth for you."

"But it's too late," she said softly, hanging her head low and staring at the tiles on the floor.

Stuyvesant tried to take her hand, but she pulled it away, looking over her shoulder at her husband. His acorn eyes were watching them. Watching her.

"It's not too late."

She weakly held up her hands to stop Stuyvesant from touching her. "I'm already married."

"You can get a divorce," he said. "Your mother did, and we can go back home together like this never happened."

His gaze was so piercing in its intensity that she had to lower her own eyes again. She felt dizzy with fatigue. "I can't just leave."

"You can get a divorce when we get back to New York."

Her broken heart pinched. "English law does not recognize American divorces," Cordelia whispered. "I would still be married to him."

"Then get an English divorce! You were married under duress. Your mother forced you into it."

"It's not that simple in England," she said, briefly looking at his dark eyes. "For a wife to get a divorce, I would have to prove that my husband was cruel or deserted me. Neither of which is true."

"Then ask Lord Farnham to divorce you," he pressed.

Casting a glance at Thomas, she saw that his gaze was still on her. On them. What would he say if she asked him? Would he beg her to stay? Or would he finally feel free of an obligation he never wanted to have in the first place? He would be free to marry Penelope.

Thayne opened the door and announced dinner. She had to go. She couldn't think about Stuyvesant now.

"You're Lucy's escort." She left Stuyvesant without another word, or a look, to find Thomas. She needed to be by his side for the procession into dinner. It was another British tradition that you entered the dining room according to your rank. But when she saw Thomas, his aunt Lady Oxenbury was already holding on to his arm.

Cordelia bit her lip, unsure of what to do or whose arm she was supposed to hold. She felt a small push in the middle of her back. She turned to see Lois on the prince's arm. She pointed for Cordelia to go to Lord Oxenbury at the front of the procession. As a duke, he held the highest rank of any man present (for Prince Albert Louis was only the heir to a duke). Cordelia walked quickly to his side. Lord Oxenbury offered her his arm with a kind smile. He was a portly man, with a shock of white hair and a long gray beard.

Lord Oxenbury led the procession with dignity that Cordelia hoped one day to possess. He assisted her into her seat at the center of the table, for the Prince and Princess of Wales adopted the custom of sitting at the center of the table, instead of the ends. He sat on her right and Lord Grimsby sat on her left. Stuyvesant was at the end of the table, sitting next to Lucy and Penelope, who was smiling behind her fan at him. She sighed. She was stuck sitting between two old men for no better reason than birth. In every other way they were most unsuitable dinner companions, based on age, interests, and even personalities. It was going to be a quiet dinner.

She consoled herself with the fact that the long dining room table looked exquisitely lovely with a dozen vases of pink Malmaison flowers. It made the room feel fresh and airy, like a spring garden. Interspersed between the flowers were pyramids of succulent fruits: peaches, raspberries, pears, and grapes. In the center of the table was a silver epergne statue, which quite blocked her view of Thomas, who was sitting across from her. The two women at his side were both of his aunts: Lady Grimsby and Lady Oxenbury.

"How did I do?" she asked Lord Oxenbury.

He grinned. "Splendidly. Not a person out of place. Quite a feat in this company."

"I studied the Table of Precedence for hours to plan the table setting."

He laughed. "No one would guess that."

Thayne served the wine. The footmen served the two soups simultaneously; one was hot and one was cold. Cordelia managed a few bites of each, but her stomach rolled nervously. The next course was two fishes with sauces; again, one fish was hot and the other one was cold. The footmen cleared their plates and served the meat dish, followed by an orange sorbet. The next course was pheasant, which was followed with a hot savory and port wine. At last, it was time to eat the beautiful fruits that decorated the table. Cordelia took a few grapes and bit one.

She was still chewing, when she saw Lady Grimsby stand up and start to walk toward the door. Other ladies stood but looked at Cordelia.

Lord Oxenbury touched her arm. "Never have I seen anything so rude; don't move. Lady Grimsby's trying to undermine you as hostess."

The hostess was supposed to give the signal for the ladies to leave the room, never a guest. For a moment, Cordelia sat as still as she would have if she had an iron rod strapped to her neck and shoulders—which her mother had used on her as a child to improve her posture. The ladies in the room sat back down in their seats. Cordelia then stood up and walked to the door where the Marchioness of Grimsby was standing.

"Are you ill, Lady Grimsby?"

"No, certainly not. Why should I be ill?" she said imperiously.

"Then there is no other polite excuse for your hasty exit."

Lady Grimsby blushed from her pointy chin to her beak-like nose. Cordelia did not flinch but waited for Lady Grimsby to sit back down at the table before sitting down herself. Lois caught her eye and winked at her. Cordelia finished eating her fruit and looked around the table to make sure that every other lady was done. She then stood up and gave the signal to the other ladies that it was time to retire to the library, while the men stayed for a half hour longer to drink coffee and liqueurs and smoke cigars.

She was nervous to take the lead but kept her head high, her mother's training coming back to her. Lois linked arms with her and Lucy, and together they led the other thirteen women in yet another procession.

"You're doing brilliantly," Lois assured her.

"You were so brave," Lucy agreed.

The footmen opened the door to the former dining room turned parlor, where Mr. Perkins, a professional organist, was playing Brahms on the grand piano. She was fond of Brahms, but not as fond as she was of Chopin or Beethoven. She watched his fingers move competently over the keys. Perhaps she was biased, but she thought that her fingers were just as proficient. If only women could be professional pianists like men were. She would be able to take care of herself without her father's money or her mother's social position or her husband's title.

Mr. Perkins played continually for a half hour, while the ladies chatted. It seemed a travesty to Cordelia that his polished performance merited so little attention. Her mother-in-law moved next to her.

"A very creditable dinner, Cordelia."

"Thank you, Blanche."

"You sat me in the correct position, but I confess, I am used to a more prominent seat at the table. It makes me feel quite low to no longer be important."

Cordelia put a hand over her mouth. "I am so sorry."

"No, you did right," Blanche said, and patted her shoulder in a motherly way. "But I was wondering, are there many countesses in America?"

She blinked. "Uh, no. There are no titles in America, so the only people with titles are visitors."

The dowager licked her lips. "So, if I were to go to America, then *I* would be the most important person at parties?"

"Yes," Cordelia said, finally catching on to her mother-in-law's idea and finding it a marvelous one. "I am sure there would be no end to hostesses wishing for you to grace their parties, and they would seat you in the most prominent place at the table."

"Are there handsome young men in America?"

She thought of Stuyvesant, who was a great deal too young for her mother-in-law. "Yes, yes, there are many handsome young men."

"I shouldn't wish for Penelope to marry a plain man. They might have ugly children," Blanche said with a visible shiver.

"Of course not," Cordelia agreed. "Are you planning on taking Penelope to America?"

"I am thinking of it," she said. "Are all the handsome young men as rich as you are?"

Cordelia opened her mouth before she had words to speak. She didn't want to lie, but she also didn't want to discourage this delightful plan. Cordelia was already weary of their forced foursome. "Yes, there are handsome young men who are as rich as me."

"I think Penelope would like to be rich."

"I am sure she would," Cordelia agreed. "I would be only too happy to write letters of introduction for you both to scores of New York hostesses. Just say the word. You could even stay with my mother, if you'd like to."

The dowager patted Cordelia's hand. "You're a good girl. I could almost imagine you were my own daughter if you weren't an American."

Cordelia held in her laugh and politely thanked her.

Mr. Perkins finished his last piece, and all the ladies clapped, Blanche the loudest of all. She stood up and said, "My daughter-in-law is also an accomplished pianist. They have pianos in America, you know."

"Why doesn't Lady Farnham play for us as well?" Lady Grimsby asked snidely. "Perhaps a duet?"

Her suggestion was met with universal approval. Cordelia loved to play the piano, but she was hoping to be less of the center of attention. She stood and gave a false smile and walked over to the piano bench where Mr. Perkin's sat.

"Do you have any duet music?" she asked quietly.

"I only have Beethoven's 'Sonata for Piano Four Hands in D major, Op. 6,'" he replied. "But it is too difficult for an amateur."

"I've played it before. Would you like to play primo or secondo?"

He scooted over for her on the piano bench and took out the music and placed it on the stand. He'd chosen the base part. Cordelia took off her long blue gloves and laid them across her lap.

"One, two, three," she whispered, and they started, three staccato notes and then the beautiful trills and runs. Cordelia lost herself in the ethereal music and the pleasure of playing with an accomplished partner. She glanced briefly at Mr. Perkins during the rondo and he smiled at her. They continued to play in perfect precision. Music was truly transcendent. Together they played the last chord. The applause that met it was greater than before. Cordelia turned to see that the gentlemen had entered the room during their duet. Thomas clapped the loudest of all, and Stuyvesant didn't clap at all.

"Thank you for the duet, Mr. Perkins," she said, and held out her hand.

"It was truly my pleasure, Lady Farnham," he said, and took her hand and bent over it. "You are a worthy player."

Cordelia stood up and found Lady Oxenbury by her side. Thomas resembled his aunt more than he did his own mother. They had the same shade of acorn-brown eyes and brown hair. She was slight like Thomas, but her chin was receding.

"Well done," she said, and appeared pleased without smiling. "You'll do for Thomas and for Ashdown."

Stuyvesant's offer to run away with him flashed through her mind, and she blushed for even considering it. "Thank you, Lady Oxenbury."

"I haven't seen Ashdown look so well since I was a little girl," she said. "But where is Hibbert? I hope he is not ill."

Cordelia was put out of countenance a second time. She was not about to tell the duchess that her old butler was in jail, though probably innocent. Or that someone else was trying to kill her. "He's retired."

"Ah, well, I shall have to visit him," Lady Oxenbury said.

"Who are you going to visit, Aunt?" Thomas asked.

"Hibbert," she said. "It's strange; I never thought he would retire, but he must be at least seventy."

Cordelia gave a speaking glance to Thomas, and he responded by putting his arm around her shoulders. "I am sure we could manage that, but Cordelia's arranged card tables in the sitting room. Shall we lead the way?"

Thomas moved his arm from her shoulders to her waist, leading her away from his aunt and out of the room. She looked over her shoulder and their guests were following them.

"What are we going to do about Hibbert?" she whispered.

"I don't know," he admitted. "I'll confess the whole to my aunt tomorrow morning and ask for her advice. She loves to give advice. Whether you ask for it or not."

She nodded and wondered if he'd put his arm around her to comfort her or to claim her. He led her to a table for four and sat across from her. The Duke and Duchess of Oxenbury joined them, the rest of the guests making groups of four. The only ones that looked uncomfortable were the foursome of unmarried persons: Lucy, Prince Albert Louis, Penelope, and Stuyvesant. Her old love was not watching his partner, Penelope, but her. *It would solve all of my and Thomas's difficulties*, she thought, *if Stuyvesant would fall in love with Penelope and take her to America, with Blanche in tow*. But she saw Penelope's eyes wander as often to Thomas, her heart shining through them. Penelope's heart was still taken.

Cordelia played a queen of hearts card.

What a dreadful, romantic tangle they were all in, and she was afraid that it was about to be cut.

36

The next morning Oliver led the shooting party. Each man was dressed from head to toe in tweeds and required three guns, with two servants to work as loaders. The persistent sound of gunshots gave Thomas a headache, and he was relieved when it was time to join the ladies for the midday meal. Per custom, luncheon was served in a tent near Ashdown, and all the ladies were dressed in similar tweeds.

Cordelia's tweed jacket emphasized her narrow waist, and the green color brought out the reddish tints of her hair. She was in the center of a group of women, telling a story that they must have found amusing, for the women were laughing. He walked up to the group, longing, as always, to be near enough to feel the sunshine of her presence.

"How was your morning, ladies?"

"We spent it reading the papers," Lady Oxenbury said.

"And gossiping," Lois added with her tigerish smile.

"A very productive morning, then," he said.

The ladies laughed and dispersed to greet their husbands, leaving only Cordelia, Lucy, Penelope, and Thomas. The light, humorous atmosphere was gone in an instant, replaced by an awkward restraint.

"Did you bag many birds?" Penelope asked.

"At least a hundred, between all of us."

"You have always been such a good shot. Even your father said so, and he was a well-known sportsman."

He turned to Cordelia and Lucy. "My father always boasted of a year when he, Mr. Ryse, and three other friends bagged over seven thousand rabbits in one season."

"I bet everyone was tired of eating hare by the end of that year," Lucy said.

Thomas laughed and so did Cordelia. He had never before made the connection between the hunt and the table.

"The late Lord Farnham shared the bounty of the hunt with his tenants and the poor in the village," Penelope said stiffly.

"I am glad to hear it," Cordelia said. "I have seen much need in the villages around Ashdown. The recent poor harvests have hit them the hardest."

"It is not Thomas's responsibility to feed them."

"We are not feeding them. We are simply providing employment opportunities so that they can feed themselves," Cordelia said, linking arms with Lucy and walking to a table to sit down next to Stuyvesant.

Penelope lifted her nose. "Cordelia forgets her place as well as yours when she pays her American friends more attention than is their due."

"I see nothing wrong in her behavior," Thomas said. "She is talking to all of her guests. Please refrain from criticizing my wife."

He strolled to the opposite end of the tent and took a seat next to his aunt Lady Oxenbury.

"My lady's maid had quite a story to tell me about Hibbert."

"I am sure she did," Thomas said. "I was hoping to have a private word with you about it."

"Hibbert would never have tried to harm your wife. His devotion to our family is the stuff of butler legends. I don't believe it for a moment."

Thomas sighed. "I don't know what to think about it, but he was the only one besides me with access to the gunroom."

His aunt took a large drink from her glass. "Since Hibbert was apprehended, have there been further accidents?"

"Yes, only yesterday," he said. "Cordelia likes to walk through the ash grove, and a tree she always passes by had a branch that had been partially cut. The person must have waited for her to arrive and then pulled on the branch at the opportune moment."

"Sinister."

"What am I to do, Aunt?"

"You're to leave for the London Season soon, I expect."

"Early next week."

"Then leave here as soon as the weekend party breaks up."

"We could. I even asked Cordelia to go before the party, but she refused to."

Lady Oxenbury nodded in approval. "She has the makings of a great hostess. You did better than I expected."

Thomas paused. "Then, you didn't expect me to marry Penelope?"

"I hoped you wouldn't," she said. "One's first love rarely lasts, and it was obvious from the outset that her dowry would never be enough for this estate."

"I never raised any expectations," Thomas said slowly. "But my parents did. I don't know how to politely..."

"Tell her to back off?"

"Yes," he said. "I avoid her as often as I can, but when we are in company, her attention is—"

"Marked," she said. "Is Cordelia aware of it?"

"Yes." Like a fool, he'd told her himself.

"That is unfortunate, and since your mother is her guardian, it is difficult to find her a place elsewhere without causing the sort of gossip that I am sure you are trying to avoid."

"That's why I asked for your advice."

"Your mother talked last night of visiting America with Miss Hutchinson," she said. "I would send them on the next boat."

"America?" Thomas said incredulously.

Lady Oxenbury gave a haughty smile. "Your mother wants to go to America because your wife assured her that there are no other countesses. I do not know if she plans to marry herself or Penelope off to a rich American man, possibly both."

Thomas laughed but sobered. "My mother, Penelope, Cook, Mrs. Norton, and Thayne are the only people who could have shot at Cordelia besides Hibbert. They are the only people who live at the abbey and had access to the guns."

"I don't mean this unkindly, Thomas, but I doubt my sister-in-law has the brains or temperament for premeditated murder."

"I don't think it was my mother either," he said softly. "Which makes me fear that even if Cordelia and I leave the abbey for London, we may be bringing the murderer with us. Our senior staff, of course, will be accompanying us."

"Then your wife may still be in harm's way."

"Yes."

His aunt took another drink from her glass. "If Cordelia died, what would happen to her money?"

"I received two million dollars as part of the marriage settlements. Her death would not benefit me at all."

Lady Oxenbury's eyebrows raised. "Then you must figure out who would benefit from it, Thomas."

"I've been trying," he said, and raked his fingers through his hair.

"Try harder."

His uncle came up to them, and Thomas relinquished his seat to him. He looked around the tent, and the footmen were preparing to serve the food. The only seat left was between Penelope and Cordelia—Stuyvesant sat on her right. *It is going to be a long luncheon,* he thought as he sat down. *A very long luncheon.*

Once Thomas was seated, Thayne signaled the footmen to start serving the food. He was grateful for the distraction they gave. He stole a glance at Cordelia, but she was looking determinedly at her plate. He took a bite of the cold meat, but it was tasteless in his mouth.

"Are you going to shoot again after luncheon?" Penelope asked.

"Er, yes," he said. "All the gentlemen are."

"And the ladies will go inside and change our dresses in time for tea," Cordelia said, an edge to her voice. "Then we will change our dresses again in time to eat dinner. It seems that all ladies do is eat and change their clothes."

"At least our dresses are all pretty," Lucy said.

"It is important to wear the appropriate clothing," Penelope said. "It's what distinguishes the aristocracy from the rest of the world."

"I couldn't agree more," Stuyvesant said sardonically.

Penelope, obviously missing his barb, looked gratified at his assent. Cordelia gave a tight smile and took a drink of her punch. "I confess that I am excited to dress up tonight for the masquerade."

"You could dress up in any costume and I'd still know who you were," Stuyvesant said.

"How could you?"

"I've known you your whole life," Stuyvesant said. "You couldn't possibly fool me. You've probably picked some elaborate French queen to portray, with a dress designed exclusively for you by the house of Worth in Paris, and you'll be dripping in jewels."

Thomas watched Cordelia's face, and he saw her eyes glance down to her plate before smiling back at Stuyvesant. He must have guessed correctly.

"Would you like to make a friendly wager, Stuyvesant?" Thomas asked.

"What sort of wager?"

"Whichever one of us guesses Cordelia in costume first will win twenty pounds."

"Let's make it one hundred," Stuyvesant said. "It will be the easiest money that I have ever earned."

"And if neither of you guess who I am before the unveiling at midnight," Cordelia said, "then you'll both have to pay me one hundred pounds."

Stuyvesant laughed loudly and Thomas tried to smile, but the sound of the man's laugh irritated him too much. Everything about the large American man annoyed him, from Stuyvesant's accent to the way he cut his meat with his left hand.

"I wonder if you'll be able to guess my costume, Thomas," Penelope said, eager to stay a part of the conversation. "You've known me just as long as Mr. Bradley has known your wife."

"I can't wait to see it," Thomas lied, and turned the other direction. "Stuyvesant, my valet, Thayne, would be happy to assist you with a costume."

"I can manage," he said. "We Americans are known for our ingenuity."

"And humility," Lucy said from his side.

Penelope snorted.

"My humility is one of my attributes that I am the most proud of," Stuyvesant said, and laughed as if he were a great wit.

"Miss Hutchinson will be able to experience American ingenuity and humility firsthand," Thomas said. "My mother means to take her on a visit to America."

Stuyvesant grinned broadly. "Well, it is churlish not to be proud of one's own country, and I can't deny that I think America is in the forefront of the world in technology and industry. The New World leaves the old one in the dust."

"Perhaps the old one is perfectly fine with the way things have always been," Penelope said with a touch of asperity.

"This century is coming to a close, and I wonder what great changes the next one will bring," Cordelia said, clearly trying to lead the conversation away from an argument.

"I daresay all sorts of new technologies and inventions," Lucy added.

"Sometimes I fear our way of life is coming to an end," Thomas said. "And I am not sure if that is a bad thing."

"Why would it be a good thing?" Penelope asked.

"Because so few enjoy the privileges denied to so many," Thomas said. "A comfortable house, plentiful food, and good health."

"I think it is our duty to provide those opportunities for everyone," Cordelia said, looking at him with rare approval.

"A man should earn his own way," Stuyvesant said. "And take care of his own. No one can do it for him."

"But what of the elderly, or poor women?" Cordelia asked. "If they are unable to provide the necessities for themselves or for their children, surely we should help them."

"If you help them, then they won't learn to help themselves," he said.

Thomas took a large bite of ham. Perhaps he had been wrong in trying to keep Stuyvesant and Cordelia apart. The arrogant young man didn't even realize how much he was angering her. Or how much her volunteering in the village meant to her. He finished his lunch and returned to the hunt with renewed spirits. Stuyvesant might have known Cordelia as a child, but she was a woman now. A woman with a mind of her own and the largest heart of any person he'd ever met.

37

*M*iss Vaughn was waiting for Cordelia to change from her tweeds to an elaborate tea gown, with a lovely V-neck and elbow-length sleeves. It was a soft pink that brought out the color of her cheeks. She picked up an exquisite pearl-handled fan painted with little flowers. Her father had purchased it for her in France. Cordelia felt a pang of homesickness. She missed her father. She missed the life she'd lived with him, where she never had to worry about anything. Life was one endless stream of lovely parties, beautiful yachts, and the next exotic city to visit.

But she wasn't sure those lovely trips would be the same now. Even if she went with Stuyvesant, Cordelia was not the naïve girl she'd once been. If she saw those cities again, she would not only see the beautiful buildings but the poverty that they were built on. The hunger that hid behind every corner. The desperation that disguised the indignities suffered by thousands, and their glittering leaders who wore golden crowns and expensive tailoring, dripped with diamonds, and ate a feast every night while so many around them went hungry.

Cordelia looked in the mirror at her third dress of the day and the five-strand pearl necklace at her throat. Was she any different than the others? Her tea gown was made in Paris and her jewels were worth a king's ransom.

She walked down to the green sitting room, where a Viennese orchestra was playing while her female guests listened politely. The music was lovely, but her mind was not on it. Her thoughts were on her home in America and her life there. As a child, she'd assisted her mother in many charitable projects. Sometimes they raised funds with a concert or sewed for the poor, but it wasn't until she came to Ashdown that she'd really seen poverty face-to-face. And the face of poverty frightened her. Charity at Ashdown was not the simple give-your-money variety; Cordelia went inside of these people's homes. She saw their dreadful living conditions and the lack of proper sanitation. She knew their names. They were not "the poor" —some vague term that had no meaning. Their names were Nancy, Mrs. Brooks, Mrs. Partridge, Phillip, Jenny, and so many more whom she longed to help. To use her own two hands to make their lives better. To give the children, especially, more opportunities for education and financial advancement. Helping in the village had brought her more joy and satisfaction than attending a hundred parties in America.

Cordelia simply could not go back to New York with Stuyvesant and pretend that the last six months hadn't happened. That she hadn't changed, and that on some level, she was ashamed of who she had been. At her own selfishness and self-pity. She'd been the little rich girl who had everything money could buy, except happiness.

Except freedom.

But she was no longer that girl. She was no longer forced to be obedient to her strong-willed mother and her inflexible dictates. Cordelia now had the freedom to do what she wanted to, and she wanted to help people wherever she lived. Whether she chose to stay with Thomas or divorce him to leave with Stuyvesant.

The Viennese orchestra finished their set, and Cordelia signaled Thayne to bring out tea. The footmen pushed in carts full of cakes, crumpets, muffins, and scones with jam and Devonshire cream. The ornately decorated teapot and cups were part of her wedding gifts, made of priceless bone china. Cook had outdone herself again. But Cordelia felt a pang of remorse. She was feeding people who already had so much and, in a few hours, would sit down for an eight-course dinner.

Her refraining from drinking tea would not help the poor in the village. She shook off these thoughts and carefully poured the hot beverage into the teacups. She made sure that every lady was amply provided for before taking a seat next to Penelope and smelling her sweet, lavender perfume.

"May I speak to you for a moment?"

Penelope gave her a wan smile. "Of course, Cordy."

Cordelia looked around her to see that the other women were still near enough to hear. Penelope had never called her by that nickname before. "I was wondering if you would be willing to wear one of my costumes. My mother bought several as a part of my trousseau, and we could fool the younger members of the party."

Penelope almost smiled as she took a bite of a crumpet. "I should think it would be quite droll."

"So, you will do it?"

"Why not?" Penelope said, and actually smiled. "What harm could it do?"

Cordelia thanked her and went to Lucy. "I have a masquerade gown for you as well, if you'd like to wear it."

Lucy grinned. "I would love to wear *any* of your clothes. They are always exquisite."

Cordelia laughed. Together they made their way around the room, talking to each of the guests. Lois made a joke that nearly caused her to snort tea out of her nose, and Lady Grimsby was unhappy with her bedroom accommodations. They moved to talk to her other guests Mrs. Bracken and Lady Esher, when she noticed Lady Oxenbury was watching her. She felt self-conscious under the duchess's scrutiny but made pleasantries and continued around the room until she and Lucy were standing near her.

"And how are you doing, Lady Oxenbury?"

"Well enough."

"Is there anything I can do for your comfort?"

"Be wise."

Cordelia blinked. "I am not sure what you mean."

Lady Oxenbury looked intently at her again. "You'll reflect on this weekend for the rest of your life, and the decisions you make will determine whether you become one of the great ladies of England or fall into obscurity and disgrace."

She had no response to this enigmatic speech. She blinked and tried to—but couldn't—fake a smile underneath the duchess's hawk-like gaze. "I'll try to be wise."

"And trust your instincts. They are more correct than you know."

"Very good—uh—thank you for the advice."

Lucy pulled her back to a sofa. "That was a very strange conversation."

Cordelia could only nod.

"I can scarcely wait to put on my costume," Lois said from the chair beside them.

"Shall we be able to guess who you are?" Cordelia asked.

"Probably," Lois said with a low, seductive laugh. "It is a trifle shocking, but I couldn't resist purchasing it."

"I am intrigued already," Lucy said.

Lois grinned tigerishly. "Then I am already a success."

The tea things were cleared away. Cordelia led both Lucy and Penelope to her room, where Miss Vaughn was waiting with three ballgowns displayed on dummies. Penelope gasped when she saw the first gown. It was pink and truly exquisite, with a dog collar necklace that had belonged to the unfortunate dead queen Marie Antoinette. Her mother purchased it for an enormous price from Tiffany's.

"I think you have chosen your costume," Cordelia said, and pulled the interesting hairpiece out of the trunk. "There is even a wig."

"Are you sure?" Penelope asked. "I've never worn anything so fine."

"It's only a costume," Cordelia said, glad to see a smile on the ever-serious Penelope. "Miss Vaughn, can you help Penelope into the gown? And put the French perfume on her—a dab on each wrist and one on her neck."

"Why the perfume?" Penelope asked.

"I always wear it. It would have given me away."

"We'll have to add a bit of padding to the bosoms," Miss Vaughn said matter-of-factly.

Penelope giggled—a sound that Cordelia had never heard before.

"Now, Lucy, which dress do you want?"

Her friend shook her head. "You should choose first. You are the hostess. The most important person at the party."

"And you are my best friend and I insist."

"You are as stubborn as your mother," Lucy said with a reluctant smile. "Very well then, I would pick to go as the Statue of Liberty."

The dress was decorated with glass pearls in a lightning-bolt pattern and made of yellow satin. The ensemble came with a torch-like light with a built-in battery that, when you pressed the button, lit up.

"That leaves me with Queen Elizabeth I," Cordelia said. "Although, Lucy's red hair would go better with the costume."

"I am sure your mother bought a wig to go with the dress," Lucy said. "She never misses even the smallest of details."

It was true. Cordelia wondered if Lucy realized how often she mentioned Cordelia's mother. Her friend had not grown up with her own mother, a famous opera singer. Nor with her father because she was illegitimate. Was Lucy trying to help Cordelia reconcile with her family? Was she in communication with Cordelia's mother? It was something her mother was entirely capable of.

She forced herself not to think about that now. She helped Miss Vaughn dress Penelope first. Cordelia clasped together the dog collar diamond necklace around Penelope's neck, and Miss Vaughn pinned the curly white wig onto her hair, with the pearls already strung through it, then powdered her face in the style they did in the 1700s. Cordelia brought the mask from the same trunk—it was porcelain, delicately painted. She tied it behind Penelope's head, while Miss Vaughn put on the French perfume. Penelope looked as if she'd walked out of an old painting. She was more beautiful than ever.

Cordelia swallowed—her throat dry. She almost wished that she hadn't lent her dress to Penelope so that Thomas would not see her in it. Suppressing the petty feeling, Cordelia couldn't help but admit to herself that *she* wanted Thomas's admiration. She wished for her husband's love because he held her heart.

She still cared for Stuyvesant, she probably always would, but the connection between them had weakened—over time or distance. Could it be renewed? Would she love Stuyvesant as she now did Thomas?

Did she stay with a husband who didn't love her? Or leave with a man who did and that she no longer loved? It was an impossible conundrum, as both paths seemed littered with heartbreak for more than her.

Miss Vaughn brought out the matching slippers, but Penelope's feet were too large for them. Cordelia couldn't help but be a bit pleased that there was one area in which she was daintier.

"The skirt is so large that no one will ever see my feet."

"You look exquisite," Lucy said.

"Queenly," Cordelia made herself add.

"Thank you," Penelope said. "But you two haven't gotten ready yet yourselves."

"Why don't you go down to the great hall, and Lucy and I will join you as quickly as we can."

Miss Vaughn had to open the door and Penelope edged through it sideways—her skirt was so enormous. Cordelia felt relieved to see her go.

"You're next, Lucy," Cordelia said, and went to unbutton her friend's day dress.

Miss Vaughn reverently carried the gorgeous yellow gown and they put it on Lucy. It was the perfect shade to compliment Lucy's bright red hair. Cordelia helped her put on her gloves and head-dress. The matching beaded mask covered her friend's eyes, but there was no mistaking who Lucy truly was. Her friend picked up the torch and held it above her head, pressing the button so the light turned on.

"You look magnificent!" Cordelia said, forcing a smile to match her enthusiastic words. "Now all you need is Prince Charming."

Lucy giggled and blushed. "Prince Albert Louis is very handsome and quite charming, but I am sure if he knew the circumstances of my birth, he would not be interested in me."

Cordelia took her friend's hands and focused her mind on Lucy's needs. "You are not responsible for your birth, and in my opinion, you are worthy of anyone, including princes."

"Here, here," Miss Vaughn said. "Now, my lady, no more dawdling. We need to get you dressed."

"Luce—you should go down without me, otherwise you'll give me away."

Lucy pointed the torch at Cordelia and pressed the button to light it up. "Yes, Your Majesty."

They both giggled and Lucy left the room.

Miss Vaughn helped Cordelia put on the high-collared dress that represented the noble English queen. The gown wasn't as striking as the dainty pink one of Marie Antoinette, but it was made of dark crimson velvet, and the skirt did not require a crinoline to form it. Miss Vaughn put the large, curly red-haired wig on her. The collar around her neck was enormous! She glanced at her reflection and nearly laughed; still, she hoped that Thomas cared for her enough to recognize her in it.

Cordelia knew her husband was fond of her, but fondness paled in the face of love. She wanted it all. Maybe if Penelope went to America with Blanche, Thomas could finally let go of his feelings for her. Maybe, like Cordelia's for Stuyvesant, they would fade to only caring or dim in comparison to the relationship that he had with his wife. For the life they had together.

Or Thomas might continue to love Penelope, and Cordelia

would be between him and the woman he loved. Maybe she would always be a stranger in her own home. A foreign interloper whose ways did not belong.

Cordelia did belong in America. If she left with Stuyvesant, he would love her. She had friends and family in New York City. She knew that she could be happy there again. Perhaps she would grow to love him like she did Thomas. Stuyvesant was breathtakingly handsome and he radiated strength. She would also be close enough to see her sister, Edith, often. Maybe even repair her damaged relationships with her parents.

"I'll powder your face," Miss Vaughn said. "I heard once that, when Queen Elizabeth I died, she had over an inch of powder on her face."

Cordelia sneezed and white powder dusted the air. She laughed and Miss Vaughn did too. Although, there was nothing to laugh about. Her life was a complicated disaster. Miss Vaughn continued to powder her face until Cordelia couldn't see any of her freckles. She then placed the black velvet mask over her eyes. Cordelia didn't recognize herself and she was sure that Stuyvesant or Thomas would not either. Not until the unveiling at midnight. More time for her to process her own feelings. To make her choice.

After wanting to go home for so long, she felt reluctant to leave England. To leave Ashdown Abbey, after she'd worked so hard to make it feel more like a home and less like a mausoleum.

Her silliest concern was that her successor would not separate the food into different tins for the poor but continue the precedent of putting them all together mishmash. She'd already purchased new books for the school children, but she didn't want to miss their spring music concert that they'd been preparing for. There was so much she could do to improve the lives of the people who lived near Ashdown. So much that she wanted to do.

Cordelia was no longer interested in a purely social life, a life of endless parties and social engagements. She looked forward to the London Season, but she was excited to return to Ashdown and her philanthropic works. She wanted to make a positive difference in the world. She wanted to be remembered for more than her jewels and her exquisite wardrobe. She wanted to be a woman who made a difference in the world. Who made her community a better place for everyone, not just the wealthy or well-born.

Truthfully, most of her hesitation was because of Thomas. She realized now that she loved him. But he didn't love her. Would staying with him bring her more misery than leaving?

Miss Vaughn added some lavender scent to Cordelia's wrists. "Do you need anything else, my lady?"

"No, you did marvelously, as always, Miss Vaughn," Cordelia said, and hugged the older woman, whom she viewed as a strict but loving granny.

Miss Vaughn blushed fiercely and was fighting a smile. "My lady, you're not supposed to hug the staff."

"Are we not friends yet?"

Miss Vaughn lost the battle and allowed the smallest of smiles. "'Tis not proper, my lady. What would Mrs. Norton say if she saw?"

"I am never entirely proper, Miss Vaughn," Cordelia said, and left the room.

38

*C*ordelia walked the long way to the ballroom, the one that passed by all the visitors' rooms. She saw the Marchioness of Grimsby dressed as Hebe. Even in a mask, she held her head so much higher than anyone else that she was easy to distinguish. She also spotted Lois, dressed as an Egyptian queen.

The ballroom that had always felt rather empty was, for the first time since she'd come to Ashdown Abbey, almost half full. But instead of being lit by the bright electric lights for the ball, she'd decided to use candles one last time. To keep with the historic atmosphere. Even the footmen, in their livery uniforms, looked as if they'd stepped out of a history book.

She saw several men dressed as knights, kings, and Romans in togas. One man was dressed as a monk, and his black habit not only covered his entire body but obscured his face. She gave an involuntary shiver. The monk reminded her of the bones that she and Thomas had found. The skeleton was now buried in the Petersley cemetery; hopefully, the ghost of Ashdown Abbey had finally found peace. If only she could find peace of her own.

Penelope was smiling underneath her mask. Stuyvesant, poorly concealed, was dressed in a cowboy hat, with a mask, and paying her court. Cordelia could not help but smile to herself. So far, her plan was working brilliantly and she didn't feel so much as a pang of jealousy. The small orchestra struck up a tune and an elderly Roman asked for her hand. Cordelia made the mistake of speaking with her American accent to the elderly gentleman, but she wouldn't make that mistake again. She spoke softly, with an English accent. She found that it was easy enough to imitate. It'd been drummed in her ears since she arrived in England.

Stuyvesant stopped in front of her and her heart dropped. "Queen Elizabeth I, may I have the honor of this dance?"

"You may, sir."

He placed his hand on her waist and took her hand with his other. She felt the familiar warmth of his touch, but not the tingling in her belly that she felt whenever Thomas was nearby. She looked over her shoulder for him but couldn't identify him among the guests.

"Tired of me already, Your Majesty?"

"If you're going to be impertinent," she said in her crispest imitation of an English lady, "I am going to have to cut off your head."

"I'm fond of my head exactly where it is."

"I'm sure that you are not the only one who is fond of your head."

He spun her around and she closed her eyes and tried to recapture the joy she'd once felt while dancing with him. She wanted to feel that way again. He'd travelled halfway across the world for her and her heart was not fickle.

But divorce?

She tried not to shudder just thinking of it. He hadn't guessed who she was. Cordelia inclined her head and bowed formally. She was not about to give her disguise away yet. Stuyvesant barely waited to acknowledge her nod before walking to Penelope's side and bowing to her. Cordelia could no longer hold in her smile. She grinned. Her strategy was working marvelously.

"Might I 'ave this dance, m'lady queen," a gruff voice said beside her. She turned to see a masked man dressed like a seventeenth-century pirate, with an elaborate red coat, high-heeled boots, and a real sabre worn at his slim waist, complete with an enormous, curly black wig and a wide-brimmed hat with a tall white feather. He swept off the hat and bowed to her with a great flourish.

A laugh bubbled from her and she held out her hand to him. "Yes, I would be happy to dance with a pirate," she said in a slight British accent.

"Privateer," he said with another familiar smile. "The legal kind of pirate."

"That's rather less dashing."

"Nonsense," he said in the same gruff, disguised voice. "I am Sir Francis Drake, a privateer for my queen. You, Elizabeth Regina."

"And what do you intend to steal for me?" Cordelia asked in the same crisp English accent.

"Not for you, but from you," he said as he took her into his arms for the waltz. He leaned in by her ear and whispered, "The greatest treasure of all—your heart."

She felt a delicious shiver down her spine. Two could play this game. "But perhaps my heart is already taken by another rogue."

The privateer released her hand and touched his sword hilt. "Then the scallywag will have to answer to my sword."

"Your sword speaks? How very singular," she snapped. "Does it dance as well as you?"

"Better," the privateer said, and threw his head back and laughed. A laugh that warmed her stolen heart. A laugh she recognized—the privateer was Thomas. She wondered how she hadn't known him instantly, but he was wearing those ridiculously heeled boots, so he appeared taller than usual. And the large red coat made him look broader in the shoulders. But how could she have not recognized his smile, or the warm comradery she felt in his presence? The aching need to be closer to him?

"If you are going to flirt so outrageously with all the ladies," she said theatrically, "more than one husband will want to dance with your sword."

"I only intend to flirt with one lady," he said softly, no longer speaking with a gruff voice. "The only one who holds my heart."

She felt tears come unbidden to her eyes and a sharp stab of pain in her chest near her heart. He must have thought she was Penelope. Thomas *still* loved her.

"I'm not who you think I am," she said softly, forgetting for the first time to speak with an English accent.

"You're the woman that I love."

How she had longed to hear him speak those words! But not when he thought she was someone else. She stumbled in her steps. Dancing this close to him was agony.

The music ended and she pulled away from him. Being in his arms, while his heart still held another, was unbearable. She didn't curtsy; she wouldn't. Cordelia walked a few steps and, before she knew it, found herself in Stuyvesant's arms again. She leaned her aching head against his broad shoulder, seeking the familiar refuge of their friendship, the relief from revelations that were destroying her carefully constructed world.

"I am tired of waiting for your answer, Cordy," he said, and stopped in the middle of the dance floor.

"How do you know I am Cordelia?" she said in the same English accent.

"Because I have loved you all my life, and no one else has the same perfect posture as you, no matter what you're wearing."

Cordelia's heart finally fluttered with the delight she'd been waiting for. Stuyvesant did know her truly! "You win the wager. Thomas owes you one hundred pounds."

"He can keep the money," Stuyvesant said. "He can keep all of your money. We don't need it. Once you are divorced, everything will go back to normal."

Her mother's divorce had nearly destroyed their family and ruined their social position. The only thing that had saved them from social ostracism was Cordelia's marriage to an earl. If Cordelia were to leave Thomas, would her family be cast out again? Would Edith be ridiculed at school? Would they no longer be welcome at

Mrs. Astor's home and the parties of the social elite of New York? It would be a lie to tell herself that she cared only for the poor. She did care for the poor, but she also loved beautiful dresses and brilliant parties.

"But I worry that it won't go back to normal," Cordelia said. "You don't understand how people treat someone from a broken marriage. The cold stares and insolent looks. I don't think you understand how dreadful it is. I don't think I could endure it again."

"You don't need to think," Stuyvesant said. "I can do the thinking for the both of us."

Cordelia shuddered as she remembered her mother speaking similar words to her. *I don't ask you to think, I do the thinking... You will do as you are told.* Cordelia was tired of being told what to do. What to think. From the servants. From the aristocratic ladies. From her mother. From Stuyvesant.

"I don't want you to do my thinking for me," she said. "I am perfectly capable of thinking for myself."

"I didn't mean to offend you, Cordy," he said. "But a woman needs to trust the man in the relationship to make the important decisions."

"That's not how my marriage works," she said, standing taller. "My husband listens to me and respects my opinions. We are equal partners, and we make all of our decisions together."

"That's because he's only half a man."

"Treating me as an equal does not make him less of a man," Cordelia said, her posture more rigid than ever. "It makes him more of one."

"You prefer that pale snipe to me?" he said incredulously. "Have I come all this way for nothing?"

Her head ached and her heart constricted. Did she prefer Thomas? She didn't want to love a man whose heart belonged to somebody else. But she knew, without a doubt, that Stuyvesant no longer held her heart. The tender feelings she had for him were now all in the past. There was no future for them.

"I have changed in the time since we've been parted, Stuyvesant," she whispered, her chin trembling with every word. "I think we both would no longer be happy together."

"I will leave immediately."

"You don't have to leave. It's almost midnight and the unmasking."

"I no longer have a reason to stay."

Cordelia grabbed his wrist to stop him. "Please do not make a scene. Stay until the unmasking and you can leave first thing in the morning."

He bowed his head. "As you wish it."

But nothing was as Cordelia wished it to be.

39

The Viennese orchestra started to play a lively tune and the crowd all counted down.

Ten.

Nine.

Eight.

Seven.

Six.

Five.

Four.

Three.

Two.

One.

A row of footmen let off exploding crackers and streamers. Thayne turned on the electric lights.

Cordelia slipped off her mask, even though she wanted nothing more than to hide behind its lace. "It is time to unmask and for us to see who you truly are!"

Lois was the first to tear off her mask.

"Everyone knew it was you, darling," Oliver said, removing his own.

The Grimsbys, Oxenburys, and Eshers all pulled off their disguises, not that Cordelia hadn't already recognized them all by their shapes, followed by the Grimsbys, Whitbys, Hawkinses, and Brackens. She watched Prince Albert Louis take off his own mask and then delicately remove Lucy's. Cordelia could see that her friend was blushing and that she'd never looked more beautiful. Stuyvesant hovered near them—his expression as cold and haughty as any aristocrat. Blanche giggled and pointed like a schoolgirl with Viscount Brinkley and Mrs. Stewart.

The orchestra began to play another song.

Cordelia fanned her hot face, partially hiding behind it. Only Stuyvesant knew why she was so embarrassed. She walked to the refreshment table and took a glass of punch. She sipped it slowly, trying to regain a measure of her composure. Stuyvesant had stayed for the unmasking and hadn't caused a scene. She saw Thomas dancing with his mother. Cordelia had never before seen Blanche so animated and happy.

Save for Stuyvesant, everyone in the room was smiling and having fun. Except Penelope. Cordelia choked on her punch. She hadn't seen her at the unmasking. Perhaps she had left with another guest for an assignation?

No. Penelope still loved Thomas; she wouldn't kiss another man.

She had probably gone to use the water closet. That was the only reasonable excuse. Cordelia's nerves were simply overactive since the afternoon incident with the ash tree. Penelope was probably happily chatting in some nook.

Except Penelope had worn Cordelia's dress, her most expensive diamond necklace, and her French perfume.

Had someone mistaken her for Cordelia behind the mask?

Was it the same person who had tried to harm Cordelia numerous times?

She forced herself to take a deep breath in and out. Setting down the tumbler, she walked over to where Thomas and his mother were dancing by the Oxenburys, Hawkinses, and Rutledges.

"Blanche, I am sorry to interrupt you," she said, trying to remain calm. "But have you seen Penelope lately? I did not see her at the unmasking."

Her mother-in-law tipped her head to the side. "I thought you were Penelope, dear girl. I suppose she must have been Marie Antoinette. That poor queen. What a sad ending she had. If only the French had taken her advice and eaten more cake and constructed fewer guillotines."

"I am sure that would have made all the difference, Mama," Thomas said sardonically.

But Cordelia couldn't even smile at his wit. Her nerves were on end.

"What's the matter, Cordelia?" he asked, his voice low.

Thomas didn't seem surprised at all to see who she was.

Had he known all along? Was *she* the one he loved?

Cordelia shook her head. She couldn't think about that right now.

"I am probably overreacting after yesterday's incident," she said slowly. "But I can't rid myself of the feeling that Penelope might be in trouble."

"Why would she be?" Blanche asked, tipping her head to one side.

"Because someone thought that she was me," Cordelia whispered. "Because she was wearing my jewels, and someone has been trying to kill me."

40

"Your jewels?" Thomas repeated stupidly.

"Yes."

He took Cordelia's hand and they walked to the door where Thayne was standing. "Have you seen Penelope?"

"Can't say that I have, my lord."

"Will you have the footmen search for her?" Thomas said. "And turn on all the electric lights in the house?"

"Of course, my lord."

Thayne left the room. Thomas looked around again. The only person missing from the house party was Penelope. He tore off his itchy wig and glanced down at his wife. She tried to smile, but Thomas could see the worry in her eyes and the grim set of her jaw. Cordelia believed that Penelope was in trouble, and selfishly, all he could think about was how relieved he felt that it wasn't his wife.

A terrible thought.

They stood near the door for two more dances before Thayne returned, his face grave.

"We've searched all the rooms on the ground floor and her bedroom on the first floor, and she is not there," he said. "What should we do now?"

Cordelia clutched his hand even tighter.

Thomas held up his opposite hand and the orchestra stopped playing. Everyone in the room was looking at him.

"Is something wrong?" Oliver asked.

Thomas did not know what to say or do.

"We seem to have lost a member of our party," Cordelia said, stepping forward. "Anyone who is willing to help us look for a lost French queen, please find a partner."

"Most irregular," Lady Grimsby said.

"What fun!" Lois said excitedly, taking her husband's hand. "Come on, Ollie. This is better than a penny dreadful."

Three other couples stepped forward to join the search. Thomas directed two couples to search the basement and two others to search all the rooms on the first floor.

"Come, Cordelia," he said, taking her hand again. "We will check the second floor and the roof."

"All right, partner."

He led her to the back of the house, through the kitchen, to the servants' staircase. They climbed the two flights of stairs until they reached the landing where the secret passage let out.

"Should we separate?" she asked.

He gripped her hand tighter. "No. We'll be safer together."

"All right."

They opened every door in the servants' wing. The rooms were so basic, only holding a bed and a bureau, that only a glance was needed to ascertain that no one was there. Out of breath, they ran to the other wing. Thomas opened the next few doors, but no one was inside the rooms. There was nowhere else to look but the roof.

"Maybe you should go back to the ballroom," he suggested. Cordelia was more precious to him than any house. Than any amount of money. He didn't want to risk her life for anyone else's, even Penelope's. "You are the hostess, after all."

"We're not splitting up," she said. "We're partners."

"It may not be safe, and I don't want to lose you."

"Then trust me to make my own decisions."

He shook his head. "You're right. Of course you're right. We're partners."

Thomas held out his hand to her and together they went up the narrow flight of stairs that led to the roof. Unlike the servants' quarters, there were no electric lights. Only the dim light of a waning moon and the sound of muffled sobs. He dropped her hand when he saw a shadow with a wide skirt on the end of the parapet. He stepped forward and saw another broad figure with arched shoulders pointing a gun at Penelope.

"Drop your gun," he called.

The figured turned and he saw the face of the woman who had bandaged his scrapes as a boy—Mrs. Norton. The housekeeper pointed the gun from Thomas to Penelope and back again. "Go back inside the house, Thomas, you were not supposed to see this."

He held up his hands. "Mrs. Norton, please set down the gun. We can talk about this rationally."

"She's trying to take away my home."

"How?"

Mrs. Norton waved her free hand. "She's going to sack me after all my years of hard work and dedication. It means nothing to an American."

Cordelia inhaled sharply.

"No one is going to fire you, Mrs. Norton," Thomas said slowly. "Ashdown Abbey has been your home longer than it has been mine."

"Forty-five years," she said. "I came to work as a maid when I was only eleven. A nameless girl from the workhouse, and now I hold the title of housekeeper. The highest position a woman of my class can hold, and I won't go back to the gutter."

"You won't have to," he assured her, and took a tentative step toward her.

"I'd rather die than go back to the workhouse." The gun in Mrs. Norton's hand began to shake. "It'll be better for you too when she's gone. She is a low-born American, who is not worthy to be a countess. Once she is out of the way, you can marry Miss Hutchinson and everything will go back to the way it is supposed to be. Ashdown Abbey will follow the old traditions again."

"The woman on the parapet is not my wife," Thomas said. "It's Miss Hutchinson. Please let her safely come back to me."

Mrs. Norton shook her head. "You're trying to be noble again and save her. You always were a good boy."

She pulled back the hammer and pointed the gun at Penelope's hunched and crying figure.

"Stop!" Cordelia cried, stepping out from behind Thomas. Her head was held high, and she looked every inch the queen that she was portraying. "I am right here. Leave Penelope alone."

Mrs. Norton turned the gun back toward Cordelia, aimed it only for a second, and fired it at her heart. Thomas pushed her out of the way and fell against the roof titles. The pain in his chest this time was not from his heart but from the blood flowing freely from the wound. He gasped in agony.

"What have I done? What have I done?" Mrs. Norton dropped her gun and howled in anguish. "I've killed him. I've murdered my precious boy."

"Thomas!" Penelope screamed between even louder sobs.

Mrs. Norton gave Thomas one last agonizing look before running and jumping off the roof. The poor, misguided woman!

Cordelia was finally safe.

The pain overwhelmed his senses and he shivered with cold. He felt Cordelia's luxuriant, soft hair fall across his face, her hands heavy against his chest. He hoped to hear her voice one last time.

"Stop crying, Penelope, and help me staunch the bleeding!" Cordelia yelled.

Thomas could no longer see in the darkness but heard Penelope's steps coming closer to them.

"What do I do?"

"Give me your petticoat!" Cordelia demanded. "And then run for help."

Silence.

"This isn't the moment to worry about modesty!"

Thomas heard the swish of skirts and felt increased pressure on his chest. Again, he heard the clicking sound of footsteps.

"Don't you dare die," Cordelia yelled at him. She slapped his face with a wet hand. "Stay with me, Thomas. You are my partner! Do you hear me? Don't you dare die until we've discussed it thoroughly and come to a joint decision."

He felt like he was falling into a dark world. Everything felt topsy-turvy. He didn't know which way was up or down until she pressed her cheek against his face and the world righted again. He knew who he was and where he was. He had to fight the darkness. He wasn't ready to die. It took all of his strength to open his eyes. Her face was above him, bathed in moonlight, and unspeakably beautiful.

"I-I-I love you," she whispered, and pressed a soft kiss to his lips.

If this was death, he'd gladly welcome it.

41

"Thayne, come quickly to me," Cordelia called, fighting to keep her voice steady. Her stomach roiled and she felt sick. "He's lost consciousness and a great deal of blood."

The new butler ran to her side without any pretense to dignity and knelt down beside her.

"Press down with both of your hands," Stuyvesant said, joining them with his own large hands. "Once we staunch the bleeding, we can move him to a more comfortable place."

Oliver stood watching over them in shock.

"Don't stand about. Go and fetch the doctor, Oliver!" Cordelia yelled, her voice strained from all the yelling she'd already done.

He didn't move but continued to stare at them in wide-eyed horror.

"Cordelia, you go. He's in shock," Stuyvesant said. "Thayne and I will stop the bleeding."

She hesitated for only a second before standing up and wiping her bloody hands on her fancy dress. She rushed past Oliver and nearly ran into a pair of footmen on the stairs. Both were strong, tall young men, over six feet.

"Gerald and Tim, please make a stretcher to carry Lord Farnham down from the roof."

They turned around and went back downstairs. They stopped at the servants' landing, where Lois was comforting a sobbing Penelope. Cordelia continued down the last two flights of stairs to the ballroom, where the rest of the servants and the guests waited. They watched her entrance in astonishment. She looked down at her bloodied hands and her wild hair. Her appearance did not matter. She did not care what these people thought. Catching her breath for a second, she ran through the room until she reached the kitchen. It was just as full and busy as the ballroom. She spotted the head groom.

"Mr. Rowell, you need to go and tell the doctor that he needs to come immediately. Then visit Constable Hawes and ask him to come at once. There's a body on the east side of the house."

"Yes, Lady Farnham." He bowed and took long strides out of the room.

Cordelia turned to Hattie. "Lord Farnham has been shot. We need his room prepared immediately and fresh bandages."

"Yes, my lady."

She next turned to Cook. "Please prepare hot water for the doctor and perhaps a broth or tea for Lord Farnham."

Cordelia's stomach turned and she nearly lost all of its contents. With a great struggle, she managed to return to the ballroom. Her guests crowded around her, all talking at the same time.

She held up her bloody hands for silence. "There has been an accident. If everyone would please return to their rooms, I will give a full explanation in the morning."

"I demand to know what is going on," Lady Grimsby said.

"You heard what Lady Farnham said, Augusta," Lady Oxenbury snapped. "We are to go to our rooms."

Lady Oxenbury walked out of the ballroom, and slowly the rest of the guests, with their servants, followed. Lady Grimsby was the last person to leave the ballroom.

Miss Vaughn rushed into the room and put an arm around Cordelia. "Let's get you cleaned up. Lord Farnham needs you."

Numbly, Cordelia allowed herself to be led to her bedchamber. Miss Vaughn helped her wash off the blood and change into a simple dress. She walked through the dressing room to Thomas's room. The footmen were carrying in Thomas's body. He was no longer wearing the red jacket or his sword. His face was devoid of color, but his bandaged chest moved up and down ever so slightly. Stuyvesant, Oliver, and Thayne followed them into his chamber. Thayne threw back the coverlet and told the footmen to place the stretcher on the side of the bed. They carefully lifted Thomas off it and into his bed.

Hattie arrived with bandages, and Cook herself brought the hot water. Cordelia watched in amazement at the coordinated effort of the staff in cleaning and caring for Thomas.

The doctor arrived a half hour later. He undid their makeshift bandages and examined the wound.

"Lady Farnham, would you be so kind to leave the room?" the doctor said, shaking his head. "I need to extract the bullet."

"Doctor McKenzie, he is my husband. I am not leaving his side. So I suggest you get about your work."

"Surgery is no place for a lady."

Cordelia's whole body stiffened with anger and frustration. "I am not just a lady; I'm his wife and I will be staying."

The doctor turned to the first man in the room as if to get his permission for Cordelia to stay. It was Stuyvesant.

"Do as Lady Farnham says, and be quick about it, man," he said.

The doctor shook his head again. "Most irregular."

Cordelia watched the doctor try to dig the bullet out of Thomas's chest. It was almost like he was fishing inside him. There was even more blood, which concerned her greatly. Finally, she heard a clunk and saw the doctor had dropped the bullet in the bowl. She and Thayne cleaned the blood off of Thomas's chest, his breathing shallower than ever. Doctor McKenzie then took out a needle and thread from his bag and sewed the hole up. Thomas stirred a little, mumbling something, but his words weren't coherent enough to understand.

"We should leave," Stuyvesant said. "Let them all get some sleep."

He herded out the doctor, the footmen, and Oliver, who still appeared to be in shock, leaving only Cordelia and Thayne in the room. They each slept in a chair on opposite sides of the bed.

42

*H*er head ached terribly, and she was sleeping at a funny angle. She lifted it and realized that she'd been leaning on Thomas's bed from her chair. Instinctively, she grabbed his wrist and felt for a pulse—there was a slight but steady beat. She gently set his arm back on the bed and grabbed her own pounding head.

Thayne stirred on the other side. "If you'd like to go freshen up, I'll stay with him until you return."

A tangled curl fell into her face and she no doubt looked a fright. "Are you sure, Thayne? You could go first, and I could wait for you."

"I think Thom—Lord Farnham would prefer to see your face when he wakes," he said, and smiled at her for the first time.

"I'll be quick," she assured him before walking through the dressing room to her own bedroom.

Cordelia went to unlock her door, when she heard another door open and saw Penelope walk out from the secret passageway, holding Marie Antoinette's diamond collar necklace in her hands.

"I forgot to return this to you last night," she said. "I knocked on your door, but it was locked and I didn't want them to be misplaced, so I took the secret passageway."

Cordelia accepted the jewelry from Penelope's hands. "I am so sorry about last night. Had I any notion that lending you a costume would have endangered your life, I never would have suggested it."

"I went with Mrs. Norton because I had torn the hem of my dress and she offered to fix it for me. She said that her sewing kit was up in her room in the attic. But when we reached the attic, she pointed the gun at me and made me climb up to the roof. She told me to jump off," Penelope said, a hitch in her shrill voice. "She wanted it to look like you committed suicide because you were so unhappy here...and I am one of the reasons you have been unhappy."

"I know," Cordelia said, nodding slowly. "You've been my ghost."

Penelope's mouth opened in surprise. "I should never have done it. It was Mrs. Norton's idea—she's the one who told me about the secret passage. Not Blanche. I only wanted to scare you, not harm you. I swear it."

"I first recognized your lavender perfume when we sat together to make the invitations for the house party. And then last night, when I helped you dress, I was certain of it."

"Then, you saved my life knowing I was the one haunting you?"

"Yes."

"You are a better person than I am."

"I don't know about that," Cordelia said. "But I hope we can someday be friends despite our rather shaky start."

"There is more. I told the staff this morning that I was the one haunting you," Penelope said, her eyes on the floor. "Cook admitted that Mrs. Norton knew she was spoiling your breakfasts and she promised Cook that she wouldn't be punished for it."

"It is over and done with."

Penelope shook her bowed head. "The footmen thought they were standing up for Hibbert and Mrs. Norton by giving you small helpings at dinner. And Tim confessed this morning to the staff that he was responsible for the branch that almost fell on you and Miss Miller. It had been Mrs. Norton's idea as well, but he was the one who pulled the rope. He said that he only meant to frighten you, after seeing you flirt with your American friend. He didn't mean you or your friend permanent harm."

The footman had been in the entry when Stuyvesant had arrived and held her arms. Tim had witnessed their emotional exchange. His loyalty to Thomas and the Ashby family was commendable, but she couldn't allow someone who had tried to harm her in any way to stay in her home.

"He will have to be dismissed," Cordelia said, and then gave Penelope a penetrating glance. "And who was responsible for shooting at me?"

Penelope flushed red. "I swear it wasn't me. I suppose it would have to have been Mrs. Norton—her husband must have taught her how to shoot before he died. She clearly had excellent aim, for she hit Thomas last night. And she's the only other servant besides Hibbert who would have had a key to the gunroom."

Of course. Both the housekeeper and the butler had keys to every cupboard and room in the house. With Mrs. Norton dead, and once Tim was dismissed, Cordelia wouldn't have to worry about bringing the murderer with them to London.

"Thank you for telling me the truth."

Penelope exhaled slowly. "There is another truth I must face: Thomas doesn't love me anymore. I realized last night that he loved you, and I wish I could tell you that my feelings for him were also gone, but it would be an untruth."

Cordelia swallowed, her throat dry. "I know, and that is why I think it would be best for all of us if you were to go to America with Blanche. Experience a change of scenery, and perhaps meet other young men who are available."

She nodded and turned to leave through the now unlocked door. She paused as she opened it and said over her shoulder, "You make a splendid countess, Cordelia. Even if your American ways are different than ours."

"Thank you."

Penelope left the room just as Miss Vaughn entered carrying a breakfast tray. "You look peaky, my lady. We can't have that. Not with a houseful of guests."

"I forgot all about my guests."

"Now, don't you worry about them," Miss Vaughn assured her. "Hibbert arrived back early this morning, and he has everyone from the duchess to the servants in shipshape order."

"I believe it," Cordelia said with a laugh.

"He's a good butler, my lady."

"I realize that now and I will tell him."

"Good," Miss Vaughn said, and clapped her hands. "I'll get your morning frock ready."

Cordelia ate her breakfast and then allowed Miss Vaughn to clothe her and dress her hair before returning to Thomas's side. He was sleeping still, so she sent Thayne to his own room to take a much-needed rest. Cook brought a tray of tea and a bowl of gruel and set it on the table.

"Pull the cord if you or Lord Farnham need anything else."

"Thank you, Cook. You have been so helpful during this entire ordeal."

"I'm only doing my job."

"And I appreciate it," Cordelia said, and held out her hand to the older woman. Cook took Cordelia's hand and shook it before leaving the room.

Cordelia sat down on the edge of his bed. She placed her hand on his forehead to check for fever. His head felt a trifle warmer than it should have, but not enough to alarm her. She gently kissed his brow.

"Does this make me the sleeping princess again?" Thomas asked in a quiet, raspy voice.

She gave a sound that was half laugh and half sob. Tears of relief fell down her cheeks and she wiped them away with her hand. "No, silly. You were always Prince Charming, who rescued Rapunzel from her tower."

He tried to shake his head, but his face contorted with pain. "No, no. Rapunzel was perfectly capable of rescuing herself. She just needed a partner."

"She couldn't have asked for a better partner."

"I need to apologize."

"It can wait."

"No, it can't," Thomas said, his voice croaky. "There's nothing like nearly dying to give you a fresh perspective on life. I am so sorry for many, many things. But the most important one is that I should never have gone through with the wedding when I saw your tears. I should have stopped the bishop right there, then and asked you what *you* wanted, and I will forever regret being too cowardly to do so."

"I forgive you," she said, and caressed the side of his face.

Thomas closed his eyes. "You're making this harder."

"Making what harder?"

He opened his eyes and stared meaningfully into hers. "Cordelia, do you want to leave with Stuyvesant? Or do you want to stay with me?... Or neither? Would you rather attend Oxford University? You deserve to choose, and whatever you decide, I will do everything in my power to make it so."

"You mean a divorce?"

"We might be able to get an annulment because the marriage was never consummated."

Cordelia felt her face go red and was glad to see a little color steal into Thomas's cheeks as well. "I hadn't thought of that."

Thomas placed his hand on hers. "There is nothing in this world that I want more than for you to stay with me, but I want it to be your choice. What you want."

"I don't want the sort of marriage my parents had," she said. "I don't want a husband who has affairs with actresses and singers."

A small smile played on his colorless lips. "I have a solution for that."

"What?"

"If I were to sleep in your bed every night, you would never be in any doubt of my location or affections."

Cordelia felt a smile form on her own lips. "But you would eat all the bacon on the breakfast tray."

"Only half," he said.

"And I want a proper marriage proposal," Cordelia said. "I never got one."

"Do I have to kneel? Because if that is so, we may need to wait a few more days. I don't think I can even sit up at this point."

She ruffled his hair and then caressed his cheek.

"Very well, Rapunzel," Thomas said. "I love your hair and I long to climb up it."

"You're supposed to take this seriously!"

"I am and you're interrupting," he said. "I love you, Cordelia, with all the strength of my heart, and I vow that I will be true to you for all time, in sickness and when shot... You're richer and I'm definitely poorer... For the good and the bad, I want nothing more than to be at your side as your partner in everything. Will you marry me?"

Cordelia grinned at him.

"How did I do?" he asked.

"Not bad."

"Not bad? It was brilliant," he protested.

"You can practice on our honeymoon," she said. "You still owe me one of those too."

"I couldn't agree more."

She leaned down and kissed his lips. It was soft and lingering, with the promise of a lifetime of kisses and happily-ever-afters.

AUTHOR'S NOTE

Between the years 1870–1914, 454 American women married European men, many with foreign titles. The American brides, called "dollar princesses," brought close to a billion dollars to Britain, and unfortunately for the girls, this money became their husbands to spend as they chose (*Husband Hunters* 1). These marriages were called "cash for coronet" or, in today's language, "money for a title." European titles gave prestige to American families and allowed the nouveau (new) rich entrance into the Knickerbocker's society (old New York money). Because a young woman's marriage could move her entire family upward socially, young American women were cosseted, well educated, and often inherited as much money as their brothers. Unlike in England, where the eldest son inherited the title, estate, and bulk of the fortune.

Cordelia Jones is a fictional character; however, her story is inspired by two American teenagers who married into the British aristocracy: Consuelo Vanderbilt (1877–1964) and Cornelia Bradley Martin (1877–1961).

Consuelo Vanderbilt's mother, Alva, was determined to have her daughter marry into the British aristocracy, and nothing less than a duke would do. Alva wouldn't allow Consuelo to leave their home

(Marble House) until she promised to marry whomever Alva picked. Consuelo refused, because she loved Winthrop Rutherford and was secretly engaged to him. Alva didn't allow Consuelo to see her friends and confiscated all her letters. After five months of cajoling, yelling, and threatening to kill Rutherford, her mother claimed that her own life was in danger if Consuelo continued to defy her. Consuelo reluctantly gave in, and her mother's recovery was instantaneous. Alva wanted Consuelo to marry Charles Spencer Churchill, ninth Duke of Marlborough—"Sunny," who is mentioned in this book for being short.

The morning of November 6, 1895, Consuelo was late for her wedding because she was crying and the maid was sponging her eyes. The press reported everything about their marriage, including her lingerie to her diamond-studded gold garters. Large crowds came to the church just to catch a glimpse of their very own American princess. Consuelo's marriage allowed Alva to regain her social position in New York after her divorce earlier the same year.

Consuelo went to live at Blenheim Palace, which, thanks to her dowry (two and a half million dollars in railroad stocks), was getting much-needed renovations and repairs, including electric lights and central heating. She gave birth to two sons, but there was never any love in her marriage. The duke had been in love with somebody else and confessed this to Consuelo shortly after their wedding. He'd only married her to save his estate.

Consuelo legally separated from her husband in 1906 and eventually got an annulment. Her memoir, *The Glitter and the Gold*, is a fascinating account of not only her life but all the amazing people she met, from kings to kaisers. The story of separating the food in the tins for the poor and the dinner fiasco, with a lady guest leaving before the hostess, both come from her memoir. She was also a great humanitarian, who gave countless dollars and hours to improve the lives of those less fortunate than her, particularly women and children.

Cornelia Bradley Martin was just fifteen years old when she became engaged to Lord William Craven, fourth Earl of Craven. He was the owner of thirty-seven thousand acres and the estates of Ashdown House and Coombe Abbey. A family member recounts that one day she was playing with dolls, then she was told that she couldn't do that anymore because she was going to be married (*Husband Hunters* 220). She was married at only sixteen, and the groom was twenty-four, on April 18, 1893. Contemporaries teased Craven for snatching Cornelia up before she'd even come out (able to attend adult parties).

Her dowry was one million dollars and the Earl of Craven immediately began renovating his family estate Coombe Abbey. He used her money to reroof the building, improve the servants' quarters, and install electric lights. Together the couple had one son, William Craven, in 1897. In 1921, the Earl of Craven drowned in a boat-racing accident. Cornelia sold Coombe Abbey in 1923 to a builder named John Grey, and it is currently a hotel.

Lois's character was inspired by the first of the "dollar princesses," Jennie Jerome, who married Randolph Churchill, third son of the seventh Duke of Marlborough. Jennie is probably best known for being Winston Churchill's mother, but she was a political force of her own and wrote many of her husband's parliamentary speeches.

DISCUSSION QUESTIONS

1. How is Cordelia's life like a fairytale?
2. If you were Thomas how would you save your family and estate? Is he the villain or the hero of the story?
3. Why were American heiresses called 'dollar princesses' and why did they seek out 'cash for coronet' marriages?
4. "I promise that I will do everything in my power to be a good husband to you. To be faithful to you. To be a good partner," Thomas said. How are Cordelia and Thomas partners? How does that partnership grow into something more?
5. Why do you think the English servants treat Cordelia so poorly? Why do the upper staff dislike her?
6. "Charity at Ashdown was not the simple give-your-money variety; Cordelia went inside of these people's homes. She saw their dreadful living conditions and the lack of proper sanitation. She knew their names. They were not 'the poor'—some vague term that had no meaning." How and why does Cordelia's view of charity change? What do you think true charity is?

7. The Dowager Lady Farnham doesn't know much about America. Did you find her questions innocent or insulting? Do you have preconceived notions about other nations?

8. Stuyvesant grinned broadly. "Well, it is churlish to not be proud of one's own country and I can't deny that I think America is in the forefront of the world in technology and industry. The new world leaves the old one in the dust." How do the new world and the old world collide in the story?

9. Who did you think was trying to harm Cordelia and why? Did you guess the true culprit?

10. "She leaned down and kissed his lips. It was soft and lingering, with the promise of a lifetime of kisses and happily-ever-afters." Did you like the ending? Do you believe in *happily-ever-after*?

ACKNOWLEDGMENTS

The greatest treasure is family! I am so blessed to have each of you in my life: Jon, Andrew, Alivia, Isaac, and Violet. I have the best parents who always support me: John and Jill Larsen. And I am lucky enough to have the two most amazing sisters in the world: Michelle Martin and Stacy Moon.

I am so grateful for my friends who read early drafts and cheer on my writing: Erin, Susannah, Debbie, Irene, Dawn, Jennie, Katie, and Dannielle.

I am so thankful for the author friends who make publishing fun: Tiana Smith, Erin Stewart, Jennieke Cohen, Addie Thorley, Rosalyn Eves, Tricia Levenseller, Charlie Holmberg, Sheena Boekweg, Sam Taylor, RuthAnne Snow, Crystal Smith, Dee Garretson, L. E. DeLano, Alexander Chappell, and so many more.

AUTHOR BIOGRAPHY

Samantha Hastings met her husband in a turkey sandwich line. They live in Salt Lake City, Utah, where she spends most of her time reading, eating popcorn, having tea parties, and chasing her four kids. She has degrees from Brigham Young University, University of North Texas, and University of Reading (UK). She also writes cozy murder mysteries under Samantha Larsen.

Learn more at www.SamanthaHastings.com

OTHER BOOKS BY THE AUTHOR

Standalone Books

Secret of the Sonnets

By Any Other Name

The Girl with the Golden Eyes

The Last Word

The Invention of Sophie Carter

A Royal Christmas Quandary

Return of the Queen

The Stringham Family

The Duchess Contract

The Marquess and the Runaway Lady

Debutante with a Dangerous Past

Christmas in a Castle

Wedded to His Enemy Debutante

Lady Librarian Mysteries
(under Samantha Larsen)

A Novel Disguise

Once Upon a Murder

Nonfiction

Jane Austen Trivia

I am Made up of Words: Poems by Samantha Hastings

Made in the USA
Las Vegas, NV
29 August 2023